A plan gone awry . . .

There could be little doubt it was the earl's coach since this particular road led to only one destination, Sorrelby Hall. Scrambling backward, Olivia frantically tried to dismount from the tree. She succeeded, but not as she had planned.

Arms flailing, skirts flying, Olivia fell from the tree and landed only a few yards in front of the careening coach. Excruciating pain overwhelmed her. . . . As she slowly opened her eyes, a man's face stared down at her, horrified.

Perhaps in his early fifties, he was a rotund man, with a pleasant, though not heart-stopping, visage. He certainly did not measure up to Olivia's expectations of the sixth Earl of Sorrelby. . . .

Unthinking, she questioned, "The Devil's Darling?"

Colin had sprung from the coach. He overheard Olivia's use of his nickname and froze, astonished that his notoriety was so far-flung.

Executing a courtly bow, he dryly intoned, "At your service, my lady."

Shock ripped through Olivia, vibrating painfully throughout her bruised and battered body. In her wildest imaginings, she had never thought a man could be so breathtakingly handsome. . . .

The
Devil's Darling
Casey Claybourne

JOVE BOOKS, NEW YORK

THE DEVIL'S DARLING

A Jove Book / published by arrangement with
the author

PRINTING HISTORY
Jove edition / November 1994

ISBN: 0-515-11492-8

A JOVE BOOK®
Jove Books are published by The Berkley Publishing Group,
200 Madison Avenue, New York, New York 10016.
JOVE and the "J" design are trademarks
belonging to Jove Publications, Inc.

PRINTED IN THE UNITED STATES OF AMERICA

10 9 8 7 6 5 4 3 2 1

For my mother, Marty, who encouraged
me to read romance, and
for my dear friend, Shelley,
who encouraged me to write it

Chapter One

"CONFOUND IT, O'SHEA, must you hit every rut from London to Sorrelby?" Colin Forster, the sixth Earl of Sorrelby, good-naturedly growled at the driver perched above him on the coach.

O'Shea, reins in one hand, apologetically turned to the dark head protruding through the coach window and answered, "I'm doin' the best I can, man, but this road dunna look as if she's been traveled since the days of good King James."

"Oh, never mind. I should have ridden Dublin instead of hiding here inside the coach like a fox gone to ground," Colin answered, his deep baritone softening.

"Hah," O'Shea barked with laughter, "that's ye, for sure, the fox gone to ground."

Colin chose to ignore his coachman's guffaws and carefully drew his head back inside the coach. O'Shea's irreverence stemmed from nearly thirty years of caring for first the boy Colin, and later the man. He'd put the infant on his first horse, taught the youth proper Gaelic, and then followed the man into war. Each had saved the other's life a dozen times over.

"Damn," Colin repeated, "a fox hiding in his burrow."

Generally, when traveling, Colin preferred to mount his stallion, Dublin, rather than to ride inside an uncomfortable, dusty coach. An experienced horseman, he enjoyed the rigors of a long journey. But, under these unusual circumstances, he had chosen to travel incognito as he left London's most rapacious group of hunters—the marriage-seekers.

Since his seventeenth year, Colin had known tremendous

popularity with the *ton*'s dissatisfied wives and bored widows. His prowess in the boudoir was well touted. In fact, his numerous liaisons over the past dozen years had earned him the dubious moniker, "The Devil's Darling," for it was said that not even the devil himself, or herself, could resist Colin's rakish smile and violet eyes.

After a sojourn on the Continent under Lord Wellesley's command, Colin had returned to London in even greater demand by the love-starved ladies, and obligingly, he had picked up his reputation exactly where he had left it prior to his turn in the army. His years in the military had merely honed him into a sharper, stronger, and more appealing man than the daredevil youth who had charmed haute society.

If Colin felt genuine affection for his paramours, the emotion went no deeper. He enjoyed women, and from what he could tell, women thoroughly enjoyed him and his lovemaking, but none of his relationships had endured more than a handful of months. He had yet to experience the kind of love he had seen his parents share and had begun to despair that he ever would. Once the initial thrill of a fling began to fade, he quickly moved on, reluctant to give his current ladylove false hope of a more enduring relationship. Thus, his much-maligned and much-envied celebrity.

However, last week, fate intervened. Horace Forster, the fifth Earl of Sorrelby, succumbed to lung fever, leaving his entire estate to his sole grandson, Colin. Fortunately for Colin, he was not ill-prepared to take control of such vast holdings, having wisely invested a few thousand pounds many years ago in a shipping venture and, time after time, reaping a healthy return on each new expedition. Although he had not been wealthy prior to inheriting his grandfather's fortune, by necessity, he had learned the intricacies of commerce and, gifted with business acumen, had earned an income sufficient to support his family comfortably.

Colin had felt little regret upon learning of his grandfather's demise. Often, as a lad, he had silently cursed the phantom patriarch who had disowned his only son, Colin's father, Reginald, rather than consent to Reginald marrying an Irish-woman. Naturally, Colin had known that his father was in line for the title, but the quiet country life that the family led in remote Shropshire kept them far removed, both in locale and in mind, from the world of wealth and privilege. Only after venturing to London, a young man determined to make his fortune, did Colin begin to understand all that his father had given up for love of his wife and children.

Although emotionally unaffected by Horace's death, the social ramifications stunned the otherwise worldly Colin Forster. Within forty-eight hours of his ascendancy to the earldom, no less than fourteen overly eager London mamas arranged for their unwed daughters to make the acquaintance of the new Earl of Sorrelby. His recently acquired wealth and title catapulted Colin to the top of the "suitable for marriage" ranks. Where two days previous he had been a wickedly handsome man with few material prospects and a scandalous reputation, suddenly the *ton*'s unmarried daughters were materializing at every function where Colin was in attendance, be it a raucous polo match or an intimate tea party.

As the carriage bumped along toward Sorrelby Hall, Colin recalled the previous night, during which one young lady, the buxom Beatrice Haverland, elevated the pursuit to a higher, and more devious, level. Returning late from his club last evening, Colin was informed by the butler that a young lady awaited him in the town house garden.

"She was most insistent, my lord," Graves said, his tone clearly indicating his unfavorable opinion of the caller.

"What the devil?" Colin exclaimed. "At this hour?"

Striding purposefully into the shadowed courtyard, Colin discovered the tantalizing Beatrice perched calmly on a stone bench looking for all the world as if she regularly made calls on unmarried gentlemen of the *ton* at one in the morning.

Colin had imbibed a bit too freely that evening, and unfortunately for him, his reasoning slowed to a snail's pace upon viewing the moonlight reflected off Beatrice's showcased endowments. One dark curl lay seductively on her breast, inviting his gaze. Her eyes cast down demurely, she quickly arose.

"Good evening, Lord Sorrelby," she said, her voice unnaturally loud in the hushed courtyard. The overpowering scent of her musky perfume floated toward Colin as she approached him. His liquor-induced confusion held him in place, although the impropriety of her visit did register in one small corner of his clouded consciousness.

Before he could respond to her greeting, Beatrice stopped directly in front of him, grabbed his hand, and thrust his callused palm into her décolletage.

The feel of warm, feminine flesh abruptly aroused the earl from his muzzled state, as did the theatrical shriek from the direction of the town house's French doors.

Standing there, ostensibly to witness this intimate scene, was Nellie Osborne, a dear friend of the calculating Beatrice. Nellie, a very poor actress, splayed both hands protectively across her chest, trying her best to appear properly shocked.

Colin instantly recognized the gravity and implications of the incident, retrieved his fingers from Beatrice's front, and without a word, pivoted on his well-polished heel and exited through the garden door.

Acquainted with Beatrice and her overbearing father, the Earl of Wotbane, Colin prudently decided to retire immediately to his country estate, a few miles north of the tiny village Mossgate. Informing O'Shea that it was high time he examined his new holdings, they departed for Sorrelby at dawn. It remained to be seen how Beatrice would now proceed with her plot. Undoubtedly she would endeavor to force him to offer for her; however, Colin had no intention of chaining himself to the conniving Miss Haverland for the remainder of his days.

Colin and O'Shea had been on the road nearly four hours and had passed through Mossgate approximately ten minutes previous. During this time, Colin had reflected on his recently acquired popularity and cursed the fates that had brought him this deuced inheritance. If not for his mother and sisters, he might have chosen to cast it all aside.

Logically, Colin had long ago accepted the inevitability of marriage. The continuance of the Sorrelby line rested on his shoulders. Now the wisest course of action would be to locate a suitable wife as quickly as possible—a manageable young woman to reside at Sorrelby and breed an heir. Once safely wed, he could return to London to manage his business and personal affairs, no longer the target of avaricious, unmarried ladies.

Satisfied with that resolution, and determined to find himself such a bride, Colin allowed himself to relax against the squabs as the coach bounced and lurched along the rough country road.

Suddenly O'Shea shouted hoarsely from his seat, a scream echoed across the valley and the coach pulled up sharply, throwing Colin to the far side of the cabin.

Olivia Knowles congratulated herself as she shimmied along the branch of the ancient oak tree. Her plan was progressing to perfection. That morning word had reached Mossgate from a traveling wares salesman that the new Earl of Sorrelby was en route to his ancestral home. The salesman had been departing from an inn, a couple hours outside London, when the earl and his man arrived to break their fast and to change horses.

Once the news circulated Mossgate and reached Olivia's ears, she instantly put her plan into motion. Although loath to confront the earl, Olivia had been coerced by her cousin, Margaret, into speaking with Sorrelby's new master regarding the acquisition of a physician for their tiny village. Olivia grimaced with chagrin recalling the ease with which Margaret had persuaded her to intervene on the townspeople's behalf.

"Now, Olivia, please look at this logically. Who better than you to address the earl on this issue? He's widely known as a rake of the first order, and I'm convinced that once he looks upon your beauty, he will be unable to refuse you anything."

Olivia had frowned, her auburn brows meeting menacingly at the bridge of her pert nose. "I will *not* go begging to the new earl, Maggie. If it weren't for his grandfather having been such an insufferable miser, we wouldn't be in this pickle."

Margaret had reminded her, however, that the situation was especially dire now that the estate physician had returned to London following Horace Forster's demise. Although forbidden by the hard-hearted earl to treat the Mossgate villagers, the doctor had surreptitiously tended the seriously ill while he had been in residence at Sorrelby. With his departure, the citizens had not even a midwife to care for them. Olivia had occasionally assisted Sorrelby's physician, and due to her voracious reading, she had some knowledge of medical practice, but she also knew her limitations. She could not be responsible for every illness or accident that befell her neighbors.

Therefore, she had devised a plan. Her low opinion of the aristocracy, coupled with her fierce pride, had prevented her from approaching the earl with a direct request. So she had concocted a scheme, one not well received by Margaret's brother, Henry.

"Quite naturally," Olivia had explained, "the earl will discover me along the road with a turned ankle. When he stops to assist and then inquires about a physician, *voilà*, there we are."

"But, really, Olivia," argued Henry, the practical member of the family. "Accosting gentry on the side of the highway isn't altogether proper, you know. Just not the thing."

"I concede that it departs from Dr. Trusler's *Principles of Politeness*," she countered, "but I prefer that the earl believe our meeting a circumstance."

"I would still feel much more comfortable if *I* were hiding beside the roadway," Henry had persisted. "The man has the deuce of a reputation, you know. For gossip of his philandering to reach as far from London as Mossgate, you can rest assured that he has earned that outrageous nickname, 'The Devil's Darling.'"

Despite Henry's remonstrations, Olivia had insisted on carrying out her plan alone—the very same plan that now found her perched among the branches of the gnarled oak.

Upon initially taking her post, she had anxiously paced back and forth awaiting the earl's arrival. She had selected this particular location as it afforded her a view down the valley, and was far enough outside of town that the earl could not simply abandon her in the hopes that another rescuer would happen by.

However, as the morning progressed, she had grown concerned, wondering if perhaps the earl might have opted to stop in Mossgate to acquaint himself with the villagers.

"Blast it! If he stops at Mossgate, I might be out here all afternoon," she grumbled irritably to herself. Impulsively she had decided to climb the tree to see if she could spot the earl's carriage.

Inching cautiously along the oak limb, Olivia moved farther and farther, craning her neck for a view of the village. Her progress was arrested as a prickly branch snagged the hem of her skirt. She stopped to disentangle herself when suddenly the sound of pounding hooves reached her ears. She looked down on the road to discover a coach quickly approaching her location.

"Oh, no," she said, panicking, "he's here! How could he arrive so quickly!" contradicting her impatient thoughts of only a minute earlier.

There could be little doubt it was the earl's coach since this particular road led to only one destination, Sorrelby Hall. Scrambling backward, Olivia frantically tried to dismount from the tree. She succeeded, but not as she had planned.

Arms flailing, skirts flying, Olivia looked like a fledgling chick attempting its first aerial assault as she fell from the tree and landed only a few yards in front of the careening coach.

Excruciating pain overwhelmed her as did the dirt from the dry roadway. Flat on her back, she gasped for breath, sucking in the grimy cloud swirling around her. Coughing, she silently prayed not to lose consciousness as she slowly opened her eyes, blinking away a fine film of dust. A man's face stared down at her, horrified.

Jowly, pink-cheeked, and balding, he kept opening and closing his mouth like a trout out of water. Perhaps in his early fifties, he was a rotund man, with a pleasant, though not heart-stopping, visage. He certainly did not measure up to Olivia's expectations of the sixth Earl of Sorrelby.

Forcing her blurry eyes to focus, she willed her head to stop its uncontrollable spinning that she might regain a small measure of her wits. Pain radiated from every limb, but still she struggled to her elbows, attempting to sit.

Unthinking, she questioned, her hoarse voice expressing her doubt, "The Devil's Darling?"

Colin had sprung from the coach fast on the heels of O'Shea. He overheard Olivia's use of his nickname and froze in his tracks, astonished that his notoriety was so far-flung.

Lips quirked in a humored smile, Colin approached the prostrate figure. Executing a courtly bow, he dryly intoned in his deepest baritone, "At your service, my lady." As he straightened from the salutation, his eyes met those of Olivia.

Shock ripped through Olivia, vibrating painfully throughout her bruised and battered body. In her wildest imaginings, she had never thought a man could be so breathtakingly handsome. Thick, curly blue-black hair topped a lean, powerful physique that would tower a good six inches above her tall frame. Broad shoulders seemed to block out the morning sun while the square jaw and shadowed planes of his face contributed to his remarkably rugged masculinity. His teeth were brilliantly white and shone brightly in his darkly tanned face. Hypnotic violet eyes held her spellbound, compounding her dizziness and weakening her trembling arms.

Unaccountably, neither he nor she could tear their eyes away although Olivia felt light-headed from his mesmerizing effect upon her. Her breathing was harsh and rapid. A relentless pounding inside her head grew louder and louder until without warning, darkness descended, obscuring her vision and hurtling her into a black abyss of unconsciousness.

Chapter Two

COLIN REMAINED TRANSFIXED, caught midway between standing and bowing. The physical jolt that had electrified him upon first laying eyes on Olivia receded, leaving him frozen in the awkward position. His thoughts were traveling in circles as he madly searched for an explanation to the astonishing sense of recognition he felt upon viewing this country lass. Unquestionably, he had never made her acquaintance and yet . . . had he?

O'Shea, misinterpreting his master's look of stupefaction, assured him quickly, "She's only fainted, Colin. I didna run her over." To confirm his statement, he knelt beside her and picked up her limp wrist, searching for a pulse.

Shaking his head as if to clear it, Colin stepped forward. The girl was seriously injured, he determined, and in need of immediate care. Her skirt was tangled halfway up her thighs, revealing a pair of astonishingly long and lovely legs. Colin swore under his breath he'd never seen a more beautiful set of limbs.

O'Shea followed Colin's gaze and, blushing, leaned over to arrange the girl's clothing more modestly. Her skirts were too entangled for his self-conscious tugging to be effective. Colin impatiently pushed O'Shea's hands aside and gently wedged his arms beneath Olivia's back and knees. Effortlessly he picked her up and strode to the coach, shouting behind him, an edge to his usually silky-smooth voice, "Hurry, O'Shea. We'll take her on to Sorrelby—it must be just ahead."

He carefully stepped inside the coach, mindful not to jar his fragile cargo. As he eased back against the bench, he searched her face, hopeful that the memory of some distant meeting between the two of them would surface.

A thick fan of dark auburn lashes now concealed the unbelievably large emerald orbs that had stared up at him, bewilderment and pain reflected in their translucent depths. Colin noted how the exotic tilt to her eyes mimicked the slant of her high cheekbones, although the square and slightly stubborn jaw suggested strength amid the delicate features. Abundant red-gold hair contrasted starkly against the porcelain of her skin as the wavy tresses fell over his arm.

Good God, she's lovely, he mused. Almost without volition, he reached out and stroked her hair from her forehead, revealing an ugly purple abrasion. He winced at the bruise, not relishing the thought of her pain.

No, he reflected, if ever I had met this exquisite creature, I would not likely have forgotten her. But then, why did she seem familiar? And she, too, prior to losing consciousness, had reacted as if she recognized him. Furthermore, what reason would a young, gently bred woman have for dangling from a tree on the outskirts of Sorrelby? He vowed to have an answer to that puzzle before they parted company.

Colin frowned at the prospect of parting company with such a lovely being and then frowned anew. What was wrong with him? he berated himself. He had left London to escape the gender, and now this titian-haired bit of femininity, literally fallen from the sky, had entranced him with one look.

The coach slowed in front of a massive stone structure, its impressive gray turrets and towers silhouetted against the crystal-clear spring sky. The circular driveway surrounded a cherub-embellished fountain whose waters reflected the hundreds of mullioned windows gracing the manor's facade. Acres of rolling lawn bordered the estate on the west side, and on the east a large greenhouse sparkled in the bright rays of the April sunshine.

Colin, however, had little opportunity to appreciate his inheritance, for his eyes never left the unconscious girl on his lap. O'Shea drew up the horses and hopped down to open the carriage door. Colin gingerly stepped down, cradling Olivia in his arms. She lay so lifeless in his embrace that for a brief moment he experienced a sharp pang of alarm. Then her head fell to the side, exposing her long, swanlike neck. A pulse beat there, allaying Colin's fears.

A pencil-thin man awaited their arrival at the top of the enormous stone entryway. Dressed plainly in an old and tattered blue-and-gold uniform, he stepped forward and back, as if he were uncertain whether to rush down the stairway to greet them or to await them at the door. Colin decided the matter.

Climbing the steps, three at a time, he glanced briefly into the servant's pale face and ordered sharply, his voice well-honed from his years in the military, "Send for the physician. This woman is injured."

Charging past the startled butler, Colin entered the main hall. His step faltered as his eyes took in the magnificence of Sorrelby Hall. An immense crystal chandelier hung from the vaulted and frescoed ceiling, its many-faceted prisms reflecting prettily off the grand marble staircase that curved gracefully to the second story. The intricately detailed fresco depicted a Bacchanalian rite, which despite his concern for the girl, brought an ironic grin to Colin's handsome features. Above each doorway, ornate alabaster carvings of cupids, satyrs, and centaurs welcomed visitors through their decorative portals. Seventeenth-century Mortlake tapestries blanketed the walls, their scenes of nymphs cavorting at harvest's festival, echoing the fresco's theme.

Colin privately thanked the ancestor who had built the manor with an eye for subdued refinement and quiet elegance. As a guest of the Regent, Colin had visited Carlton House on more than one occasion, and although many of his peers thought the royal palace unequaled in its beauty, Colin considered it ostentatious. He did not care for overblown gilded opulence and found his new home to be much to his taste.

He quickly ascended the staircase, striding past the portrait galley of his ancestors, and opened the first doorway to his right. A well-kept, but now well-seasoned, bedroom was within. Crossing the sadly frayed Aubusson carpet, Colin laid

Olivia on the bed's blue silk coverlet. Her head fell back against the pillow and her eyelashes fluttered, but she did not awaken.

Sitting beside her, he gently ran his large hands along her shoulders and then her arms, to check for any fractured bones. As he ran his hand down her sleeve, he noted that her dress was neither new nor stylish nor of exceptional cloth. Her hair spread about her, dusty and in disarray. Even smudged with dirt and marred by the goose-egg bruise, she was exquisite. Like the interior of a rose petal, thought Colin, unconsciously trailing a finger along the velvety softness of Olivia's inner wrist.

A polite clearing of a throat arrested Colin's hand in mid-caress. The butler stood ramrod stiff at the doorway, his eyes discreetly averted.

"Yes?" Colin snapped, his voice unintentionally harsh as he tried to cloak his chagrin at being found in such an intimate position. He rose abruptly from the bed, frowning with annoyance.

"My lord," the servant greeted nervously. His head bobbed up and down, sending a few white hairs floating atop his sparsely covered pate.

He waited while Colin adjusted the coverlet over Olivia. When Colin finally turned again to the door, his usually pleasant countenance was once again restored. Sighing with relief, the butler made the introductions.

"Smythe is the name, my lord," he proudly declared, puffing out his nearly concave chest. "For over a century a Smythe has served the Earls of Sorrelby. I, myself, served your father Master Reginald. If I may, my lord, you favor your father, and a handsome lad, he was." Smythe smiled, revealing a row of yellowing, crooked teeth.

"On behalf of the entire staff, allow me to say that we're very pleased to have you here, my lord."

"Thank you, Smythe." Colin nodded graciously.

"In regard to your request for a physician . . ." Smythe paused, unwilling to bring that dark frown he witnessed earlier back to his master's face.

"Yes, what of it?"

"I regret, my lord, that there is not a physician available."

"What do you mean, 'not a physician available'? Surely, my grandfather did not perish away without seeking medical attention?"

"Oh, no. The late earl retained an attendant for the estate; however, the physician returned to London the day following your grandfather's . . . demise. . . ." Smythe trailed off uncomfortably. "Our condolences, my lord."

"Well, then, send to Mossgate." Colin waved his hand dismissively, becoming a little exasperated with the obtuseness of the well-intentioned Smythe.

Colin turned to look at Olivia, who still lay resting quietly. The deep blue of the coverlet set off her brilliant golden hair and emphasized her unusual pallor. One hand lay open as if in supplication. She appeared so young and so very vulnerable, thought Colin. An unusual, and somewhat disturbing, feeling of protectiveness washed over him.

"Again, my lad, I am sorry, but there is no physician in the village, either."

Colin slowly spun around, the intensity of his gaze causing Smythe to shift nervously from one ostrichlike leg to the next.

"There is no one?" Colin questioned, his voice expressing his growing irritation.

"No one, my lord."

Closing his eyes with vexation, Colin fought to remain calm. "All right. We will retain someone immediately. Locate the steward and have him await me in the study in ten minutes. Also, send up two maids with hot water and bandages. And Smythe, find a nightdress"—he waved his hand in the air like a magician conjuring—"or something, for the young lady here."

Pleased to see that the newest Earl of Sorrelby had matters under control, Smythe clicked his bony heels together sharply. "As you wish, my lord."

A few minutes later two flushed and harried-looking maids came scurrying into the bedroom, heavily laden with the requested supplies. Colin arose from the bed and turned to the servants, his hand outstretched to take one of the heavy pails of water from the younger maid. As he reached out, the girl looked up and gasped.

Discomfited by Colin's uncommonly good looks, she tripped over her feet, spilling half the contents of her bucket. The warm water sloshed over onto the Aubusson carpet, and worse, onto Colin's boots, eliciting another, more horrified, gasp. Both wide-eyed girls watched Colin, fear stamped across their pink-and-white features.

Colin smiled reassuringly.

"Never mind. The boots were in need of cleaning."

"Oh, I'm ever so sorry, my lord," the guilty one ventured, her voice trembling.

Surprised by her timidness, Colin reiterated, "It's of no import."

"Y-y-yes, my lord. Thank you."

"As for our guest here"—Colin gestured to Olivia—"she has taken a bad fall. I would like you to bathe her and change her into a suitable garment. Handle her gently. When you are finished, fetch more hot water and leave it with the bandages beside the bed."

The two bobbed curtsies and murmured their "yes, my lord's."

With one last look at Olivia, Colin exited, the sound of muffled whispers following him out the door.

Striding down the stairs, he wondered at the maids' fearful attitude. Grandfather must have run his household with an iron fist, he thought to himself. And tight pursestrings, as well, he added. Glancing about him, he noted that on closer inspection, the opulence of the manse showed evidence of its age. Although the house appeared to be meticulously maintained, his discerning eye found the faded velvet draperies at the hall's large windows and the frayed tapestry upholstery on the huge Elizabethan chairs. The silk wallcovering had been neatly patched in a number of areas.

He stood irresolutely in the main hall, realizing he did not know how to find the study where the steward must be awaiting him.

"This way, my lord," Smythe spoke at Colin's elbow. Startled that a man of Smythe's years could move so quickly and so quietly, Colin studied his butler with newfound respect as they continued down the hallway and entered a dark, mahogany-paneled room. The drapes were drawn, casting the already dark room in deep shadows.

"Open the drapes, Smythe. This room resembles a mausoleum."

Moving across the room to see to his master's bidding, Smythe passed by a burgundy leather wing chair. Only after Colin's gaze found him did the occupant of the chair rise to meet the new earl.

Stepping out of the shadows, the man mumbled a greeting, his voice deep and gruff. In his early thirties, hard work and hot sun had aged him prematurely. A threadbare coat encased his stocky figure, stretching tautly across thickly muscled shoulders. His brown, weather-worn face revealed little, although his large hands were tightly clenched against his sides. He stood with his legs widespread and his chin raised high, his stance challenging while his face remained impassive. Sorrelby's steward impressed Colin as a carefully guarded man prepared to do battle.

Since the steward showed no intention of introducing himself, Smythe stepped forward.

"Jack Whitehead, the steward, my lord."

"Sit down, Whitehead," Colin instructed, walking past the man to seat himself behind the enormous mahogany desk. The steward's covert hostility intrigued Colin. He picked up a pen from the desk and reached for a sheaf of paper. He began to write, quickly slashing the words against the parchment. He stopped from time to time, tapping the quill against his temple while he openly studied the overseer.

As the mantel clock loudly ticked off the minutes, Whitehead tried not to reveal his mounting agitation. He stared straight ahead at a point over Colin's shoulder, refusing to meet his eyes. Colin, however, noted the small muscle twitching involuntarily in the man's jaw.

"Military training?" Colin questioned abruptly.

"Aye, m'lord," he answered, his black eyes darting a suspicious look at Colin.

"Good. So you've learned to follow commands, hmm, Whitehead?"

Again, the black eyes briefly pierced him.

"Aye, I have."

"Fine. There is some urgent business in London I want handled immediately. You will need to leave within the half hour."

Colin watched Whitehead digest the information, the steward unable to conceal his bewilderment.

"I am sending you with a letter of authorization," Colin continued brusquely, "to retain a physician. When you arrive in London, contact Lord Preston Campton on Hyde Park. He will assist you in finding someone suitable. It is a four-hour ride to London. I expect you to return, with a physician, within twenty-four hours. Is that understood, Whitehead?"

Rising to his feet, Whitehead curtly nodded. He leaned across the desk and took the letter Colin handed him, looking curiously at his new master. Colin returned the assessing look with equanimity.

Wordlessly Whitehead turned to leave.

"And Whitehead—"

The steward twisted around to face Colin.

"You'll need this." Colin tossed a pouch of coins at the man, who deftly caught it open-palmed.

"Yes, m'lord." He bowed and left.

Running his hand through his jet-black hair, Colin scratched the top of his head. Something was amiss at Sorrelby Hall. He did not need to rely on his espionage experience to deduce as much when chambermaids looked upon their employer with terror and the estate overseer regarded him with thinly veiled hostility.

Thinking of the girl upstairs, Colin wondered if perhaps she was a player in this curious drama. It certainly was most unusual for her to be lurking in tree branches so close to the estate. Squaring his broad shoulders, he arose from the squeaky leather chair, determined to find some answers to the mysterious climate pervading Sorrelby.

Opening the study door, Colin was not surprised to find Smythe standing in the hallway.

"I've taken the liberty of placing your trunks in the master suite, my lord. Mr. O'Shea"—Smythe pursed his lips sourly—"has installed himself in the servants' quarters."

Familiar with O'Shea's cantankerous moods, and certain that the mishap on the road had probably put his manservant in an especially ornery state of mind, Colin hid a lopsided smirk behind his hand in the guise of a cough.

"Hrmph. Very good, Smythe. I am going to see to our patient upstairs. Have O'Shea meet me there posthaste.

"Also, arrange for some broth to be sent up. Oh . . . and a meal for myself as well. I'm famished."

Entering the bedroom, Colin was pleased to find that the maids had finished bathing the young woman. One maid was plaiting Olivia's hair while the other tended the freshly lit blaze in the fireplace.

Completing their tasks, the younger one meekly asked, "Is there anything else you'll be needing us for, my lord?"

"Not now, thank you. You may go."

As they left, O'Shea entered.

"Well, O'Shea, it seems that we're going to have to make use of our battlefield doctoring until the genuine article arrives from London," Colin stated as he removed his dusty coat and began rolling up his white shirtsleeves.

O'Shea groaned loudly in objection but followed Colin's example, moving over to the basin to wash his hands.

The two men worked quickly, determining that the gravest injuries were a swollen, possibly fractured, left ankle and the head contusion. Bandaging the ankle and a scraped knee, Colin was careful to concentrate on Olivia's injuries and not on her silky, coltish legs. Glancing across to his companion, Colin noted that O'Shea's usually ruddy complexion seemed even ruddier as they administered to their exceedingly lovely patient.

After binding the final bandage, Colin walked across the room to the dinner tray which Smythe had brought in earlier. After pouring two glasses of wine, Colin handed one to O'Shea, and the two men sank into the chairs facing the fireplace.

Colin drank deeply from the crystal goblet.

"What is your opinion of Sorrelby, my friend?"

O'Shea tossed back the contents of his glass.

"She's a beauty but in need of work, that's for sure. Ye ought to see the servants' quarters. Newgate must be more comfortable than the cell I'm to be sleeping in. No wonder the house is barely staffed; the conditions are none too inviting."

"Who is on staff?" Colin inquired, raising the silver cover to his plate. Sniffing appreciatively at the enticing meal, he commented, "The chef seems to be worth keeping."

"Aye, the chef is one of Smythe's sons, an agreeable sort, not like his persnickety father."

Colin chortled. "I gathered from Smythe that you two were rubbing each other the wrong way."

O'Shea frowned. "That nervous old hen! Fussin' and fidgetin' about. If ye ask me, the entire household seems to be borderin' on a nervous crisis. Never seen such a jumpy group of characters."

"Yes, I've noted the same. Rather unusual, isn't it?"

Colin swirled the last drops of wine, staring into the bottom of his goblet as if reading tea leaves. If only the future could be so easily forecast, he wryly reflected.

A low moan from the bed arrested his attention. He jumped up from the chair and came to stand beside the bed.

"Oh, please, Henry, cease that infernal hammering," Olivia groaned to herself, one hand moving tentatively to her temple. Her eyelids felt weighted as she struggled to lift them, suddenly realizing that the pounding came not from Henry's mallet but from within her own head.

Running her fingers along her forehead, she found the goose egg responsible for her cranial distress. A lump on my forehead, she mused, too befuddled to recall the circumstances surrounding her fall. She was on the verge of abandoning her efforts to open her eyes, when a low, husky voice quietly asked, "Would you like a drink of water?"

The sound of that voice was a shot of adrenaline to Olivia's nervous system. Her eyes snapped wide as the memory gates flooded open. Visions of hypnotic violet eyes masked behind ridiculously long, dark eyelashes swam before her. A white broadcloth shirt lay open at the neck contrasting sharply against tan skin and black springy curls. As Olivia began to focus more clearly, she saw that it was no vision.

She tried not to stare, but she was feeling extremely disoriented and this man seemed to be the only recognizable feature in the room. Those eyes, that face . . . a dusty road . . . the coach . . . heavens, she had fallen from a tree! And this was Colin Forster, the earl! Olivia closed her eyes again, grimacing as she pieced it all together.

"Are you in pain?"

Olivia dared not shake her pounding head. She looked up to find that the earl had leaned over more closely to catch her response. His face hovered only a foot above hers and she could not stop her involuntary sharp intake of breath.

His eyes narrowed with concern.

"Can you understand me? Are you in pain?"

Biting her lower lip, Olivia took control of herself. She breathed deeply.

Gaining command of her voice, she croaked, "Yes, I understand you, and yes, I am a tad uncomfortable . . . and yes, I would like that drink of water, please."

Colin reached over to the bedtable and poured a glass of water from the pitcher. He then slipped his arm behind Olivia's back and helped her sit up. She felt for a moment as if she were going to lose consciousness again, but after a few seconds she regained her equilibrium. Fleetingly, she wondered if her dizziness was caused by the bump on her head or by the nearness of the earl. Colin brought the glass to her lips and she drank eagerly.

Sitting up, Olivia was able to get a better look around the bedroom. She recognized O'Shea sitting by the fireplace. Colin gently lowered her, stacking the pillows to prop her up into a semi-reclining position.

"Where am I?" Her voice sounded more familiar to her ears now that the water had eased away the dust clogging her throat.

"You're at Sorrelby Hall." Colin towered above her, carefully watching her face for a reaction. She did not appear surprised.

Olivia's kelly-green eyes, clear and candid, looked directly at Colin. "Then you must be the Earl of Sorrelby." She made it a statement of fact. "And who is he?" She did not turn, but pointed a finger toward the fireplace.

"That is O'Shea: valet, coachman, confidant, and family friend. You might not recall that we were unable to complete the introductions on the highway. May we have the pleasure of your name, my lady?"

Olivia found it odd that although the earl's tone of voice was light and humorous, he studied her with a vaguely disquieting intensity.

"My name is Olivia Knowles. I am from Mossgate."

Unconsciously Olivia raised her chin a couple of degrees.

Bowing, Colin intoned, "A pleasure, Miss Knowles."

"O'Shea"—Colin half-turned—"see if you can find some brandy for Miss Knowles."

Swiveling back to address Olivia, he continued, "Unfortunately, we do not have laudanum, but I assure you that brandy works quite nicely."

Colin picked up the bowl of broth as he spoke and came over to sit next to Olivia on the bed. Olivia felt warmth steal into her cheeks as his thigh accidentally grazed her hip. He adjusted his position so that they were no longer touching, but Olivia was not able to forestall the telltale blush.

He raised the spoon and coaxed, "Let's have some broth before O'Shea returns with the brandy, hmm, Miss Knowles?"

Obediently Olivia opened her mouth. After swallowing the nourishing liquid, she peeped at him from beneath her sweeping lashes.

"I am very grateful for your hospitality, but please, my lord, isn't there someone else who can act as nursemaid? I am certain that you must have very important matters to attend to."

"What could possibly be of greater importance than dabbing broth from this delectable chin?"

His purple gaze glittered with humor as he picked up a napkin from the bed's sidetable. She watched his long, bronzed fingers approaching, and then the crisp linen fabric brushed across Olivia's sensitive lower lip causing goose bumps to race up and down her forearms. Olivia recoiled from his touch, distinctly uncomfortable with the unbidden sensation, as previous to this, napkins had never had such a profound impact upon her sensibilities.

Intrigued by her apparent skittishness, Colin continued spooning the broth. Was it shyness or guilt that caused her to pull away from him? Deciding to cut to the heart of the matter, Colin broke the heavy silence.

"By the way, Miss Knowles, I cannot help but wonder as to your reason for scaling that treacherous old oak. Are you perhaps an ornithologist?"

Olivia raised her luminous eyes and looked directly into Colin's chiseled features. Birdwatcher, indeed. Instinctively she knew that he did not believe her to be an ornithologist for even a single second. He had merely tossed it out as an excuse for her to employ if she so desired.

She stated matter-of-factly, "I was spying on you, of course."

The silver spoon paused halfway between the bowl and Olivia's lips. She gleefully congratulated herself on setting the imperturbable earl back a few paces. He was altogether too smug, in Olivia's opinion. Colin, on the other hand, discerning her self-satisfaction, allowed a reluctant smile to drift across his features.

"Of course. How obtuse of me. Perhaps you could enlighten me as to the purpose of your espionage."

Gaining strength with each mouthful of broth, and emboldened by her ability to catch the earl off guard, Olivia's spirited nature began to assert itself. In a syrupy sweet voice, she replied, "Perhaps."

While on the Continent, Colin had viewed Da Vinci's popular *Mona Lisa*, and at this moment he could not help but compare her famous smile to that of the bewitching lass facing him.

Olivia was saved from further elaboration by the entrance of O'Shea.

"Here's your brandy, though I didna have an easy time gettin' it from Smythe. He acted like I was plannin' to sneak off to the stables with it."

He set the tray down on the fireside table.

"Give a shout if ye want me," and he left.

Colin got up and poured a liberal amount of brandy into a crystal snifter. Crossing over to Olivia, he raised the glass to her lips and urged, "Drink this now. It will dull the pain."

Delicately wrinkling her nose at the noxious fumes, she gulped half the contents of the glass. Coughing and sputtering, she gasped for breath, casting an accusing scowl at Colin.

"*Dull the pain?*" she croaked. "By sending liquid fire down my throat?"

Colin's eyes shone with suppressed mirth.

"I apologize," he said, his rich voice heavy with sham solemnity. "I should have realized that you're a novice to the pleasures of brandy. Here, finish it up."

Olivia narrowed her eyes speculatively, a mysterious grin lurking about her mouth.

"I doubt that the vicar would approve of this. Alone in a bedroom with London's most infamous rake who is intent on plying me with drink."

Glancing down, she took note of the heavy cotton nightgown she had been provided. "And in my nightclothes, no less. For shame."

"You need not worry that I will inform the vicar of your current situation," he promised with good humor.

"Oh, but you must!"

An ebony eyebrow shot up with surprise.

"You see, I reside with the vicar and his family." A tiny frown gathered at Olivia's brow. "They must be terribly concerned that I have not yet returned home."

"I will send a messenger immediately."

He proffered the goblet once again, and Olivia finished its contents, albeit with a sour expression.

"Would you like to pen a note, or shall I take care of the missive?" he asked solicitously.

Olivia frowned again and cradled her palm against her aching forehead.

"If you wouldn't mind . . . I am beginning to feel a bit light-headed."

Glad to see that the brandy was taking effect, Colin ordered, "You rest. The physician will be here tomorrow."

Even though sleep was quickly descending upon her, Olivia opened her eyes groggily. "Physician? From where?"

Attuned to her sudden interest, he peered at her curiously and replied, "From London."

As she succumbed to the welcoming arms of Morpheus, Olivia giggled and mumbled half-asleep, "A physician. Isn't that funny?"

Colin stood watching her for a minute or two as she dozed off. He could not shake the feeling that he knew her from somewhere.

"Funny, indeed."

When next Olivia awoke, the room was dark save for the light of the fire and a lamp upon the table. Snoring lightly in the fireside chair was a young maid, her cap askew atop riotous brown curls.

Olivia did not wish to disturb the apparently exhausted girl, but the maid awoke almost immediately, perhaps sensing Olivia's gaze upon her. She hopped out of the chair and scurried to the bed, curtsying as she came. After seeing to Olivia's needs, she excused herself, hurriedly explaining that the earl had given her "strict instructions."

Olivia would have called her back, but the maid was out the door before Olivia realized that she was leaving. Within two minutes the door opened again, and Olivia knew intuitively that the Earl of Sorrelby was entering. She could not begin to comprehend her reaction, but her body seemed to respond to his proximity in the most unsettling fashion. A faint tingling ran across her flesh, warning her of his presence. She felt a trifle annoyed by her reaction, and her expression reflected this annoyance as Colin walked in.

Olivia scrutinized the arrogant planes of his face, the inky-black brows slashing over violet eyes and the sensually molded mouth. He always seems to be vaguely amused, Olivia thought. She generally tended to think the worst of the *ton*, so, rather than attribute his humored countenance to good temper, she preferred to believe it was due to a condescending sense of superiority. She had to admit, though, that he was a magnificent-looking man.

Colin stood impassively while Olivia examined him, absorbed in her thoughts. Only when he spoke did she realize that she had been staring at him from the moment he had entered the room.

"I would ask if I pass inspection, but I fear that the manner in which you are glowering at me is sufficient answer."

She blushed to the roots of her hair, mortified by her ill-bred behavior. Whatever was wrong with her, she groaned to herself.

Stammering like a schoolgirl, she tried to make amends, "I-I-I am so s-s-sorry. I didn't mean to be rude. M-my thoughts were elsewhere."

Colin, in feigned distress, brought his hand to his chest as if he had received a blow.

"Ah, my poor masculine ego is crushed by your indifference."

Olivia realized she was not going to win in this exchange of words and threw up her hands in mock surrender. Laughing, she replied, "My lord, I meant no insult to your ego."

In a more serious tone she continued, "On the contrary, if I appeared displeased, it was directed toward myself, not you."

Colin quickly seized upon that statement. He held up his palm to stop her words, his look warm with appreciation.

"No, my lady, I must object. To my eye, there is nothing displeasing about you."

Flattered, Olivia hid her pleasure behind a jest. Teasing, she replied skeptically, "Oh, yes, I understand that you are quite the connoisseur of women."

Colin shrugged eloquently. "Which renders me eminently qualified to judge."

Prepared to speak, Olivia hesitated. She really did not wish to continue this farce. She seriously doubted that a man like Colin Forster, the Earl of Sorrelby, could be beguiled by her, a naive village girl, ignorant of the ways of men.

Abruptly Olivia decided to confess her earlier plans to the earl. "Well, I believe that you have reason to be displeased with me." Taking a deep breath, she launched into her explanation.

"I am here by design. Well, actually, it was an accident, but there really was not supposed to be an accident, only you were to think that there was. Falling from the tree was an accident, but our meeting was not."

Attempting to follow her story, Colin questioned, "Is this pertinent to your reason for spying on me?"

"Oh, yes," Olivia assured him, nodding. "I was waiting for your coach. I was going to pretend that I had turned my ankle, and when you stopped to assist me, you would discover that Mossgate needed a physician."

Pursing her lips regretfully, she said, "But I guess that you have discovered as much already. You did say that you have sent for a physician, did you not?"

Inordinately pleased, as well as amused, by her blunt confession and her forthright attitude, Colin smiled.

"Yes, I have sent for a physician. But tell me, why the need for all this deception? And how were you elected to bring the matter to my attention?"

Even as the words left his mouth, Colin realized why this lovely country lass was chosen to speak with him— Apparently, the villagers of Mossgate believed they knew his weakness. They probably searched three counties trying to find this beauty to plead their case. But why was all this necessary? Certainly, a request for a physician was a reasonable one. Or did they have cause to doubt that he would approve their appeal?

"I volunteered . . . in a way. And I sincerely apologize for the half-witted plot to enlist your sympathies."

With a heavy sigh she explained, "My greatest shortcoming is pride"—dipping her head to one side, she thoughtfully amended—"or perhaps impetuousness."

"At any rate, I did not relish the idea of begging you, an earl, a nobleman, a peer of the realm—" Olivia's tone sharpened with scorn until she brought herself up short. "Well, I was too proud to speak with you directly."

"I take it you are not enamored of the nobility?" Colin questioned mildly.

Olivia rolled her eyes expressively.

"What good have any of those strutting peacocks you call lords, or their pampered, self-indulgent ladies, ever done for anyone?" Raising her finger, she corrected, "Oh, no, I am forgetting your vast contributions to the realm of fashion."

Invoking her best upper-crust accent, Olivia mocked, "I say, Sherbourne, what an absolutely smashing neckcloth. You must have your valet share his technique with my man. Or—"

Colin's laughter interrupted Olivia in the midst of her performance. She certainly had a gift for mimicry, he thought. Tossing her head just so and gesturing in that imperial manner, she could be mistaken for any number of duchesses or countesses of his acquaintance. And what a changeable creature!

Two minutes ago she was meek as a lamb, begging his pardon for her attempted deception, and now the saucy girl was ridiculing both him and his compatriots. One hardly knew what to expect next from the minx.

Still chuckling, Colin gestured to his own sober attire.

"Surely, we are not all thick-witted dandies. Has the Quality no redeeming qualities?"

Delighted that her playacting had amused instead of offended, Olivia shook her head sadly with mock regret. "I am afraid it's a matter of breeding, my lord. Once born to the aristocracy, you cannot escape it."

Colin dropped his chin to his chest, crestfallen. "I shall endeavor to overcome my patrician imperfections." Raising his head, his eyes twinkled. "Let me begin by inquiring as to your health."

Involved in their witty repartee, Olivia had not been aware of her throbbing ankle or of the headache burgeoning behind her forehead.

"Now that you mention it, I would appreciate another glass of that foul-smelling brandy."

"As you wish. However, I have ordered a meal to be sent up for you. I would recommend dinner first since brandy does not sit well on an empty stomach."

"Thank you for your consideration." Olivia paused. "Ah, my lord . . . I would have you know that my strength is returned and I am quite able to feed myself."

She squirmed slightly under his penetrating gaze. He bowed perfunctorily.

"I am glad that you are improving."

A knock on the door heralded the entrance of the chestnut-haired maid. After the servant set down the tray, Colin quietly instructed her to stay with their patient until she fell asleep for the night.

Addressing Olivia, Colin said as he quit the room, "I will have the brandy sent up for you. I pray you rest well. I shall see you on the morrow."

Chapter Three

"Excuse me, miss, you have a visitor. Miss Margaret Nicholson. Shall I have her sent up?"

Carefully pushing herself up on the pillows, Olivia answered enthusiastically, "Oh, yes, Polly, right away please."

Although it was not yet noon, Olivia was growing weary of her sickbed. Unaccustomed to lounging about, she generally filled her free time with gardening and swimming, riding and long walks. Glaring down at her swollen ankle, Olivia grudgingly resigned herself to the fact that her active lifestyle would have to be curtailed for a few days.

She had awoken early, feeling much refreshed from her long sleep. After Polly had brought breakfast, Olivia dug into the pile of books Colin had thoughtfully selected for her. Although she had already read many of the titles provided, nearly half of the books were new to her, and after some consideration she opened Rousseau's *Emile*. She had learned that at the time of *Emile*'s publication, Rousseau had been forced into exile in Switzerland. So, naturally, any book that could cause such scandal piqued Olivia's curious nature.

She glanced out the window, appreciating the view of the tiny picturesque pond nestled against an oak grove to the south of the manor. Watching the sunlight glint off the blue-green water, Olivia yearned to run across the fields and jump into its welcoming depths, though icy they would be in April.

Her wistful reverie was broken by a knock at the door. Margaret entered the room like a miniature pink whirlwind. Bustling across the room, she fairly flew to Olivia's side and sank onto the bed. The two girls presented a charming contrast—Margaret, a diminutive study in pastels, whereas Olivia was a tall, vibrant splash of color.

Reassured by Olivia's rosy cheeks and calm expression, Margaret grasped her cousin's hand and sighed. "Thank heavens, you're in one piece. When Father received the message last evening, I wanted to come right away, but he said I should wait until this morning. I could hardly sleep last night worrying about you. Whatever happened, Liv?"

Olivia smiled warmly. Goodness, wasn't she lucky to have a family that loved her? She also felt a twinge of guilt that her recklessness could result in poor Maggie losing sleep. Patting Margaret's hand, she briefly related the story of her introduction to the earl.

Margaret made a receptive audience, groaning in sympathy and squealing with delight as the narrative demanded. After Olivia had finished her tale, Margaret observed that her friend had omitted some extremely pertinent details.

"So, is he handsome?" she asked excitedly. "At the very least, he must be tremendously charming to have so many women head over heels about him."

"Yes, he is devilishly handsome and oozes charm from every pore of his aristocratic being."

Margaret frowned at Olivia's sarcastic tone.

"My, but you're cross. It doesn't sound as if you like him very much." Suddenly alarmed, she asked anxiously, "Has he been forward with you?"

Olivia sighed. "No, he has not made any unwelcome advances. In fact, he has been nothing but solicitous of my health and well-being.

"Frankly, Maggie, I think I like him *too* much. I was positively determined to despise him, but I . . . I just can't. I mean, I don't even know him, and yet he . . ." Olivia trailed off helplessly.

Margaret's sky-blue eyes searched Olivia's averted face. In a reassuring voice she pressed, "What do you mean, Olivia?"

Turning trustfully back to her friend, Olivia tried to explain. "I only met him yesterday, but it seems as if I have known him before. We laugh and talk together easily. I feel comfortable with him." Gently biting her lower lip, she added, "And at the same time frightfully uncomfortable. He makes me feel strange—a funny, prickly feeling. I don't like it. Especially in light of his reputation."

Nodding her blond head, Margaret assured her that she understood completely.

"Oh, yes, that does sound ominous. Certainly, no one has ever made me feel prickly." Her eyes widened to the size of small saucers, and she asked in a squeaky voice, "Liv, you aren't attracted to him, are you?"

Olivia looked thoroughly horrified at the suggestion, and before she could muster up a proper protest, there was a sharp knock at the door. A frisson of anticipation ran up Olivia's spine, virtually announcing the person knocking before his satiny baritone rang out, "Miss Knowles, the physician is here. May we enter?"

"Ah, yes, please do."

Colin entered, accompanied by a youngish, bespectacled man carrying an enormous black leather bag. Colin introduced him as Mossgate's new physician, Mr. Leonard Browning, and Olivia then introduced Margaret. Maggie shot Olivia a quick, comprehending glance.

Colin cut a most dashing figure this morning in a charcoal coat, black riding boots, and black breeches clinging snugly to his muscled thighs. Only his pristine white cravat and piercing purple eyes offered any colorful relief to the somber attire.

Margaret and Colin discreetly moved over to the fireplace to seat themselves while the physician made his examination. Removing bandages and tools one by one, Mr. Browning put on an elaborate show of laying them out single file on the coverlet. He explained to Olivia that his instruments were of the latest and most innovative designs to be obtained. He questioned her as to pain here and there while gently poking and prodding with a variety of the unfamiliar instruments. Olivia watched him with interest, while also straining to hear the muffled conversation between Colin and Margaret in the background.

After a few minutes Mr. Browning cleared his throat, prepared to announce his diagnosis.

Encompassing both Margaret and Colin in his delivery, he began, "It appears that Miss Knowles's head injury will heal with rest. A painful contusion, but aside from headache, I do not predict any complications. However, the ankle is more difficult to assess." Studying his twiddling thumbs, he adopted a rather professional-looking scowl of concentration.

"The ankle, I fear, might be fractured. I suggest two weeks of complete rest. After that time, I should be able to determine if it be strained or broken."

"May she return home?" Margaret asked with concern.

The physician shook his head vehemently. "I could not possibly recommend a ride across that pothole-laden road. The jarring might worsen her condition." Rubbing his eyes beneath his wire-rimmed glasses, he added, "I, myself, am still somewhat dizzy from the coach ride here."

Margaret murmured something sympathetic about the terrible state of the roadway, when, standing, Colin took command.

"Well, then, it is decided. Miss Knowles will convalesce here. Mr. Browning, please accept my hospitality, also, until a house can be readied for you in Mossgate. Miss Nicholson has kindly offered to assist in preparing a cottage for your use."

Margaret lowered her lashes bashfully as the physician thanked her for her kindness.

Colin looked directly at Olivia as he spoke to Mr. Browning. "Let me thank you again for agreeing to take up residence in our small part of the world. You cannot imagine the enthusiastic welcome awaiting you in Mossgate."

The good doctor picked up his leather bag, replying, "London did not really suit me." With a fleeting smile at Margaret, he added, "And I believe I shall enjoy the country life."

Colin spent the afternoon with the steward, Whitehead, closeted in the study, poring over the books. He found the accounting to be less than organized and the steward to be less than helpful. Hedged answers such as "I don't remember" or "I'll have to check" were his responses to the majority of Colin's inquiries regarding the deplorable condition of the accounts. Colin would have sent him packing then and there if not for the fact that he sensed Whitehead was hiding something. He knew Whitehead to be an intelligent man, thus Colin found his pleas of ignorance unacceptable. Experienced in ferreting out closely guarded secrets, Colin was disinclined to terminate the steward until he had unraveled the mystery.

Furthermore, he could not understand how his grandfather, a penny-pincher to the end, would allow his financial records to fall into such a muddle. From what Colin had learned from his grandfather's solicitor in London, Horace's sole pleasure in life had been money. After having banished his son, Reginald, from his home, Horace had become embittered and obsessed with wealth, living in seclusion at Sorrelby Hall. According to the solicitor, Horace Forster had not once left the estate in over three decades.

After Whitehead's departure, Colin opened the safe behind his grandfather's portrait. Deeds, promissory notes, a vast jewelry collection, and numerous bank vouchers evidenced the staggering riches Horace had accumulated over the years. At a time when the country's economy faltered, Horace had succeeded in doubling his assets. Reflecting on the poverty so evident in Mossgate, Colin surmised that many must have suffered so that Horace could prosper.

Colin had already instructed Smythe to hire twenty or so additional servants from the village and four times that many had applied for positions. The existing servants, though admirably loyal to the estate, were sadly overworked. The laundress was doing the job of three women, while only one assistant was available to the master cook. Smythe, assuming the roles of both head butler and housekeeper, had only four footmen and three maidservants to assist him in the running of the formidable estate. The manse, comprising eight bedrooms, four sitting rooms, three parlors, a study, a library, a state drawing-room, a ballroom, a small chapel and cloister, the greenhouse, servants' quarters, and a servants' hall, demanded, at a minimum, Colin estimated, forty to fifty houseservants.

As for the steward, Colin ordered him to double the number of farmworkers currently laboring in the fields, and to retain three additional groomsmen, four more gardeners, a falconer, a gameskeeper, and a blacksmith.

Another pressing issue involved the refurbishing of Sorrelby Hall. It was Colin's desire to return the gracious manor house to its previous brilliance. Although most of the materials would have to come through London, he could utilize Mossgate's labor force, which would have the additional benefit of improving the villagers' severe economic situation.

The amount of work and money involved in his proposed renovation was staggering, but Colin relished such a challenge. Upon returning to London, he could personally select the fabrics, the furniture, and the art best suited for Sorrelby's palatial presence.

Returning to London, however, meant returning to the matrimonial foxhunt, and Colin was not eager to fling himself back into the fray. Mentally cursing himself for his cowardice, he nonetheless decided to delay his return to London until after the arrival of his mother and sisters. They were scheduled to arrive within the fortnight, and he was eager to see them, as it had been many months since he had last visited his childhood home. Although he knew that his mother would object to such generosity, he intended to purchase a London house for her. His sisters were coming of age, and he wanted each of them to experience a proper Season in London, including the requisite frippery and gowns mandated by the endless parties and balls.

Katherine, the oldest of the sisters, should rightfully have been presented last season, but his mother rejected Colin's offer to finance her coming out. Deirdre Forster had refused, arguing that Colin's earnings should be funneled into his expanding trade.

But now, thanks to his grandfather's fortune, Colin could provide handsomely for his family.

Upstairs, Olivia was also thinking of her family: both the parents she had lost as a child, and the family who had lovingly adopted her. Orphaned at the age of seven, Olivia had arrived in Mossgate twelve years ago to take up residence with the Vicar Nathan Nicholson, Olivia's father's first cousin. The vicar and his wife, Joan, had welcomed Olivia as a daughter, raising her with the same unquestioning love they bestowed on their own two children. Henry and Margaret had been equally accepting of their new cousin, and the three had proved to be inseparable over the years, forging a bond as close as any siblings.

Having been gently raised by loving and tolerant parents, the Nicholson children, and Olivia, had enjoyed a measure of freedom not generally afforded in English households. Nathan and Joan encouraged the development of each of their charge's individual interests and talents. They spoke freely between themselves and often heatedly debated subjects ranging from politics to art.

As Olivia grew, Uncle Nathan had furnished her with a history of her father's family, but on her mother's side, she knew little. Her mother had also been orphaned at a young age and had been raised by a fisherman and his family who had found her half-drowned on the banks of the Shannon River. Aunt Joan had told Olivia that she bore a remarkable likeness to her mother, a fact that secretly warmed Olivia. Unable to recall many memories of her parents, at the very least, she was glad that she carried a likeness of her mother in her own face.

Shrugging off her brief melancholy, she turned her thoughts to the Nicholsons. Although she was delighted that the earl had retained a physician, the doctor's presence would now present a void in the family's small income. In the past Olivia had earned a shilling or sixpence here and there plying her limited medical skills. Now, she thought, she would need to find another way to contribute to the household coffers. Although the Nicholsons were better off than most of the villagers, Olivia would not consider residing with them unless she could pay her way. A position as a private governess or schoolteacher might have to be investigated since there was little else Olivia was qualified to do.

Maggie would be disconsolate if Olivia left Mossgate, but they both must look to the future. Recalling the surreptitious glances exchanged earlier between Maggie and Mr. Browning, Olivia thought she wouldn't be the least bit surprised if Maggie were a physician's wife within the year. In fact, Maggie had chattered away the entire afternoon, enthusiastically praising the young physician's insightful diagnosis of Olivia's condition.

The crimson sunset had just yielded to the deep indigo of evening dusk when Polly entered carrying a supper tray. Olivia was surprised to see her then lay the small fireside table for two, setting out the Waterford crystal, Limoges china, and family-monogrammed silver. The luxurious setting was surpassed by the succulent aroma of roast duck wafting across the room to whet Olivia's appetite. She was about to ask Polly to bring her a plate when Colin entered, a chess set under his arm.

"Miss Knowles," he greeted, his deep, masculine voice caressing Olivia, "you are looking much improved from this morning."

Intent on suppressing the ever-present "prickliness" assaulting her senses, Olivia answered somewhat coolly, "Lord Sorrelby."

Colin gestured to the linen-clad table. "I hope you do not mind if I join you for supper. We have had so little opportunity to talk."

"I am honored."

Measuring at a glance the distance from the bed to the table, Colin shook his head, "This won't do. Polly, bring over that footstool there."

A slight frown of annoyance flitted across Colin's face as he noted the way Polly nearly tripped over her feet, rushing to his bidding. Placing the footstool where indicated, she curtsied no less than three times before nervously raising her face to the earl. Exasperated by the staff's constant show of timidness, he nonetheless offered the maidservant a smile prior to dismissing her. The girl eagerly scuttled out the door.

Moving to Olivia's side, Colin bowed. "Miss Knowles, may I take you in to supper?"

Olivia scowled up at him in confusion. "What do you mean, my lord?"

Bending over, Colin flipped back the silk coverlet and picked up Olivia as if she weighed no more than the goose-down pillow on which she lay. Olivia squawked in dismay. Prepared to protest his casual handling of her person, the words died on her lips as he set her down in the chair and gently placed the injured ankle upon the tapestried footstool.

Colin stoked the fire while Olivia mentally castigated herself for her adolescent overreaction to his touch. Of course, it meant nothing to him; he was only assisting her. How was he to know that each and every fiber of her being came alive at his touch? Vowing to remain relaxed, Olivia reached for her wineglass and took a fortifying drink. Dinner was superb and Colin acted the perfect host, serving her from the covered dishes and inquiring as to whether she found the meal to her taste.

Olivia discussed her impressions of *Emile*, as well as other reading she had recently enjoyed, and the two had a lively discussion regarding censorship and the role of government. Colin found himself laughing half a dozen times at some outrageous comment on her part.

"You certainly speak your mind, don't you, Miss Knowles?"

"Better I speak my own thoughts than merely echo someone else's, wouldn't you agree?" she asked, cocking her head in an unconsciously coquettish fashion.

Raising his glass to her, he concurred, "I do."

The firelight cast a warm glow to Olivia's alabaster features, and Colin felt hard-pressed not to reach out his hand to her petal-soft cheek. Enveloped in the snowy-white nightgown, she appeared to him to be nothing short of angelic. There was a purity and innocence to her features that belied the sensual promise hidden in the emerald depths of her eyes. And in that moment Colin knew that he wanted to awaken that slumberous passion. He wanted to hold her in his arms and kiss her until her breath came fast between those ruby lips. His wayward thoughts were creating havoc in his tightly molded pants, and he shifted uncomfortably in the overstuffed chair.

Reining in his imagination, Colin inquired, "Do you play chess?"

"Yes, I love to play," Olivia answered with delight. "My uncle adores chess and is forever coercing one of us into a game. However, I should advise you," she teased with an admonishing finger, "that I am an above-average player."

A sly grin spread across Colin's face, reminding Olivia of a fox in a henhouse. "So, you think you're that good, eh? Well then, how about a little wager?"

Immediately on guard, she asked cautiously, "Such as?"

Shrugging his broad shoulders, he responded casually, "Oh, nothing really. Let's just say a favor. The loser will owe the victor a favor, agreed?"

Olivia thought the prize innocent enough and assented.

After the first dozen moves, she realized that she would need to play masterfully to best her astute opponent. While she played with verve and daring, his stratagem was cold, precise logic. Even though she tried to confound him with her slightly unorthodox style, he seemed to uncannily anticipate her every move. She played valiantly, and actually had him on the ropes at one point, but he recovered to win.

As he checkmated her king, Olivia clapped her hands. "That was wonderful! I have rarely had such a good game."

Colin smiled and accepted her congratulations. "Thank you for the fine competition. You are most gracious in defeat."

"I enjoyed myself tremendously."

Eyes glinting, Colin reminded her, "I will collect that favor at a later date, agreed?"

Although a spark of apprehension recalled their wager, Olivia smiled confidently. "Agreed."

Over the next few days, Olivia established a routine in her confinement. In the morning she read until her visitors arrived. Either Maggie, the vicar and his wife, the physician, or a friend from the village would call on her each day. They brought news from Mossgate, including rumors of Lord Sorrelby's altruistic plans to resurrect the town's sagging economy. All were curious about the earl and plied Olivia with as many questions as they could politely pose. Much was made of Mr. Browning's arrival, and Olivia deflected any credit for her part in procuring the physician. She stated time and time again that all thanks were due the earl. She enjoyed the visits but found it difficult to respond to the queries regarding her host.

Gossip surrounding him was widespread. All of Mossgate knew of his reputation with women. Olivia tried to minimize that side of his character by emphasizing his gentlemanly behavior with her, but the majority of people were too fascinated with his almost legendary philandering to heed her opinion. In truth, Olivia did not like to think of the other women in his life. A tiny kernel of jealousy stirred in her breast whenever some visitor reminded her of Colin's infamous past. Although she had yet to overcome her disdain of the upper class, she preferred to set Colin aside from his irresponsible and fun-loving peers. In doing so, she was also inclined to pretend to herself that his rakehell reputation was more fantasy than fact.

He joined her for dinner each evening, and they talked, laughed, played chess and cards. Olivia found herself eagerly awaiting Polly and the dinner tray, deceiving herself that the deliciously prepared meals were the attraction. When Colin entered, dressed in his conservative, yet elegant, dark garb, his hair invariably tousled from impatient fingers, Olivia felt inordinately pleased to see him. She did not choose to examine her feelings too closely, but instead simply enjoyed his company and their time together.

One evening the conversation turned to London, and Olivia proceeded to interrogate Colin about life in the capital. His satirical description of the Regency and its gilded trappings, while reinforcing Olivia's low opinion of the aristocracy, also made her laugh.

He described one truly elaborate fete at Carlton House where the two-hundred-foot-long tables were decorated with miniature streams, complete with sand, moss, and rocks. Swimming in the tiny rivers between the serving dishes were live gold and silver fish. Unfortunately, Colin explained, before the dinner was complete, the oxygen-starved fish began floating belly up, spoiling many of the diners' appetites. Some of the more inebriated guests, however, mistakenly confused the deceased fish with the fourth course.

Wiping the tears from her eyes, Olivia laughed. "It all sounds magnificent and completely mad! Do not tell me you frequent that type of soiree regularly?"

Colin shrugged good-naturedly. "Although it is difficult to refuse an invitation from the Regent, I am not really one of his crowd. Even if I can avoid the palace, I cannot stay away from London due to my shipping business."

"I never thought I would pity you, my lord, but I almost begin to." She sank back into her chair smiling, exhausted from the constant laughter.

Over the rim of his wineglass, Colin watched Olivia arrange the wool shawl over her swollen ankle propped carefully upon a footstool. He wanted her. He could not escape that fact. The past five evenings in her company had increasingly whetted his sexual awareness of her. She laughed so easily, throwing back her head to expose her creamy throat. Witty, bright, and well read, he often took a controversial stand on an issue merely to enjoy her intelligent counterargument. When vehemently arguing a point, she had a tendency to gesticulate in such a manner that her bosom heaved up and down, ultimately causing Colin to lose his train of thought. But as much as he desired her, she was an innocent, and Colin was too much the gentleman to seduce a young girl. If only . . .

Colin's head shot up with surprise as an idea dawned. Of course, he thought, how perfect the solution! It was so obvious he was amazed that the idea had not come to him before. The answer to all his needs.

"A game of chess tonight, my lord?" Olivia asked in her soft, melodic voice, interrupting his contemplation.

"What? Oh, yes. I'll get the board."

Distracted, Colin did not play well, and Olivia capitalized on his lack of concentration. Moving her queen across the board with a flourish, she exclaimed with ill-concealed glee, "Checkmate."

Smacking his palm against his knee, Colin grumbled half-serious, "I, unfortunately, am *not* a gracious loser."

Picking up his now defunct king, Olivia waggled it back and forth under his nose. "Come now," she teased, "you cannot begrudge me one game after you've taken at least six from me. Or have you had so little experience with defeat?"

Colin's eyes twinkled as he surveyed his opponent.

"I urge you not to press your luck, brave one." He spoke softly, the lighthearted teasing voice deepening, becoming hypnotically seductive. "I almost always achieve what I desire."

Wondering what the earl desired, Olivia held his mesmerizing stare. Fleetingly she pictured a small golden field mouse cornered by a sleek ebony cat. Colin Forster was certainly more dangerous than any tabby she had ever known. His smooth black hair and feline grace reminded her more of a panther, cunning and powerful.

Colin read the apprehension in her face and was pleased. She is not afraid of me, he thought, but of how I make her feel. Taking that as a good sign, he smiled and arose slowly from the chair.

"Good night, my lady. And congratulations on your victory."

Colin spent the greater part of the next day formulating his plan. Once decided on his course of action, he felt certain that everyone involved would benefit. The trick, of course, would be convincing Miss Olivia Knowles of the validity of his proposal. The time they had spent together this past week had been enjoyable, he felt, for both of them. She appeared to welcome his company, and he was man enough to sense that she was not indifferent to him physically.

Resting the pen upon the desktop, Colin linked his fingers together and cradled them behind his head as he leaned back in the burgundy leather chair. He glanced at the clock perched on the mantel and saw that it was almost teatime. Time to make his opening move on the lovely Miss Knowles.

Rising, he walked over to the portrait of Horace Forster and moved it aside. A large, black velvet box lay atop a pile of papers inside the wall safe. Colin removed the box and rang for Smythe.

Within seconds Smythe appeared.

"Smythe, Miss Knowles and I will take tea on the garden patio. I presume her guests have departed?"

"Yes, my lord, the last left about twenty minutes ago."

"Fine."

Ascending the grand marble staircase, Colin noted that his heart beat a little more quickly than the norm. Deriding himself for his foolishness, he slowed down. He knocked upon the door, and Olivia answered, "You may come in, my lord."

He entered to find her sitting at the window, her needlepoint in hand. Wearing one of her own dresses that Maggie had brought from home, she looked enchanting. Colin could not fathom how a simply made, green cotton gown could look so lovely. Perhaps it was the way her kelly-green eyes matched the color of her dress? Or was it the sunshine kissing her golden hair as it curled gracefully down her back?

Smiling with obvious pleasure, he asked, "Have you magical powers that you knew it was me at the door?"

Lowering her eyes, she joked, "Well, I am half-Irish and perhaps a bit fey."

Colin leaned casually against the door, his muscled legs spread wide, his arms folded across his broad chest. "I am half-Irish, also, and I have never been able to see through oak doors."

An impish smile was Olivia's only response.

Straightening from the door, he asked, "Would you care to join me for tea downstairs?"

Olivia's face brightened. "I would dearly love to leave this room!" Her face fell slightly as she remembered the physician's warning. "But won't Mr. Browning object?"

Colin walked over to Olivia, his tall form dwarfing her as she sat in the tiny boudoir chair.

"He said that your ankle should not be jostled, but I promise not to jostle you in the slightest." Bowing slightly, he asked softly, "May I?"

Without a word Olivia innocently raised her arms to him so that he could lift her, and Colin felt something turn over in his chest. She was so open and free; so entirely different from the women he had known. He lifted her with care and carried her downstairs. Neither spoke, both too conscious of the other's warm, unfamiliar body pressed against their own.

Colin carried her down the hallway and out to the patio, where Smythe had arranged a table under the shade of a small maple tree. The courtyard patio was laid out in a detailed pattern, boxwood forming a neat hedge and brilliant green backdrop to the freshly bloomed spring blossoms.

"How lovely!" Olivia exclaimed as Colin carefully deposited her upon the chair and lifted her ankle to the cushioned ottoman placed there by the efficient Smythe.

Glancing around, Colin concurred, "Yes, it is, isn't it? Excuse me a moment, I have forgotten something."

Olivia admired the beautifully kept garden and felt a tiny stab of homesickness thinking of her aunt's flower-filled garden at home. Closing her eyes, she lifted her face to the warm spring air and breathed deeply of the fragrant lilac perfuming the patio. Although she was momentarily homesick, she felt unaccountably happy.

Colin returned carrying a large box and a sheaf of paper. He seated himself, his expression somewhat abashed.

"I was hoping that you could assist me in a project for which I am ill-suited."

Her eyes wide with surprise that the capable Earl of Sorrelby would need *her* help, Olivia answered quickly, "Of course I will help. I do owe you that favor after all," she added, dimpling. "But what is it?" she asked curiously, craning her neck to look into the box as Colin opened the lid.

She gasped as he revealed a collection of stones that would rival the crown jewels. Emeralds, diamonds, rubies, and sapphires sparkled blindingly in the afternoon sun. Ropes of pearls commingled with brooches, earrings, and necklaces.

"Good heavens, it's a king's ransom! Perhaps two kings," she amended.

Colin noted that her apparent amazement was devoid of greed or envy. She seemed impressed by the display, but not covetous.

"Would you please assist me in cataloguing this mess? I'm afraid that my description of this here"—he held up a sapphire pendant—"'blue thingamabob' would not suffice for my solicitors."

Olivia took a sip of her tea and chewed distractedly upon a cucumber sandwich.

"Well, yes," she offered hesitantly, "but you must know that I am not too knowledgeable in this field."

Handing her the paper and quill, Colin shrugged in an

offhanded manner. "Any help you could lend would be deeply appreciated."

Still holding the pendant, he asked, "Now, what would you call this?"

Olivia pursed her lips and thought for a moment.

"Emerald-cut sapphire on gold filigree chain."

Sitting back in his chair as if well satisfied, Colin exclaimed heartily, "Now, that's much better! Nice work."

As Olivia examined another necklace, Colin drained his teacup.

"I have another *small* problem," he began slowly. Olivia mumbled a vague "hmm?" under her breath as she studied the ruby and diamond necklace and scrawled a description on the ledger.

"Since inheriting my grandfather's title, and especially his riches, I have encountered . . . some difficulties."

Glancing up, Olivia grinned. "Ah, that we should all be so afflicted."

"I do not deny the many advantages; however, I have paid a price for this title," he related soberly, his voice carefully laced with a touch of regret. "My freedom.

"Morning, noon, and night, I have been besieged by the most mercenary fortune hunters. My quiet, well-organized routine has been completely disrupted to the point where my business is suffering. Everywhere I turn, unmarried ladies have been shamelessly pressing their attentions upon me, rendering me a virtual prisoner in my own home."

Olivia's chin jutted up. "How unfortunate for you," she retorted sarcastically, unaware that jealousy threaded her voice. She returned her attention to the jewelry case and selected another piece.

Studying her annoyed little frown, Colin struggled not to burst out laughing. Maintaining his serious mien, he continued, "I know what you are thinking. 'The Devil's Darling' would welcome such attentions, but the truth of the matter is, I do not."

Olivia purposefully kept her gaze fixed upon the sapphire brooch.

"I am reluctant even to return to London, the situation is so intolerable."

Olivia glanced up as Colin ran his fingers through a wealth of black, silky curls, his expression one of consternation. She had rarely seen him so somber; no laughter sparkled in his eyes and he appeared truly troubled. Although Olivia privately thought he overstated the direness of the situation, she felt moved to sympathy by his downcast countenance.

She lay her small, white hand upon his and teased, "Come, it can't be as bad as that. I cannot imagine you running from anyone, much less a pack of panting females. Surely, you can find a solution to your problem."

"What would you recommend?" he asked with knitted brows.

"Well, you could renounce your title and wealth," she proposed.

"Yes," Colin slowly drawled, as if weighing her proposition, "but would it be fair of me to saddle some distant relative with the same predicament?"

Wrinkling her nose, Olivia shook her head. She doubted that anyone, unless blessed with Colin's famously good looks, would be nearly as desirable based only on a silly title and some money.

"Hmm," she thought aloud, "you must think of something to make you less appealing."

Colin, sneaking a peak at her from the corner of his eye, fought to keep his lips pursed together.

"Quite right. Less appealing."

They both sat silent for a long minute, contemplating Colin's predicament. Abruptly Colin smacked the side of his head with his flat palm. Olivia's eyes flew to his expectantly.

"The answer, of course, is simply to remove the carrot of my bachelorhood."

In the face of Olivia's befuddled expression, he picked up a stunning emerald-and-diamond ring from the box and held it up to the fading sunlight. She followed his movement, her eyes riveted upon the glittering ring. The garden was unusually quiet save for the whisper of a hummingbird's wings hovering about the shrubbery.

Colin's granite features were darkly serious in the shade of the maple tree as he extended the ring to Olivia. His deep voice reverberated throughout the garden.

"Would you do me the honor of becoming my wife?"

Chapter Four

RARELY IN OLIVIA's life had she been shocked speechless. She desperately wanted to laugh. In fact, she needed to explode with laughter, but her voice had temporarily abandoned her. Without warning, the tiniest of giggles erupted, shaking her slender shoulders. Another was quick to follow, and as she clapped her hand over her mouth to stifle the inevitable guffaws, she noted from the corner of her eye that Colin did not appear to share her amusement. He watched her with disquieting intensity, the expression on his devastatingly handsome face so serious that Olivia abruptly choked on her laughter.

The smile faded from her face and her humor slowly evaporated to be replaced with growing dismay.

"Surely you jest?" she ventured hesitantly. When he did not respond, but maintained his expressionless composure, she asked again, "It *was* a joke, was it not?"

On the other side of the table Colin fought to subdue his irrational, yet mounting, indignation. To think that the first honest proposal of marriage he had presented a lady should be met with a laugh in his face! Unbelievable! His cronies at White's would love to hear of this! Ruefully Colin had to admire the irony of the situation. After evading the altar these past dozen years, the proverbial shoe was now on the other foot. He wished to wed, and his chosen bride was, at the moment, staring at him as if he had suddenly grown horns and sprouted a tail.

Colin drew himself up a bit as he answered with a slight smile, "I assure you that I am not in the habit of tossing around marriage proposals in jest. My offer for you is most sincere."

Olivia was nothing short of appalled. Her jade-green eyes widened perceptibly and she asked herself if perhaps the blow to her head had altered her hearing. She could not begin to fathom playing the role of a countess! Hobnobbing with those phony folk who considered themselves "high society"? Egads, did she look like someone who would enjoy that type of nonsense? The only question she could think to pose was a strangled "Why?"

"Why?" he repeated. "There are a number of reasons I should choose to marry. As I explained, I need a wife. I cannot tolerate the constant interruption of having young misses thrust at me left and right. I need to see to my business in London and get on with my life."

"But why *me*? I know virtually nothing of your social circle, and what I do know of it, I abhor!"

"Your lack of social training matters little to me. I do not plan to entertain frequently in London, and as my wife, your primary residence would be here at Sorrelby.

"Besides," Colin added almost as an afterthought, "you are a singularly beautiful young woman. Any man would be proud to call you his own."

Blushing and stammering, Olivia tried to voice her strongest objection, her voice faltering on the edge of panic. "But . . . but I am not in love with you. And I am quite certain that you are not in love with me, either!"

Colin dismissed her protest with a shrug. "Very few couples of my acquaintance are in love at the time of their marriage. And I believe that we would get along well together." Pausing, he questioned, "Unless . . . have you already a beau, Olivia?"

"I'd say that's none of your affair!" she exclaimed heatedly. Good Lord, he was talking about marriage as if it were a business proposal! Honestly, the nerve to presume . . . She did not even like the aristocracy, and the last thing she desired to do was marry into it! Gathering her wits, she decided to conclude this foolishness before she lost sight of her barely contained temper.

With more force than she intended, she responded, "But just

because I am not in love with someone else does not mean that I am going to marry you! Really, my lord, I intend no offense, but the answer is *no*!"

With an emphatic little shove, she pushed away the diamond-and-emerald ring he had held out to her.

Colin narrowed his eyes thoughtfully as he concentrated upon the next tack to take with the redheaded spitfire facing him. Instinctively he had known that she would not accept his proposal gracefully, but his ego had not anticipated such a vehement refusal.

Casually pocketing the ring, Colin inquired, "Since marriage does not seem likely, may I ask what are your plans for the future?"

Olivia winced as he unknowingly hit a nerve. That very subject had been troubling her these past few days. She was nineteen, a grown woman, with no plans to wed. Realistically the only option available to a gently bred woman, aside from marriage, would be to take a position as a governess. However, she had remained uncertain whether or not to pursue that path as it would mean leaving Mossgate. But she adamantly refused to reveal her niggling little insecurities to His High-and-Mighty Lordship!

"I have been giving my future much thought, my lord," Olivia began, her haughty little chin set stubbornly. "I have decided to pursue a position as a governess."

Colin leaned back against the cushioned chair and allowed a ghost of a smile to drift across his face. Steepling his fingers together in a thoughtful manner, he observed the young lady he had selected for his wife. With her head held high, she feigned a sudden fascination with the flowering lilac bush to her left, avoiding his gaze. Her cheeks were bright pink with confusion, and her deep green eyes sparkled angrily. The stiffly erect posture she held thrust into evidence the alluring curve of her breasts, generating in Colin a painful ache of desire. No, he said to himself, she did not resemble any nanny he had ever had the good fortune to meet.

"My dear, I do not wish to seem pessimistic; however, I seriously doubt that you will be able to find a position as a governess looking the way you do," Colin said, gesturing toward her with a wave of his hand.

Self-consciously Olivia looked down at her dated, green gown. Granted, she thought, the dress is not in the height of fashion, but it still was not yet ready for the rag pile.

"I would like to think that my credentials would be of greater importance than my meager wardrobe," she countered lightly.

"No, my sweet, you misunderstand me," Colin answered with a cynical chuckle and a shake of his dark head. "Your wardrobe is of no detriment. It is your beauty. I do not know many women who would hire you to live in their house as a constant temptation to both husbands and sons. Most nannies' appearance is less, shall we say . . . appealing. And, you, Olivia, are most appealing. Silken, willowy, and graceful. Like this lily," and he gently stroked the petals of the flower growing to the side of the table.

In spite of herself, Olivia turned to him, to watch the softly spoken words fall from his lips and the strong, sensitive fingers trace the curve of the lily's petals.

"And if, lovely lily, by chance you are hired by the man of the household instead of the mistress"—he paused, his voice growing colder with each word—"you will most likely find yourself deflowered before you are even shown the way to the schoolroom."

Olivia gasped at his callous prediction and drew back slightly. Colin had not purposefully spoken so harshly, but the mere idea of Olivia in such a situation ignited a fury within him the likes of which he could not explain.

Bringing his hand to rest lightly upon hers, he murmured contritely, surprised by his own volatile reaction. "Forgive me, Olivia, I did not wish to frighten you. I only fear that being raised in the country, in a vicarage, no less, you have little understanding of the darker side of the world."

Her eyes troubled, she withdrew her hand and laid it in her lap.

"You are correct, my lord. I have had little experience with the baser side of human nature." She set her jaw firmly, declaring, "But do not think me naive. If your exalted peers are ruthless ravishers of innocent employees, I will forgo a career that places me at the mercy of the upper class. I will become a schoolmistress then. In the country," she emphasized, "with people of my own ilk."

Colin groaned to himself. Now he had done it, blast it! He had unwittingly set her even more staunchly against the aristocracy. Whereas most women of his acquaintance would leap at the chance to wed an earl and become a countess, his title was proving a handicap in his courtship of the headstrong Miss Knowles. Confound it, why must she be so biased against the nobility!

With a grim smile of determination, Colin crossed his muscled arms across his chest. All right, he mused, if she wants to be obstinate about this and deny her attraction to me, while hiding behind her reverse snobbery, I can play the game better than she. Patience and tenacity had always served him well, and when Colin set himself a goal, he was relentless in its pursuit.

Sipping his second cup of lukewarm tea, he carefully measured his words before throwing down the verbal gauntlet.

"Since I have no choice but to accept your rejection of my proposal, I will do so—this time. However," he warned with a suggestively wicked gleam in his eye, "as far as I am concerned, the matter is not closed. I want you for my wife, and make no mistake, I will do my utmost to persuade you to accept me."

Following suit, Olivia spunkily crossed her arms across her soft bosom, forcing the curves to swell enticingly above the neckline of her gown.

"I pray you do not exhaust yourself in futile effort, my lord. I am simply not interested."

Both amused and irritated by her show of bravado, Colin decided to remind the brazen little miss just whom she was toying with. Lowering his voice to a dangerously soft whisper, he arose menacingly from the chair to tower over her as he asked, "Then if our conversation is concluded, shall I take you back upstairs?"

Refusing to be intimidated by his overpowering masculinity, Olivia subdued the quiver in her voice and maintained a cool facade. "Yes, please."

Although her insides were churning like a whirlpool, she refused to show her agitated state to the earl. Steeling herself against the seductive warmth of his arms, she gritted her teeth as Colin reached down and lifted her from the chair.

In the past, he had always carried her impersonally, careful to transport her quickly and with the minimum of bodily contact. On this occasion, however, he cradled her high against his chest, holding her so closely that their breaths intermingled. Determinedly, Olivia kept her head down although she could feel his eyes upon her.

Looking over Colin's shoulder at the tea table, Olivia questioned, concerned, "But what about the jewels?"

With a glance backward, Colin answered, "I am not worried that I shall be robbed within the walls of my own house." She felt his gaze return to the top of her downcast head.

"I hope that I can still count on your assistance in cataloguing the jewelry?"

"Yes, of course," she declared, somewhat annoyed at his insinuation that she would now renege. Rashly she raised her eyes to meet his and instantly realized her error. He was so close that Olivia could see her reflection in the limpid violet pools of his eyes. She knew that she should turn away, but some inner force compelled her to indulge herself, if only this once, and she greedily drank in the face above her. She followed the intelligent forehead to the slash of ebony eyebrows, past those unforgettable eyes to his narrow, patrician nose. Her gaze then fell in innocent invitation to the curves of his sensuous mouth, and Colin could not deny the unspoken request.

Lowering his head, he watched as Olivia's lashes fell in acquiescence to his kiss. Their lips met in a feather-light kiss. Determined to proceed cautiously, Colin was nonetheless overwhelmed by her soft, sweet response. He increased the pressure, gently sliding his mouth across the velvety surface of Olivia's slightly parted lips.

When she brought her hand around to caress the nape of his neck, Colin experienced an explosion of need that rocked him to his toes. His kiss became more demanding, and Olivia instinctively met that demand.

Reason fled as she responded to the passion Colin aroused deep within the core of her being. The tingling sensation that she always experienced when he was near was now multiplied a thousand times over as Olivia felt her body vibrating under the force of his kiss.

After a long moment Colin was the first to gain control of himself realizing that they stood in full view of the house. He raised his head with reluctance and smiled mockingly as he listened to the loud hammering of his heart echoing in his ears. *I feel like a schoolboy sneaking my first kiss out in the stables,* he thought, laughing to himself. He watched with pleasure as Olivia, struggling for composure, slowly opened her eyes.

Invariably honest in the most unusual situations, Olivia could not hold back the words as she burst out with emotion, her eyes locked to Colin's, "That was simply wonderful!"

Colin's smile became one of complete male satisfaction.

"Yes, it was, wasn't it?"

Not the least embarrassed by her outburst, Olivia laid her hand against the soft cloth of Colin's jacket. With surprise she felt the answering pounding of his heart and was reassured to discover that her unsettling response was not one-sided.

Still carrying her in his arms, Colin strode down the hall toward the staircase, thinking it might be an opportune moment to press forward his case, while Olivia remained slightly dazed from the force of his desire.

"Olivia, it is pointless to deny the attraction between us," he spoke reasonably over her head. "I think if you evaluate the situation logically, marriage holds substantial benefit to both you and me."

Olivia's passion-inspired fog lifted as the words *logic* and *marriage* came to her ears. She did not answer as Colin carried her into her room and deposited her upon the bed. She was grateful for his silence as her own thoughts were in turmoil necessitating what Aunt Joan would call "a good sorting-out."

Hesitantly Colin broke the still quiet of the room.

"Unfortunately, I will not be able to dine with you this evening; there is some business I need to attend to. However, I will be up to see you tomorrow."

With one last, lingering look at her golden head, Colin left the room. He would undoubtedly have been surprised to see Olivia launch a pillow at the door as soon as it had shut. Of course, she had no intention of actually hitting Colin with the soft missile, but it helped to relieve her anger.

The pillow fell harmlessly to the floor with a quiet thud, and Olivia seethed. *Aaagh,* she grumbled to herself, *who does he think he is? Wanting to marry me because it would be convenient for him?! A mutually beneficial arrangement!* Olivia pushed a few loose curls off her forehead, and as she did so, she suddenly recalled the crisp feel of Colin's hair at the back of his neck when she wantonly pulled his head down to increase the pressure of his kiss. The memory was like a bucket of icy water on her anger.

Falling back upon the bed, she half groaned, half laughed. Her fury was not for Colin, but for herself. In his world it was perfectly acceptable to arrange loveless marriages where the couple lived separate lives, each keeping his own residence, occasionally meeting at social gatherings. Undoubtedly, Colin would consider his completely proper offer unwarranted of Olivia's ire.

With disgust Olivia acknowledged that her temper had risen when Colin had casually dismissed her question about love. What had she expected? Heartfelt declarations of undying devotion? No, she could not expect love from the Earl of Sorrelby, but did she secretly yearn for such an emotion from him? Olivia quashed the question, not permitting herself to answer.

And she still needed to resolve the issue of the kiss. With that single embrace he had ignited an ember smoldering within her. The fiery passion that had resulted had robbed her of her senses, leaving her with a devastating sense that she had lost total control of herself. This was what infuriated her. She, who disdained the aristocracy and had refuted the earl's unsavory reputation with women, was falling prey to his charms. She adamantly refused to be just one more woman, in a long line of women, to become besotted with the irresistible Colin Forster, she told herself, smacking her fist into her open palm.

Insidiously a little voice whispered to her, *But you wouldn't be just another woman; you would be his wife.* Olivia thrust aside the temptation, knowing that she could never marry without love. If she were to accept his proposal, how could she ever reconcile herself to a marriage of convenience? Colin would carry on, liaison after liaison, and as his wife, Olivia would live alone at Sorrelby, valiantly pretending not to hear the gossip of her husband's latest affairs. Intolerable, she thought. She was certain that Colin would never intentionally choose to hurt her; however, if she allowed herself to become emotionally vulnerable to him, the pain would be inevitable.

Folding her hands in her lap, Olivia resolved to remain aloof. She could not allow any further intimacies between them, nor could she encourage him in his pursuit of her. She must good-naturedly, but firmly, convince him that the two of them were not suited.

The following day Olivia and Margaret sat on the patio, reveling in the afternoon sunshine and sharing confidences. Olivia was not surprised when Margaret shyly divulged her burgeoning affection for Mr. Browning, whom she described as "the dearest, sweetest, brightest man alive." Olivia was tempted to discuss the earl's proposal with Margaret, but decided it best simply to forget he had ever even broached the subject. She vowed not to give it another thought, although as Margaret waxed eloquent about her beloved Leonard, Olivia could not help but compare him to Colin. After a few unfavorable mental comparisons, Olivia concluded that it simply was not fair to the poor doctor to match him against a man like Colin Forster. Certainly, Mr. Browning had nice, thick brown hair, but of late, Olivia found jet-black locks to be uncommonly attractive. And yes, she agreed with Margaret, Mr. Browning was certainly blessed with warm, intelligent eyes. But, alas, his eyes did not sparkle with laughter nor gleam with unspoken sensual promise. No, thought Olivia, Colin Forster was simply without peer.

After lauding the merits of her beau for over an hour, Margaret yearned for a glass of lemonade and sent off to search for Smythe, leaving Olivia to bask in the fragrant spring air. She closed her eyes and lay back in the lounge, listening to the miniature operetta provided by a trio of nearby songbirds. She laughed to herself, thinking that even the birds were conspiring against her. For in her imagination they trilled and whistled a song of love.

A slight rustling stirred her to open her eyes. Olivia's chair, placed in the shadows of the maple tree, was partially hidden from the house by the low boxwood hedge, so she assumed that Mr. Whitehead could not see her as he secretly crept into the study by way of the garden's French doors.

She had been prepared to call out a greeting when something about his approach gave her pause. Glancing furtively from left to right, he was definitely sneaking into Lord Sorrelby's study. Alarmed by his stealthy manner, and recalling the fortune in jewelry she had seen last night, Olivia quickly considered her options. Due to her injured leg, she could not pursue Mr. Whitehead, nor was it likely she could overpower him if he were in the process of stealing the earl's valuables. To yell for help would allow Whitehead too much time to make his escape, with or without the stolen booty.

The most logical choice would be to remain as quiet as possible to witness the theft and hope that Whitehead would not disappear with the goods prior to Olivia's notifying the authorities.

Olivia gnawed on her lower lip, praying that Mr. Whitehead would not notice her as he exited the study. She held her breath as his head poked out from the French doors. He slowly inched out the door, clutching something to his chest and then stuffing it under his jacket, moving quickly across the lawn and out of sight.

Olivia frowned as she recognized the object he hid beneath his coatflap. Whitehead had not stolen the jewels nor the cashbox. He had absconded with the accounting ledger. How odd, she thought.

Olivia had met the steward a few days ago when Smythe had brought him to her room to remove a broken sidechair, and she had liked him. He had not been overly friendly, perhaps a bit reticent, and yet, Olivia had thought him a decent man. She certainly would not have labeled him a thief. And if he were going to break into the earl's desk, surely there were items of greater value he could take than the accountbook.

Olivia's musings were cut short by the arrival of Margaret and Smythe. On the verge of asking Smythe to fetch the constable, Olivia hesitated. Her intuition told her that matters were not quite what they seemed in this case.

Graciously accepting the glass of lemonade, she waited until Smythe had left and then turned to Margaret.

"Maggie, I need you to do me a favor. Quickly, please, go into the study and see if you can find a black velvet jewelry case. If it is there, bring it to me straight away."

Bewildered by her friend's urgency, Margaret arose and hurried into the study, casting a perplexed look back at Olivia on the chaise. Olivia urged her on with a wave of her hand, and within seconds, Margaret returned, her mouth agape as she looked down upon the wealth of jewelry displayed in the case.

Olivia held out her hand for the box. "Where did you find it?"

"It was just lying atop the desk, open as you see it now."

As Olivia began to mentally catalog its contents, Margaret asked somewhat breathlessly, "Does all that belong to the earl?"

Olivia nodded her head and without looking up, commented, "Obscene, isn't it?"

"Well, I don't know about obscene, but—"

Olivia interrupted her with a sigh. "Well, it seems to be all there, thank goodness." Except for the diamond-and-emerald ring, she amended to herself, certain that particular ring was still in Colin's possession.

Margaret looked quite taken aback as she asked, "What did you think happened to it? Did you think it had been stolen?"

Olivia answered her carefully, not wishing to implicate Mr. Whitehead. "I knew that the earl had left the jewelry out in the open and I was concerned." Eager to change the subject, she injected a note of enthusiasm into her voice and asked, "Since you're here, Maggie, you can help me inventory the jewelry for Lord Sorrelby."

Margaret squealed like a child on Christmas morning, "Can I really? How delicious!"

Margaret rhapsodized over every piece while Olivia recorded a detailed description. Although pleased that with

Maggie's help, she was able to complete the task so easily, her thoughts continued to dwell on her dilemma with Mr. White-head. Undoubtedly, she would have to inform Colin of the ledger's theft, but she wished that she could confront Mr. Whitehead first. Her instincts were rarely wrong, and instinctively she had liked the mysterious steward.

Olivia had just finished her evening meal when the bedroom door was flung open and Colin strode across the room still wearing his dark traveling cloak. Without preamble, he leaned over and grasping Olivia by the shoulders, kissed her thoroughly. Her first reaction was one of protest, but reminiscent of that morning's embrace, her mind was washed blank by the mist of passion his kiss instantly invoked. She responded fully, parting her lips to his questing tongue. He smelled richly of leather and night air, and a faint taste of rum lingered upon his lips.

Olivia had bathed earlier in the evening and had washed her hair, leaving it free to dry in front of the fire. Colin now moved his hands up from her shoulders, gliding up the long column of her neck, and lost his hands in the silken fall of her rose-scented hair.

Her head was captured between his large, bronzed hands, and only when she felt herself almost completely lost to his passion did she pull back from the kiss.

His cool hands still cradled her face as he whispered, his voice unusually husky, "The entire day I have thought of nothing else."

Regaining her sanity, Olivia tried to subdue the leap of her heart at his whispered words. She gently removed his hands from her face, silently condemning herself for her lack of willpower. No further intimacies, she had told herself. Unable to hide the quaver in her voice, she nonetheless steeled herself in an effort to sound firm. "My lord, I have not given you permission to take such liberties."

Colin wanted to laugh out loud at Olivia's painstaking attempts to deny her reaction to his kiss. Her irises were black with desire, her breath came fitfully between her swollen lips, and through the thin cotton of her gown the peaks of her breasts begged for his touch. But he did not want her to mistake his humor, so he held it in check. He begrudgingly admired her iron determination to resist him although he honestly believed it was pointless. She would be his wife if he had to cajole, tease, taunt, and seduce her to assent.

Stepping back to pour himself a glass of wine, Colin bowed in apology, although the seductive glint in his eyes contradicted his words.

"Please accept my apology. I was overcome."

At this, Olivia burst into laughter. He looked far from contrite, and he knew it. Shaking her head, she wanted to appear stern, but failed.

"Overcome, pish-posh! As if anything were out of your control." That statement brought to mind Whitehead's theft, but as she opened her mouth to discuss the matter, a loud commotion in the hall forestalled her.

A very feminine voice argued, "But of course he'll want to see us right away. It's not that late. Besides, it has been months since . . ."

Smythe could be heard, nearly shouting, "Just a moment so that I may announce—"

"Announce?" the voice scoffed, interrupting. "Is that what happens when you become an earl?"—the door swung open as the girl continued—"your family must be announced?"

And through the door strode a striking young girl, ebony curls swinging under a jaunty lavender hat. She came to an abrupt halt immediately inside the door, causing poor Smythe to literally crash into her back. Her violet eyes, the very color of her cap, narrowed as she took in the intimate scene before her. Her cool, piercing gaze settled upon Olivia, who did not hesitate to meet the intruder's stare.

The girl, unquestionably beautiful, appeared to be of an age with Olivia. She was dressed well, though not extravagantly, and carried herself proudly. Olivia knew instantly that the girl must be related to Colin, the resemblance was so striking.

Murmured voices in the hall approached the open doorway.

"Really, Katherine, what will your brother think of such behavior?" a soft voice questioned. The voice's owner was preceded by two more girls, approximately twelve and fifteen years of age. Although the family likeness was evident, the younger girls had not inherited the ink-black hair of their mother, but rather, light chestnut hair, apparently from the father.

Katherine stepped aside from the doorway, allowing the remainder of the party to enter. The two girls filed past, the younger one giggling at her awe-inspiring brother, who was in the process of rising from his chair. An older woman entered as Colin approached the doorway.

Lightly flecked with gray, her lustrous black hair was piled atop her head in an old-fashioned crown of braids that suited her. Her porcelain complexion was virtually uncreased save for a few lines about her eyes. She was not tall, and as her son reached down to embrace her in welcome, she seemed to disappear within his enveloping arms. Unlike her brash, eldest daughter and her dynamic son, Lady Forster appeared almost timid, carrying herself in a somewhat diffident manner.

Despite her demure demeanor, at the same time she embodied a certain indescribable nobility; not in the titled sense of nobility, but in the character sense. Honesty and compassion enhanced her refined visage, lending a spiritual radiance to her presence.

Conversely, Katherine stood apart from her mother and sisters, an unattractive scowl distorting her features. As a child, she had worshiped her older brother, casting him in the light of her personal protector and knight extraordinaire. She had been closer to him than either of the younger girls, due primarily to the age difference, and had maintained a possessive attitude toward her handsome brother throughout the years. Her spontaneous reaction to Olivia, an obvious rival for Colin's affections, was hostile.

Olivia arose, also, balancing on her one good leg and supporting herself on the back of the chair. She silently thanked providence that she had not already changed into her bedclothes. The intimate dinner in her bedroom was condemning enough as it was, reading the conspicuous displeasure on Katherine's face.

Colin commenced the introductions as Olivia crossed the room on her newly acquired crutches, announcing with a wicked twist to his lips, "Mother, I would like you to meet Miss Olivia Knowles, my soon-to-be fiancée."

The audible reaction from the three girls, ranging from shrieks to sighs, spurred Olivia to hastily respond with a forced smile. "What rot!" she retorted, reaching his side. She pretended to slip on a crutch, thrusting an elbow into Colin's ribs.

Colin winced ever so slightly as her pointed elbow painfully jabbed his side, and he leaned down to Olivia in the guise of assisting her with the recalcitrant crutches.

"Witch," he whispered in her ear while she smiled innocently into his eyes.

Lady Forster, unsure how to respond to such shenanigans, politely held out her hand. Not much over five feet tall, she had to look up almost eight inches to greet Olivia. As she did so, she suddenly drew in a sharp breath and would have fallen to the ground in a dead faint if Colin, with lightning reaction, had not caught her in his arms.

Chapter Five

"Now look what you've done, Colin!" Katherine accused. "You've practically killed Mother with your ridiculous announcement!"

Hurrying to her brother's side, Katherine tagged behind Colin as he lay their unconscious mother upon Olivia's bed.

"Look at her, you scoundrel," she continued. "Pale as a ghost and you're entirely to blame."

In the background the two younger girls were starting to cry while Olivia attempted to soothe them with hugs and whispers of assurance. Huddled over their smaller forms, Olivia looked up just as Katherine leveled a look of pure malevolence upon her. She was so shocked by such blatant animosity that if not for the girls, she would have marched across the room then and there to confront Katherine's menacing glower.

Ignoring his sister's harping at his shoulder, Colin arose from the bed.

"I am going to send for the physician at once."

"No," Deirdre Forster said softly from the bed, her eyes fluttering open. "That won't be necessary." Feebly she reached out to Colin, who took her hand and sank down next to his mother.

"Mother, if you are ill, I insist we send for the physician," he argued, concern evident in his voice.

Removing her hand from his, Deirdre touched a gold locket lying upon her bosom. "No . . . I am not ill. But, where—"

She turned to look around the room, her eyes anxious until

they found Olivia, then her face fell with relief as she softly finished, "There she is."

All eyes followed Deirdre's to where Olivia stood awkwardly in the corner, one arm wrapped protectively around the smaller girl, her other arm braced against one of the crutches. As Olivia met Lady Forster's gaze, she noted with alarm that tears were beginning to trickle slowly down the elder woman's face.

"Come here, my dear," Lady Forster entreated, her smile full of warmth and welcome despite the wetness upon her cheeks.

Obediently Olivia retrieved the other crutch and approached the bed. Both Colin and Katherine were frowning, although Colin's frown appeared to be one of puzzlement while Katherine seemed vastly annoyed. The crackle of the fire echoed in the room, and it seemed as if all onlookers held their breath awaiting Lady Forster's next words.

"Please, sit down so that I may have a better look at you," Deirdre asked. Colin pulled forward a chair for Olivia, who murmured her thanks.

Reaching out, Deirdre placed a slender ivory finger under Olivia's chin, lifting the younger woman's face to the golden lamplight. Olivia sensed the quiver in Lady Forster's touch and marveled that she could be so moved by her son's pronouncement. Surely, she had not so despaired of him selecting a bride! Yet as Olivia considered the blatant emotion in the face opposite, she concluded that Colin's proposed betrothal was not the cause of his mother's fainting spell and tears.

After a long moment Lady Forster broke the heavy silence.

"Fiona," she whispered. "It's a miracle that I've found you."

Deirdre spoke under her breath but loud enough that both Olivia and Colin caught her words. Olivia started visibly, and Deirdre registered the young woman's surprise.

"Does that name mean something to you?" she questioned.

Hesitantly Olivia responded, nonplussed by the near-reverence she saw in Lady Forster's visage.

"My mother's name was Fiona. She and my father died twelve years ago."

Closing her eyes to mask her pained expression, Deirdre leaned forward and caught Olivia up in her arms. Although at first unsure, Olivia returned the embrace, instinctively responding to the older woman's anguish.

Tears now flowing freely, Deirdre pulled the gold necklace over her head and opened the clasp. Holding the locket so that Olivia could view the portrait inside, Deirdre stated, her voice thick with emotion, "Your mother, Fiona McClellan, was my sister—my stepsister."

The three Forster girls gasped loudly, and Colin leaned forward over Olivia's shoulder to take a better look at the portrait, his expression stony. Olivia, her face chalk-white, clung to the arms of the chair for support and peered into the locket. The child that looked back at her could have been her own reflection in the mirror ten years ago. A young girl with huge, exotically shaped eyes and a slightly square chin smiled saucily from the oval face of the locket. Trancelike, Olivia could not stop staring at the child. Could this be her mother? The mother she had dreamed of these past dozen years?

The smart *clip-clop* of Colin's heels brought Olivia back to the present as he moved away from her back and walked over to the fireside table to pour two glasses of wine.

"I think the both of you could use a spot of this."

Mechanically Olivia took the proffered wineglass while Lady Forster accepted the second goblet.

Colin, of course, had heard the story of his young aunt's death many, many years ago from his mother. Deirdre had worn the locket every day of her life in memory of her young stepsister who had drowned in the River Shannon. Perhaps on three or four occasions, Colin had seen the portrait of the ill-fated Fiona, and it was this memory that had haunted him when he first met Olivia. She had seemed so familiar to him, and now he knew the reason.

Glancing down at the red-gold curls curling gracefully down Olivia's neck, he longed to pull her into his arms and comfort her. Instead, he laid his hand upon her shoulder and squeezed gently. His touch thawed the icy curtain of shock that had held Olivia immobile. Forcing a sip of wine past the lump in her throat, she strove to corral her thoughts.

"I had always been told that Mummy was an orphan," Olivia began.

Deirdre answered softly, "Most likely, my dear, she believed that she was an orphan."

Moving to sit upon the edge of the bed, Deirdre set her wineglass upon the nightstand. Facing Olivia, she straightened her skirts and smiled wistfully, her head slightly tilted as she transported herself back to her childhood in Ireland.

"She was a beautiful child, full of spirit and life. She laughed and played from dawn to dusk, never tiring of her imaginary games of princesses and dragons and knights on white destriers. She brought joy and sunshine by just walking into a room.

"I adored her. If she fell and skinned her knee, she would cry for me. At night she would not go to sleep until her Dee-Dee had kissed her good night. We were very close, although there were no blood ties between us.

"You see, my mother had been widowed when I was eight years old. After a year's mourning she remarried, Lord Frances McClellan, a very wealthy duke from a neighboring estate. Lord McClellan, or Papa, I soon called him, was also a widower. His wife had died in childbirth only a month previous, and he needed a mother for his baby girl, Fiona.

"So, Mother and I moved into the McClellan castle, and Fiona and I became inseparable. Even as a baby, she would reach out for me, refusing to be held by anyone else if I were in the room. Papa and Mother and I doted on her. We were such a happy family. And then . . ."

Deirdre paused to take a drink from her goblet and Olivia saw the slight trembling of her hand.

"I was seventeen and had gone for the day with a group of friends to a nearby village carnival. Fiona had begged to come, but my companions scorned the idea of bringing along an eight-year-old child. So, I had promised her a special fishing expedition when I returned home, and that seemed to appease her.

"Perhaps she wanted to wait for me in the boat and the mooring came loose. We will never know. When we discovered her missing, a gardener came forward and reported having seen Fiona near the river's dock."

Taking a deep breath, Lady Forster fought back the memory of the crushing sorrow she had known over thirty years ago.

"The boat was found a few days later. We searched for weeks but . . . I never saw my Fiona again."

Olivia brushed her hands across her eyes and then felt Colin press a handkerchief into her hand. After a few seconds to collect herself, Olivia smiled tremulously. "I can continue the story from here, but unfortunately, my history of my mother is limited.

"I know that she was found near death by a fisherman not far from Kilrush. When recovered, many weeks later, she could remember little aside from her first name. The fisherman's family circulated word of her, but no one ever came forward to claim her. Assuming that she had been orphaned in a boating accident, the Buckleys took her into their home and she was raised as Fiona Buckley."

Deirdre shook her head with dismay. "To think that she was carried as far as Kilrush. I cannot believe she survived. My poor baby."

Stepping forward, Colin put his arm around his mother.

"Come, Mother. It is late and I believe that we have all had enough excitement for this evening. You must be exhausted from your journey. Let me show you to your rooms."

Colin led the way, and the three girls followed meekly in tow. The door closed behind them, and Olivia's head fell back against her chair. She was too tired to ring for the chambermaid, so kicking off her slippers, she climbed into bed in her daygown. Spent from the multitude of surprises the evening had offered, Olivia fell asleep before her head had yet hit the pillow.

The faintest gray light filtered through the window, penetrating the shadows of the room where Olivia slept. From a deep and disturbing sleep, she awoke with a start. With the sudden arrival of Colin's family last night, and then the startling revelation of Olivia's relationship to the Forster family, she had neglected to warn Colin of Whitehead's burglary. Sitting up, Olivia smoothed the wrinkles from her rumpled dress and glanced out the window to the fields below.

Dawn crept across the meadow, illuminating the tiny rainbow dewdrops perched upon each blade of grass. The lake that had so tempted Olivia these past days shimmered, its waters smooth as glass. She only wished her thoughts were as calm as those waters below. The thieving steward, Colin's proposal, and her newly discovered heritage all combined to unsettle the usually unflappable Olivia Knowles.

She yawned delicately and stretched her arms overhead, smoothing her hand across her hair. She had also forgotten to braid her hair before she fell into bed last night, and she could just picture the chaos of curls falling from her pate. With a sigh of resignation, she reached across to the foot of the bed for the crutches.

The crutches felt awkward this morning, but after a few tentative steps, Olivia believed that she had mastered the wooden props. She quietly eased open her door and hobbled down the hallway to the staircase. Negotiating the marble stairs required some patience, and she barely escaped disaster when the crutch slipped, but within a few minutes Olivia was moving efficiently down the hall to Colin's study.

From the back of the house she could hear a servant or two scuffling about, preparing for another day at the service of His Lordship, Colin Forster, the Sixth Earl of Sorrelby.

Olivia slipped noiselessly into Colin's study and, resting the crutches against the desk, lowered herself into the oversize leather chair. Colin's scent lingered in the chair's musky leather, and Olivia could not resist burrowing her nose into its softness before beginning her search.

Surveying her surroundings, Olivia admired the richly detailed frieze bordering the mahogany molding and the walls of kid-bound books stretching from floor to ceiling. The portrait of Horace Forster appeared to be the focal point of the study, its gilt frame gleaming in the meager morning light.

Olivia studied the man whose callous disregard for Mossgate's impoverishment had forever soured her against the upper class. Bedecked in a lavish copper-colored frockcoat and tan knee breeches, Horace Forster stood, one knee bent, tricorn in hand. The artificially casual pose emphasized his unusual height, an obvious Sorrelby distinction, and classic profile. He appeared to be middle-aged at the time the portrait was painted, and the artist had succeeded in depicting his harsh and unbending character. Rigid and unyielding, he seemed to Olivia not at all like his charming and charismatic grandson.

Returning her attention to the task at hand, she scanned the surface of the desk. Although neatly stacked piles of papers abounded, the account ledger was not to be seen. She then tried to open the top desk drawer and was surprised to find it unlocked. Gingerly she tugged on the drawer.

"Dare I ask what in the hell you are doing here?"

Olivia jumped in the chair, her hand automatically flying to her chest in a startled gesture.

"Thank heavens it's you," she breathed huskily, her shoulders sagging.

"I would not thank any deity just yet," Colin warned darkly, advancing into the room. Dressed all in black, he cut an imposing figure as he stalked toward the mahogany desk. "I want an explanation."

Olivia hesitated only a fraction of a second as she considered Whitehead's plight.

"Certainly, you do," she began with a steady voice. "Yesterday, I witnessed a rather unsettling incident. Maggie and I took tea on the patio." Olivia gestured at the French doors. "Maggie stepped away to fetch Smythe, and while I was waiting, I detected a movement from the corner of my eye."

Again, Olivia weighed her words, unwilling to implicate the steward as yet.

"Straining to see through the hedge, I believe that I saw someone sneak into your study. I meant to bring it to your attention last night when you returned, but we were . . . sidetracked," Olivia finished a little lamely.

Gathering her courage, she pushed on. "At any rate, when I awoke this morning, I suddenly recalled the incident and decided to come downstairs to check if anything were missing."

Colin scowled and Olivia bit the inside of her cheek. *He doesn't believe me. He most likely thinks that I am here to make off with his cache of jewels! Oh, what a mess!* Feeling a bit cowed by Colin's glare, Olivia straightened herself and sat stiffly, awaiting his accusation.

A muscle twitched in Colin's jaw. Enunciating every syllable with iron control, he asked, "Do not tell me that you came down the stairs on those twigs!"

Confused, Olivia followed his gaze to the crutches propped against the mahogany desk.

"Oh—" she began before he interrupted bitingly.

"You could have broken your foolish little neck!"

Colin was so angry, he itched to grab her by the shoulders and shake some sense into that lovely head of hers. But he dared not touch her, for he knew that once his hand settled upon her gracefully curving shoulder, he would be unable to release her until he had caressed and kissed her breathless.

"Well, I didn't break anything," Olivia responded in a huff. "And you needn't shout at me. I have excellent hearing."

"Excellent hearing?!" Colin mimicked, his expression nearly comical in disbelief. "Excellent *hearing!* What of a modicum of common sense? That staircase is treacherous!"

Olivia remained mute, and they stared each other down for a long moment.

Something twitched at the corner of Colin's mouth. It took too great an effort to sustain his anger when Olivia sat there looking so ridiculously adorable. Her hair defied the laws of gravity as it curled up, down, and sideways, surrounding her in a crimson-and-gold halo. And the belligerent set of her luscious mouth fell barely short of a pout. She made Colin think of a strawberry-colored kitten whose fur rises on the back of its neck when riled.

His ire dissipated, "You were fortunate—this time. However, in the future, I insist that you keep to level ground on those things, understood?"

With a militant nod, in the knowledge that Colin's concern was warranted, Olivia acquiesced.

A few long strides carried Colin over to the desk where he made a cursory survey of the desk. He then opened the drawer that Olivia had been poised to investigate before his arrival. Directly in view lay the account ledger. Colin picked it up and riffled quickly through the pages. Olivia masked her surprise as she realized that Whitehead must have returned the book sometime during the night.

Colin then opened the safe behind the portrait, and with his back to her, Olivia leafed through a few pages of the ledger looking for a clue to its temporary disappearance.

"Everything seems to be in order," he announced as he spun the lock on the safe. "Were you able to discern if the intruder was a man or woman?"

"I believe it was a man."

Colin walked over to one of the chairs on the opposite side of the desk and sat down.

"Tell me, why did you not shout for Smythe once you spotted the trespasser?"

Olivia experienced a brief pang of guilt but answered, "My first inclination *was* to call for help, but then I realized that it would be pointless as the thief would be the first to hear me."

"Hmm-mm," Colin murmured noncommittally. Coming to his feet in one fluid motion, he walked to Olivia.

"Would you be so kind as to make my apologies to my mother and tell her that I will see her this afternoon? I have business that I must attend to this morning."

Colin looked into Olivia's disappointed face and added expressively, "You and I also have much to discuss when I return." Reaching down, he scooped her up in his arms.

"But for now, I will take you to your room. I'll send up Polly with your breakfast."

"Oh, please don't," Olivia protested. "I would much prefer to take breakfast with your family this morning."

Pleased, Colin smiled at her. Leaving the crutches behind, he transported Olivia to her room, neither of them aware of Katherine's head peeping out from behind a doorway down the hall.

"Please excuse my unorthodox arrival, but I have been forbidden to use the crutches on the staircase," Olivia explained, entering the breakfast room in the arms of O'Shea.

Positively lovely in her modest daygown, the lavender color enhanced the strawberry tones of Olivia's hair. Per her request, Polly had taken especial pains to arrange Olivia's hair in the current fashion that Katherine had sported last night. Although her hair was not as short as fashion dictated, the style, pulled away from her face, the curls falling high from the back of her head, flattered her immensely.

"We're honored to have you join us, my dear," Deirdre welcomed, looking regal in her own silver-gray attire.

Olivia smiled warmly at the table in general, ignoring Katherine's smirk of greeting.

"Thank you, Ma'am."

"No such formalities, please. I am, after all, your aunt. It would please me greatly for you to call me Deirdre."

Olivia hesitated, thinking how odd it would be to call your mother-in-law "aunt." But of course, it didn't matter since she had no intention of marrying Colin, she assured herself.

"I will try—Deirdre."

Shaking out her napkin, she recalled Colin's absence.

"Lord Sorrelby asked me to extend his apologies that he cannot breakfast with you this morning. He had urgent business away from the estate." The fifteen-year-old, Eleanor, cocked her head in a curious manner, and Olivia, suddenly understanding the inference drawn, hastened to clarify.

"I awoke early this morning, and we spoke downstairs prior to his departure," she amended, a slight flush to her cheeks. From the other end of the table, Katherine snorted loudly in derision.

"Katherine!" Deirdre reprimanded. Olivia pretended not to hear, although she wondered what she had done to earn the girl's instant dislike. The table fell silent for a moment, and Olivia applied herself to her breakfast.

Katherine waited until Olivia had a mouthful of biscuit and asked in a haughty manner, "What are you doing here anyway? I cannot believe that you live here. Or are you a servant of some sort?"

Olivia choked on the biscuit. Deirdre rose from her chair, placing her palms flat against the linen tablecloth. Her voice shook as she castigated her eldest daughter, "Katherine Ann Forster, I did not raise you to be so ill mannered. Apologize this instant!"

Katherine turned pink and appeared truly abashed by her mother's uncharacteristic reproof. Lowering her head, she spoke to her lap. "Kindly accept my apologies, Miss Knowles."

Olivia nodded her head to Deirdre as if to say she had not been mortally offended. Turning to Katherine, she answered, her voice gracious, "Apology accepted, and I do understand how peculiar it must seem to arrive at your brother's home and to find a stranger in residence.

"Nearly two weeks ago, I had an accident in the country and injured my leg. Lord Sorrelby and O'Shea discovered me and brought me here. The physician insisted that I not be transported, so your brother generously offered me his hospitality during my convalescence."

The littlest Forster, Victoria, chimed in, "Are you really going to marry Colin?"

Olivia felt four pairs of eyes boring into her, and she set her cup upon its china saucer. Speaking in a deliberately light-hearted manner, she answered, "Your brother enjoys teasing, as I am sure you are well aware. I have no plans to wed Lord Sorrelby, Victoria."

Of course, she amended to herself, his plans are another matter entirely. He did not seem even remotely deterred in his courtship of her, and she self-consciously conceded that she had not done much to discourage him.

Before anyone could further pursue the issue, Deirdre politely steered the conversation into other channels.

"Then you live nearby, Olivia?"

"Yes, I live in Mossgate, a few miles away, with my uncle and his family."

A wistful look shadowed Deirdre's features. "I cannot believe that my little Fiona married. What was he like, my dear, your father?"

"I was only a child, but I remember him as a prince, tall and blond. His name was Kenneth. Kenneth Knowles. He and Mother were madly in love. My memories are not too distinct, although Uncle Nathan has related much of their first meeting and their courtship to me. Father had been studying in Dublin when, on holiday, he was invited to Kilrush by a friend. Father saw her at the market and decided in that instant to marry her. When he left Kilrush, Mother went with him as his bride."

"How romantic!" Eleanor gushed. Katherine kicked her under the table, and Eleanor yowled in protest.

"Need I remind you that you are ladies?" Deirdre admonished in exasperation. "I don't see how either of you can expect to be received in London with such deplorable manners."

The lure of London had its desired effect, and both girls mumbled penitent apologies and meekly continued their breakfasts.

The meal was nearing its completion when Smythe opened the door with a flourish, formally announcing, "Miss Margaret Nicholson, Mr. Henry Nicholson, and the esteemed Mr. Browning."

Margaret shot Smythe an amused glance, then patted his arm companionably, "Why so formal today, Smythe?"

The answer was apparent as she turned around to greet the newly arrived Forster women. Introductions were made and they all returned to the table for refreshment with the exception of Eleanor and Victoria, who were excused by their mother.

"Henry, I cannot believe that you were finally able to tear yourself away from your beloved project," Olivia teased.

Henry, who had seated himself next to Olivia, sighed heavily. "I am wretchedly sorry, Liv, that I haven't been to see you before, but the timing was crucial what with the weather having been so favorable. Rain would have—"

Olivia held up her hand and laughed, "Please, Henry, spare me the scientific precipitation analysis. Seriously, though, you are pleased with its progress?"

Henry nodded. Across the table Katherine had been listening to the exchange between the two and had decided that Mr. Nicholson was the most handsome man she had met in her long nineteen years. She had not been overly impressed when she realized that he was the son of a country vicar, but after overhearing that he was a budding scientist, she revamped her opinion of the golden-haired Henry.

Due to their country upbringing, the Forster children had been tutored at home, and Katherine had exhibited an unusual aptitude for the sciences.

"Did I hear that you are a scientist, Mr. Nicholson?" Katherine inquired sweetly, two dimples flashing on either side of her mouth.

Charmed by her interest, and not indifferent to her sparkling eyes and dimpled smile, Henry launched into a lengthy and detailed explanation of his newest invention, certain to bore any layperson to tears. Olivia had hopes of cutting short Henry's lecture and rescuing poor Katherine, when she heard, at a number of intervals, Katherine pose the most intelligent questions regarding the project. Surprised by the young girl's knowledge and apparent enthusiasm, Olivia shrugged and left the two to their discussion.

As Olivia sipped at her coffee, Mr. Browning sidled over to Olivia and asked if she could find a moment for him to examine her ankle. They excused themselves, and she led him into the parlor for some privacy. After a swift examination, the physician expressed satisfaction with her progress. He admonished her to stay off the ankle for at least another few days, but judicious use of the crutches would be acceptable.

On returning to the breakfast room, Margaret approached them, clapping her hands in delight.

"Katherine expressed a keen desire to see the countryside, so Henry proposed a nature tour, followed by a picnic at the river. Doesn't it sound like fun? What say you, Leonard, shall we go?"

Leonard Browning stared into Margaret's blue eyes and, looking like a man clearly besotted, agreed. "Sounds like a jolly excursion."

"Liv, won't you please come, too? We will make a grand day of it."

"No, thank you, Maggie. I would definitely slow you down, incapacitated as I am." From across the room she caught Deirdre's eye and winked.

"Besides, I was looking forward to a day of reminiscences with Lady Forster."

Maggie's mouth pursed in a perplexed little pucker as she asked, "Reminiscences? But did you not meet just last night? What could you and Lady Forster reminisce about?"

Olivia smiled faintly.

"I am afraid that it's a very long story, but I will try to relate an abridged version."

Katherine, reluctant to witness another emotional scene between her mother and "that tart," as she had mentally labeled

Olivia, excused herself, saying she would instruct the kitchen to prepare a picnic lunch.

Olivia and Deirdre shared the telling of Fiona's story. When the tale was complete, Margaret had soaked both Henry's and Leonard's handkerchiefs plus a table napkin.

Dabbing at her eyes, she said, "Mother and Father will simply not believe it! What a tragedy for you, Lady Forster. And the poor duke! My goodness, Olivia, you're the grand-daughter of a duke!"

Olivia's head jerked up in surprise. She had been so focused on her mother, that she had not yet assimilated that fact! Her mother's father was a duke. Botheration! A blueblood. Olivia cringed inwardly when she thought of what Colin's reaction would be to that revelation after the litany of insults she had hurled upon the aristocracy.

"A very esteemed family, I might add," injected Deirdre.

Olivia studied her fingertips for a moment, unprepared to face the ramifications of her highbrow ancestry. "Maggie, please allow me to tell Uncle Nathan and Aunt Joan. I will see them tomorrow if Mr. Browning will allow." She looked to the physician for confirmation.

"If you take care," he paused a moment for effect, "I will allow it."

"Yes, I promise that I shall."

The lull was interrupted by Katherine, announcing some-what stridently from the doorway, "The lunch is packed, and I, for one, am eager to begin my tour." She tossed her head impatiently like an unruly colt eager to run.

Deirdre knitted her brows in mild distress. Katherine re-minded her very much of Colin at that age: bright, restless, and untamed. Whereas Colin, as a man, had been able to vent his wildness during his years in the army, and thus had learned how to control his passionate nature, a woman's conduct was not permitted to be so free. Nineteen years old and frustrated by society's strictures and sedate country living, Katherine had allowed pettiness and self-pity to encroach upon her once agreeable temperament. Deirdre prayed for her daughter to make peace with her turbulent nature. Perhaps, she mused, the proper husband could redirect Katherine's passion.

Deirdre waved goodbye as the foursome bid farewell, Maggie imploring Olivia to join them even as Henry playfully pushed his sister out the door. Olivia merely laughed and wished them an enjoyable outing.

Olivia and Deirdre spent the balance of the morning together, talking about Fiona McClellan and her family. Many years had been lost to them, and between the two, they tried to piece together the life of the vaguely remembered mother and long-lost sister.

When Deirdre left to find her younger daughters for their daily French lessons, Olivia decided to seek out Mr. Whitehead. The overseer's cottage, located a fair distance from the main estate, would be too taxing a trip on the burdensome crutches, Olivia decided, so she engaged a houseboy to send a message to the unsuspecting steward.

Not wishing to draw undue attention to their tête-à-tête, in her note, Olivia asked for Whitehead to meet her in the courtyard. She chose a rather secluded marble bench, reassuring herself that her intuition had to be correct. Although she had seen him steal the ledger with her very own eyes, instinct told her that an honorable man had committed what only appeared to be a dishonorable act.

The marble felt deliciously cool against her palms as Olivia leaned back, tilting her face to the toasty spring sun. She tried to rehearse her speech, but abandoned the effort, deciding that her normally forthright approach would stand her in good stead. She only regretted that she had not been completely candid with Colin that morning in the study, but she felt inexplicably obligated to protect the steward, at least until she heard his side of the story. She prayed that her judgment was not in error.

"You wanted to see me?" a belligerent voice broke into her meditation.

Olivia sat up, assessing the man's aggressive pose. His beefy arms were crossed against his chest, his legs widespread. He stood nearly ten yards away from her as if he were prepared to bolt at a moment's notice.

She motioned him forward. "Please, come sit down."

Slowly he walked over to the bench, glancing around to see if they were indeed alone.

He watched her suspiciously as he sat down, but held his tongue. Olivia took a deep breath.

"You and I have met only twice before, isn't that right, Mr. Whitehead?"

"If you say so," he begrudgingly answered.

"Yes, I do believe I am correct. Twice." She slightly tilted her head as if in serious deliberation. "And on both those occasions, I thought you to be an honest, hardworking man, if a bit on the irritable side."

A small smile faded quickly from her lips when no answering grin erupted on the stony-faced man opposite. Forsaking the niceties, Olivia cast him a shrewd look and employed her no-nonsense tone of voice.

"I witnessed your theft of the account book yesterday, Mr. Whitehead. I want an explanation."

Whitehead's jaw hardened briefly.

"I am sorry, miss, but I don't know what you're talkin' about."

Her emerald eyes gazed directly into his.

"Precisely, I speak of your sneaking into the earl's study via the French doors to remove the ledger."

Whitehead narrowed his eyes speculatively.

"Is the account ledger missing?"

"Do not play games with me, sir. You know for a fact that you returned it to the earl's desk prior to dawn this very day!"

Moving restlessly upon the bench, he asked gruffly without looking at her, "What did the earl say when you told him?"

Olivia studied the man, sensing his vulnerability.

"I have not yet informed him of your 'borrowing' the book."

The man paled slightly and then ground out between his teeth, "I haven't any blunt if that's what you're after!"

A rueful smirk twisted Olivia's full, rosy lips.

"I did not ask you here to blackmail you, but rather to help you. Tell me why you stole the book," she beseeched him.

Whitehead lowered his head into his hands and grumbled beneath his breath. Straightening, he squared his shoulders.

"Awright, blast it. I ain't got anything more to lose. I took the ledger to alter the accounts. For the past few years I've been skimmin' off the top, and the earl—damn the man and his way with numbers—was cottonin' on to me.

"I had a system whereby even the old man couldn't find the missin' money, but as soon as his grandson showed up, I knew I was in for trouble. I shoulda just run but"—Whitehead shrugged his threadbare-encased shoulder—"this is the only home I've ever had."

Suddenly he reached out and grabbed Olivia's wrist in a painful grip, his voice near panic. "But you've got to believe me. The money wasn't for me. I don't have a pot of gold hidden anyplace."

Olivia reassured him, gently tugging at his fingers until he released his hold. "I believe you, Mr. Whitehead. Tell me, what was the money for?"

Whitehead swore savagely. "That old bastard was starvin' us to death! He knew we had nowhere to go, so he gave us a few mouthfuls to keep us strong enough to do his work, but that was it. The house servants were a little better off. Sometimes they could sneak an extra portion, but if Sorrelby caught ye . . ."

"Yes?" she prodded when the steward paused, warily eyeing Olivia.

"I'll not be sayin' no more," he bit out, a glimmer of fear in his black eyes.

"What is it, Mr. Whitehead? What has you so frightened?"

The man lowered his eyes, shifting his muddy boots nervously.

"Please, Mr. Whitehead," Olivia pleaded. "You can trust me to help you."

Olivia saw the muscles in the steward's jaw spasm as he fought with himself. Clenching his fists, the man expelled a ragged breath.

"Three years back the earl caught a lad stealin' from the pantry. He beat the boy so bad that . . . well, the lad didn't make it."

Olivia's strangled gasp drew his attention.

"I tried to stop him, I swear I did, but by the time Smythe

found me and we got to the house, it was too late. The boy was too bad off."

Whitehead squeezed his eyes shut for a moment, remembering the macabre scene in the kitchen: the earl standing over the young man on the floor, his walking stick stained with blood.

"I wanted to kill the old miser. I flew at him. But he stopped me cold when he threatened to turn me in as the murderer. Smythe was right there listenin' as the earl said he'd swear that it was me who beat the boy. And who was the judge goin' to believe? Me or the Earl of Sorrelby?

"He told me and Smythe that if we ever breathed a word of it, we'd both be charged with the boy's death. So me and Smythe buried the lad. No one ever asked 'bout him 'cause he was an orphaned lad. No kin. 'Course the house servants found out, and Smythe had to keep 'em quiet. We was all on pins and needles not knowin' when the old fellow might turn us in.

"Meanwhiles, we never got enough to eat, but everyone was too scared to say anythin', thinkin' of the dead lad. So I figured a way to sneak some extra money for food every month. It weren't much money, but it kept us all alive."

Ashen, Olivia exclaimed, "In the village we knew him not to be a generous man, but such cruelty is unconscionable!

"But why, when the new earl arrived, and subsequently questioned the accounts, did you not explain to him then as you have done to me?"

Whitehead could really look quite ferocious at times, and now he leveled his blackest glare on Olivia.

"You think a gent is going to believe *me* when I tell him I've been stealing from his inheritance for years because his grandfather was a murderer and the greediest bastard that ever lived?" Whitehead snarled. "You sure don't know much about the gentry, that's fer sure. Hell, he'd probably just as soon kill me outright than to have his family's precious reputation tarnished."

"No!" Olivia protested. "You cannot believe that! Colin Forster is a gentleman in every sense of the word and that has nothing to do with his birth. He is an intelligent, moral man. I'm sure that he would believe you if you explained about the

boy's death. He would certainly understand your efforts to
ensure that Sorrelby's people not starve.

"Just consider how he has improved conditions already, not
only for the staff here, but also for the villagers in Mossgate.
You can trust him."

Whitehead pulled a cap from his coat pocket and stood. "I'll
grant he's treated us fair so far, but that don't mean I'm going
to risk my neck to confess past doin's if I don't have to. You
never know how a man will react to havin' his money stolen
from him behind his back."

He grabbed the bill of the cap and pushed it atop his head.

"So now, Miss Knowles, are you going to keep quiet about
me doctorin' the books or not?"

Olivia picked up her crutches and came to her feet. "I will be
honest with you, Mr. Whitehead. I must follow my conscience.
The death of that poor boy weighs heavily upon my mind, as
I'm sure it has done yours for the past three years. But I
promise to advise you should I decide to speak with the earl."

Whitehead curtly nodded his head in understanding and
turned, exiting the courtyard through the back gate.

From behind the yew hedge Colin moved with the stealth of
a jungle animal, following the hedge back to the study's French
doors, arriving minutes before the much slower, hobbling
Olivia.

Chapter Six

"OLIVIA," COLIN CALLED from the open doorway.

Starting guiltily, Olivia spun around and lost her balance on her left crutch. Teetering precariously on only one wooden brace, she grimaced slightly as her injured ankle bore the brunt of her clumsiness. She quickly pulled the foot from the floor, relieved to discover that although the ankle was sore, it was no longer excruciatingly painful. She was still fighting to remain upright when Colin steadied her with a muscled arm behind her back.

"I did not mean to startle you," he said, his very voice raising goose bumps on Olivia's bare arms.

"You didn't startle me," she contradicted sharply. Returning from her clandestine meeting with Whitehead, she was preoccupied and edgy and had overreacted when Colin called out her name.

Softening her tone, she explained, "It was my fault. I should not have spun around like that. I often forget that I am temporarily disabled."

Colin's expression sympathized. "Are you chafing under the physician's restrictions?"

"Perhaps I am," Olivia admitted somewhat woefully. "I am not suited to this prolonged inactivity."

Colin squeezed her shoulders, murmuring in her ear, "I promise you that once Mr. Browning clears the way, I will keep you so busy that you will become nostalgic for these days of rest."

Olivia cocked a skeptical auburn eyebrow while avoiding his

gaze. In an effort to redirect his unwavering attention, she pertly inquired, "Is that the bell for tea?"

Colin chuckled at her transparent attempt to change the subject. "Do not think you escape so easily, my pet," he teased as they strolled toward the parlor, he shortening his stride to match her uneven gait.

Matching his playful tone, Olivia questioned, her green eyes smoldering with laughter, "Whatever makes you think I wish to escape, my lord?"

After tea, Olivia offered to show Deirdre the greenhouse, modestly claiming some botanical expertise. The younger girl begged off, preferring an afternoon buggy ride with O'Shea. Once the salon had emptied, Colin retrieved the accounts ledger from his desk and headed straight for the overseer's cottage.

Only this morning, after interviewing local food tradesmen, had he pieced together the final clue to Whitehead's embezzlement. He had tracked down the estate's food merchant and had found that prior to his arrival, two separate monthly purchases had been made by Whitehead, only one of which Colin could trace back to the books.

Earlier today, when Olivia had reported her "possible" theft, Colin had been able to deduce that there was more to her story than she had chosen to reveal. Satisfied that he had nearly solved the mystery on his own, he had not pressed her to divulge her secret. Pure chance had led him to discover Olivia and Whitehead in the courtyard that afternoon. Whitehead's confession had neatly dovetailed with the conclusions Colin had already drawn regarding the missing funds.

However, his grandfather's murder of the young servant had caught Colin completely by surprise. Concealing himself behind the hedge, he had barely contained his shock and disgust upon learning of Horace Forster's barbarism. Little wonder that Sorrelby's staff had seemed to be walking on eggshells since his arrival. Most likely, they feared that Horace's heir might have inherited his grandfather's ruthlessness. Vowing to make amends for the previous earl's wrongdoings, Colin set his gaze on the overseer's cottage and strode across the vast lawn.

After a brief knock, not bothering to await a response, he marched into the small cottage. Whitehead had been poring over some estate maps, restructuring crops and fields per Colin's direction. His head shot up when the door swung open, his initial look of annoyance becoming one of wariness. Sharp, black eyes flew to the ledger book Colin held and then back again to Colin's serene expression, before he arose slowly from behind his desk.

"M'lord," he greeted.

"Afternoon, Whitehead," Colin returned amiably. "Sit down. I need to talk to you."

For a moment Whitehead cursed his own stupidity for revealing the truth about the ledger to the inquisitive Miss Knowles, but then reconsidered. She had promised to speak with him before informing Lord Sorrelby of the embezzlement, and for some reason Whitehead believed her.

Colin tossed the book upon the desk and sat down across from the steward, long legs propped leisurely upon the corner of the desk.

"I know about the kitchen boy's death."

Whitehead flinched imperceptibly at Colin's casual announcement, but Colin disregarded the man's start of surprise.

"I know that the late earl killed the lad and that he threatened to send you to the gallows should you not keep quiet about the murder." He paused, his expression unreadable as his keen eyes probed Whitehead's face.

"I am sorry that you were forced to hide his crime for him. There is no excuse for his actions, and I do not intend to offer one. I am not Horace Forster, and I do not blackmail my employees."

He maintained his calm demeanor while a note of iron crept into his voice.

"Neither do I tolerate being cheated. I expect and demand total honesty and loyalty from all those serving Sorrelby." Colin pierced the steward with a steely look.

"As I am sure you are well aware, I discovered funds missing from the accounts. I further know why those monies

were diverted and by whom. I cannot fault you for caring for
Sorrelby's people, although I strongly object to your creative
bookkeeping.

"What's past is past, but heed me well, Whitehead. You're a
good steward and I am going to keep you on. But the accounts
you keep for me will be crystal clear and balanced to the penny,
understood?"

Colin had admired the man's control throughout his speech.
Whitehead moved not a single muscle while his employer
accused him of embezzlement; his features revealed nary a
trace of emotion. When Colin stated that he planned to keep
him on, a slight release of the steward's sinewy shoulders was
the only indication of his relief.

The man's chiseled face now darkened. "Yes, m'lord. You
have my word," Whitehead assured him.

"Fine. Your word is something I hope to value."

Colin held out his hand and Whitehead shook it fervently, a
small crack evident in the man's usually impenetrable facade.

"And Whitehead"—Colin gestured to the ledger—"I expect
to see you in my office tomorrow at three o'clock with that
book cleaned up and comprehensible."

A hint of a smile flitted across the steward's brown,
weathered face. "Aye, m'lord."

Colin left the cottage, satisfied with the interview. Frankly,
he admired the man's courage in defying the barbarous Horace
Forster. O'Shea had pried enough information from one or two
servants to surmise the horrendous living conditions that the
Fifth Earl of Sorrelby had imposed upon his staff. Whitehead
had put himself at tremendous risk to care for them, for if
Horace had ever discovered his duplicity, he would have been
hanged in a thrice.

Pleased with the manner in which he had dealt with the
steward, Colin now turned his focus to the fiery-haired female
who had dominated his thoughts for the past two weeks.
Earlier, when Colin had eavesdropped on Olivia and Whitehead's conversation, Colin had wanted to rush forward and
shake her till her teeth rattled and had almost revealed himself
when Whitehead had caught hold of her wrist in a threatening
manner. The impetuous little goose might have found herself in

over her head if Whitehead had been a different man. The mere idea of confronting, on her own, a man she knew to be a thief was foolhardy at best.

Knowing Olivia as he did, Colin decided the best course of action would be to allow her to stew in her own guilt for a while. She, undoubtedly, would torment herself as to whether or not to disclose the embezzlement or not, fighting her conscience on both sides of the issue. If she informed on Whitehead, she ran the risk of bringing on his dismissal or worse. Then again, her sense of loyalty to Colin would ultimately demand that she confide her secret to the master of the house. Colin considered a few days of mental anguish appropriate punishment for the thoughtless jeopardy in which she might have placed herself.

Striding across the lush green, well-manicured lawn, Colin surveyed his new residence. The additional staff had already made a difference in the estate's upkeep, and Colin was pleased with the rapid improvement. He still found it difficult to believe that Sorrelby was now his. From the first moment he laid eyes on the manor, he had felt as if he were returning to his roots.

Instinctively, he loved the manor where generation after generation of Sorrelbys had been born and raised, he being the exception. With a silent vow he promised himself that his heir would be born here and would come to love this land as he already did.

Of course, an heir would need a mother, and the mother that Colin had chosen for his children did not seem willing to accommodate him. At least, not yet.

Increasing his pace, Colin walked swiftly toward the conservatory, where, through the opaque windows, he could see his mother and Olivia bent over a flowering bush. Entering soundlessly through the conservatory door, Colin moved on his quiet cat's feet to a point a few yards away.

". . . if you haven't yet noticed, the manor's well is fed by a natural hot springs, so that the water is quite warm, requiring minimal heating for bathing," Olivia explained, studying the magenta blossoms of an exceptionally striking flower.

"Really?" Deirdre commented. "How very interesting."

"Yes. The head gardener, Drysdale, says that the natural minerals are one reason the greenhouse plants flourish. Have you met Drysdale yet?" Olivia asked. "He's such a darling fellow. When I was bedridden the first week, Smythe would bring me bouquets to cheer me up, and Mr. Drysdale insisted on meeting the recipient of his cherished blossoms."

As Olivia spoke, an unbidden tremor ran up her spine. Since the conservatory was rather warm, she could not attribute her shivering to a draft, but instead began looking around and soon spotted Colin camouflaged behind a large palm.

"Ah-hah! We are being spied upon, Lady Forster. Over there." Olivia pointed to Colin emerging from behind the tree.

"Colin, you must leave off your military mannerisms," Deirdre chided. She turned to Olivia and asked, "Did he tell you he trained espionage units for Lord Wellesley? He received the highest decorations."

"No, he has not mentioned his training," Olivia answered, intrigued despite herself. She had difficulty reconciling her image of "The Devil's Darling" with Colin Forster, war hero.

"His French is absolutely impeccable," Deirdre elaborated, "and frequently he was sent to infiltrate enemy camps, placing himself in the gravest danger."

"You don't say," Olivia remarked, her eyes wide with interest.

Colin responded with a noncommittal grunt, reluctant to discuss his military stint, and eager to be alone with Olivia.

"Mother, I hope you have enjoyed your botanical lesson, but if I may, I would like to borrow Olivia for a few minutes."

"Certainly. Eleanor and Victoria should be returning soon, and I have some correspondence I must see to first," Deirdre answered, flashing her son a conspiratorial smile. "I will see both of you at tea, and thank you, Olivia, for the informative tour."

"Shall we sit down?" Colin proposed after his mother had left. He gestured to a nearby bench, and they sat down, Olivia careful to place some distance between them.

"How interesting that you have never mentioned your wartime activities," Olivia commented, her curiosity piqued.

"Not that interesting, really. I choose not to discuss it," he answered flatly.

"Why?"

Colin eyed her speculatively.

"Why do you think?"

Olivia grinned, recognizing that he challenged her. He wanted to see just how well she thought she knew him.

"Well," she drawled, "I would hazard that you enjoy your Lothario reputation, using it as a shield to hide behind. If people were to know of your laudable wartime efforts, they might view you in a different light, take you more seriously. And for whatever reason, you prefer to be perceived, at least by the general public, as an easygoing ladies' man without a care in the world."

Colin's expression did not indicate the shock he suffered on hearing Olivia's words and recognizing how correctly she had read him. He would not have believed she could so easily penetrate the facade he had cultivated for the majority of his adult years.

"So, am I right?" she goaded him.

"To some degree," he conceded, disinclined to further pursue this line of conversation. "But enough about me. Tell me, have you fully recovered from last night's startling revelations?"

Respectful of Colin's desire to dismiss the prior subject, Olivia pondered her answer to his last inquiry. She pursed her lips in a delightfully puckish manner.

"Well," she began, "I'm an absolute hodgepodge of emotions, both overjoyed and terrified. Naturally, I am thrilled to learn the history of my mother's family—a history of which she, herself, was deprived. To know that she was loved by her family and that she had a happy childhood, that pleases me.

"Additionally, your mother, if only by marriage, is now my aunt and . . . I cannot explain to you the intense attachment that I already feel for her. She is a remarkable woman."

Olivia tilted her head to one side, recalling their earlier conversation.

"Lady Forster and I were just discussing how odd the parallels are between my mother's life and my own. I was orphaned at the age of seven when my parents' ship went down in St. George's Channel; she was eight years old and believed to be orphaned in a boating accident. Coincidental, is it not?"

"Very interesting," Colin agreed. "So what terrifies you?"

With a shrug Olivia conceded to herself that she would have to eat humble pie on this issue.

"Well, I am sure that you're delighted, but I am horrified to discover that I am not exactly who I thought I was—the simple daughter of a country cleric.

"These many years I have staunchly clung to the belief that all that interbreeding favored by the aristocracy had dulled their highbrow wits, and now I find that I, too, by my own prejudice, am lumped into the same category as those beetle-brained bluebloods!"

Uncharacteristically abashed, Olivia continued, her voice sincere. "I, therefore, offer my apologies for the disparaging remarks I made to you the other day regarding your peers. Like it or not, by the vagaries of fate, my ancestry is as disgustingly lofty as your own."

Colin would have laughed except for the stricken expression on Olivia's face. And yet, he could not resist teasing in mock sympathy, "Oh, yes, poor girl. Such rotten luck."

Olivia finally did laugh, and Colin joined her, irresistibly drawn by the musical tinkling of her laughter. When their mirth subsided, they found themselves looking into each other's eyes, a feeling of companionship drawing them together. Within a heartbeat the companionable mood warmed into something deeper, and Olivia's brain signaled a warning as she sensed the shifting currents between them.

Reflexively she held out a restraining hand, but it was trapped against Colin's chest when he suddenly crushed her to him. He pressed his open mouth against the long column of her neck, flicking his tongue across her sensitive skin. Her eyes closed as she battled her traitorous body while Colin traced a delicious path of moist, nipping kisses to the shell-like opening of her ear. Gently nibbling upon her earlobe, he whispered endearments that caused Olivia's heart to soar.

Despite the stern lectures to herself, passion overrode her sensibilities, and she surrendered to his ardor. Wrapping her arms around his broad back, she held him close, turning her face to his. Colin, detecting her capitulation, brought his lips to meet hers, and the rapture returned in all its glory. The sweetest of fires spread throughout Olivia's veins as she met Colin's embrace, caress for caress. Her breath was labored when Colin finally raised his head, her chest rising and falling in a halting rhythm. She felt his large hand upon her back, his damp palm clinging to the sheer cotton of her gown.

Colin continued to lean over her, searching her face for the secret to his near debilitating passion. Throughout the years he had known dozens of women, many unrivaled in their beauty, some expertly skilled in the arts of pleasing a man. He had enjoyed them all in a playful, detached manner. None had ever affected him so profoundly as this emerald-eyed angel. This one kiss had almost knocked him to his knees.

"My God," he swore, "you *are* going to marry me, Olivia!"

Olivia shrank away from him, her eyes round with the realization of the liberties she had allowed him. She held out her arm, her hand extended, warding Colin away. In a placating, yet shaky, voice, she responded, "N-n-now, Colin, let us not be hasty. I regret that my wanton behavior has encouraged you, but I made myself quite clear the other day: I shall not wed you."

Alarmed by his darkening scowl, she hastily added, "I cannot condemn your conduct, for I know that I am equally to blame, but a kiss or two does not a betrothal make."

Colin bit his tongue to keep from shouting his disbelief. "My dear Olivia," he began, his tone that of a schoolmaster speaking to an especially obtuse pupil, "if I had allowed our embrace to run its course, we would have left this greenhouse in search of a minister. Do I make myself clear?"

Olivia bobbed her head nervously. "And I appreciate your . . . restraint, my lord, and again, I can only apologize for my behavior. Most unladylike, I am sure." Her tone brightening, she added, "But since no damage was done, and, in my opinion, I have not been . . . er . . . compromised, all's well that ends well, wouldn't you say?"

For a man who was famous for his iron-controlled temper,

Colin felt like smashing his fist into the garden wall. *When would she ever relent?*

"Olivia," he spoke, his teeth grinding together. "Some might say that our recent embrace has most certainly compromised you." He rested his forefinger upon her lips to forestall her protest. "However, since no one witnessed the incident, aside from the two of us, I will not force your hand. But you must understand that I am determined to make you my wife."

With a sigh and a rueful smile, Olivia answered him. "Please, Colin, believe me when I say that I have considered your offer, and after thinking upon it, I am honored. Unfortunately, I do not believe I am suited for such a logical and sensible union. I understand all your rational arguments, but I am afraid that both of us might come to regret such an act."

Colin froze. Logical, sensible, and rational. Is that how he had proposed? Granted, he liked to approach a situation in a pragmatic manner, but perhaps he had erred in his choice of words with his intended bride. What had happened to his legendary suavity? While contemplating a more complimentary tack, the door to the greenhouse opened and Smythe entered.

"My lord, Miss Katherine, Miss Margaret, and Mr. Nicholson have returned and have requested tea. Lady Forster asked if you could join them in the parlor."

"Lovely!" Olivia exclaimed, hopping up and reaching for her crutches, leaving Colin little choice but to accompany her.

"You seem to have a habit of slipping away when I wish to talk with you, minx," Colin grumbled on their way to the parlor.

Olivia beamed up at him, innocent as a lamb.

"Had you anything further to discuss with me, my lord?"

"You know perfectly well this discussion is not over."

"Ah, look, everyone is here!" Olivia exclaimed as Smythe held open the parlor door for them to enter.

"Everyone *is* here," a strident voice rang out from behind them, startling them on the parlor's threshold.

Ten paces back a trio of newcomers stood, still clad in their traveling gear. Two women, dressed opulently in the height of fashion, stood side by side, their appearance indicating that they had only their dressmaker in common. The dark-haired woman was beautiful, her chocolate eyes bright and flashing, her figure amply curving beneath her cloak. Her face had been finely molded by a master craftsman, its artistic features enhanced by a small beauty mark to the left of her pouting mouth.

Her smaller companion, a pale, mousy young lady, faded in the other woman's shadow. She hovered nervously by her comely friend's side, while the third member of the party watched them with bored amusement.

Blond and blue-eyed, his features were striking, although the sardonic twist to his lips detracted slightly from his Adonis-like appearance. Almost as tall as Colin, he stood apart from the two women, yawning behind his hand.

The dark-haired woman, who had obviously spoken before, stepped toward Colin, her hips sashaying, a heavy cloud of expensive perfume wafting in her wake.

"Colin, my pet," she purred, "it was very naughty of you to leave London without informing me. I worried so until I learned of your whereabouts."

"Beatrice," Colin greeted her with a perfunctory nod of his head, his face expressionless. He looked over to the blond-haired man, who slowly sauntered forward, shrugging his wide shoulders.

"Sorry, old man," he said, "but when I discovered that she was planning on making the trip, I decided I ought to join the two ladies"—he drawled out the word *ladies* in a manner just short of insult—"for their safety." He scowled pointedly in Beatrice's direction and added, "We let ourselves in."

Although Colin's face remained impassive, standing beside him, Olivia could sense his leashed tension. She had rarely seen him without that teasing glint in his eyes, but now his violet eyes were glacial.

Katherine, arriving at the parlor door, asked impatiently, "Aren't you coming in for tea?" Her curious gaze scanned the crowd outside, alighting enviously upon Beatrice's lavish toilette.

"Tea? Marvelous," Beatrice cooed, strolling past Olivia without even a glance in her direction. The mousy woman scurried to catch up with her friend, darting a frightened look up at Colin as she passed.

"Shall we?" Colin inquired, gesturing to the parlor.

Olivia hobbled in, followed by the blond guest and Colin, while Smythe hurried off for additional tea service. The parlor overflowed with people, and Colin, quickly and curtly, made the introductions, hesitating when he reached Henry Nicholson, as the two had not previously met.

The new arrivals, Beatrice Haverland, Nellie Osborne, and Preston Campton, greeted the Forsters and Nicholsons with varying degrees of politeness. Lord Campton saluted each lady with a peck upon the hand, soliciting giggles from Eleanor and Victoria, and offered a hearty handshake to Henry. Lady Beatrice, on the other hand, straightaway assessed each person's social position by their dress and was thus rather cool toward the more plainly adorned Nicholsons. She neglected to address Olivia at all.

To alleviate the strained atmosphere, Lady Forster offered to pour, and the group took their seats. Beatrice pointedly sat beside Colin on the sofa and then leaned over to whisper into his ear.

Recalling the sweet nothings Colin had been whispering into her own ear a mere ten minutes ago, Olivia felt her blood slowly begin to boil. She did not wait for Colin's reaction, but turned to Henry and Katherine, sitting at her right, and asked with forced enthusiasm, "Tell me about your outing."

Henry, uncommonly effusive, answered, "We had a first-rate time. Enjoyed myself immensely. What about you, Miss Forster?"

Katherine confirmed Henry's opinion, adding, "It's unfortunate, though, that Mr. Browning could not join us for tea. As we were returning, a gentleman met us on the road, claiming that the physician was needed immediately in Mossgate. The man thought it might have been a case of lung fever. Horrid disease, I understand. Grandfather died of the very thing, didn't he?"

Olivia nodded affirmatively, amused to note that Katherine's attitude toward her had softened a bit. She could not help but wonder if Henry's presence prevented Katherine from acting the harridan.

Olivia tried to follow Henry and Katherine's conversation as they waxed enthusiastic about their picnic, but she was often distracted when, from the corner of her eye, she saw Beatrice lay her hand upon Colin's arm or lean into him, laughing huskily.

Finishing her tea, Olivia had decided to excuse herself, when Lord Campton walked over and seated himself in the chair to her left.

His voice low and intimate in the crowded room, he asked, "How has Colin managed to hide such a captivating creature as yourself here in the country?" His turquoise eyes gleamed as he spoke, appreciatively assessing Olivia from her richly hued hair to the tips of her small feet.

Olivia smiled, knowing that she ought to appear insulted by his forwardness. The proprieties would demand that she take offense and protest his obvious perusal of her form, but frankly, she was not offended. Instinctively she knew that Lord Campton's flirtatious manner was merely a game. The teasing glint in his eyes reminded her of Colin. Both men, she thought, presented a front of devil-may-care insouciance, but Olivia suspected that Lord Campton, like Colin, hid a more serious and intelligent character behind that fun-loving facade.

"The Earl of Sorrelby has not been hiding me. Mossgate, the small village you passed through, is my home. I live with my cousins, Henry and Margaret." She nodded in their direction.

"I see," he answered, his gaze roaming Olivia's face. "Do you know that you have the most stunningly magnificent hair I have ever seen? Botticelli must have been dreaming of you when he painted his Venus."

Olivia's laughter bubbled forth, arresting Colin's attention.

"Honestly, my lord! Venus, indeed. I thought Lord Sorrelby an outrageous charmer, but you, sir, are yet even more incorrigible!"

Although Colin had not a clear view of Olivia's face, he recognized all too clearly the lascivious intent in Preston's eyes and felt his jaw stiffen in anger. Damn it, the man might be his closest friend, but the seduction of his fiancée was insupportable!

Beatrice, also, paused in the midst of her mindless chatter to study the attractive pair across the room. She had been none too pleased upon her arrival to discover the uncommonly lovely Olivia at Colin's side. Beatrice considered herself to be the most beautiful woman in England and disliked any competition. All to the good if Lord Campton should dishonor the country wench before she captured Colin's interest.

Turning to Colin to resume her gossipy one-sided conversation, Beatrice's next words froze on her lips. Raging jealousy immobilized Colin's refined features, except for his brilliant amethyst eyes, which were shooting lethal daggers at the unsuspecting Lord Campton. Beatrice quietly released her breath in a hiss of anger.

Only two weeks away from London and he had already found some country lass with whom to dally. Not that it signified one way or the other, she thought. He had compromised her, Nellie had witnessed the act, and now she would bring him to heel.

The Earl of Wotbane had never denied his demanding young daughter anything she desired, and over the years Beatrice had grown accustomed to getting that which she desired. If she wanted Colin Forster, the Earl of Sorrelby, she would have him!

Nonetheless, it would not hurt her cause to discredit the redheaded chit, she thought. Perhaps the girl needed to be reminded of her place.

Beatrice waited for a pause in Olivia and Lord Campton's discussion, and then in a voice loud enough to carry, inquired with obvious insinuation, "Miss Knowles. You and Lord Campton seem to be getting along famously over there. I, sadly, have no brothers and am at such a loss when it comes to male conversation. I wonder, have *you* known many men?"

Olivia, unflustered by the assault, hesitated not a second before responding sweetly, "I regret that having been raised in the country, my acquaintances must be far fewer than your own."

Then, injecting as much sympathy into her voice as she

could muster, she added solicitously, "I hope that you have made up for your lack of brotherly companionship?"

Lord Campton suddenly choked on his tea, and Beatrice's dark brown eyes squinted in outrage.

"Quite," she managed from between her tightly compressed lips.

Lady Forster quickly rushed in, hoping to forestall any further unpleasantness, as she addressed the room at large.

"Unseasonably warm weather lately, wouldn't you agree?"

Margaret automatically picked up her lead, and the two were energetically engaged in their meteorological discussion, when Beatrice interrupted loudly.

"You, undoubtedly, must have lacked for"—Beatrice paused, encompassing the room in her joke as she shrugged in a helpless gesture—"to put it delicately . . . genteel diversion in your provincial little village. Tell me, Miss Knowles, how does a country girl entertain herself?"

Olivia forced down a knot of fury that threatened to close her throat. She knew the woman was deliberately baiting her, and it took every ounce of her self-control not to let loose her temper. With biting emphasis, she answered.

"*Not* at the expense of others, Lady Beatrice."

"Touché," Lord Campton whispered across from her, saluting her with his empty teacup. Olivia arose, her bearing regal despite the crutches.

"If you will all please excuse me."

Bested, Beatrice watched her nemesis hobble out the door, and then, as if on cue, murmuring of appointments to be kept and letters to be written, everyone arose, save herself and Nellie.

Colin, mindful of his uninvited guests, coolly offered, "Since you are here, Smythe will show you to your rooms. Campton, I'd like to speak with you in my study."

Lord Campton charitably acquiesced, and tea was adjourned.

Chapter Seven

"Blast it to hell, Pres, have you taken leave of your senses?" Colin rounded on his friend as soon as the heavy study doors closed behind them.

Preston raised one eyebrow in surprise, nonplussed by Colin's ire. All the years that Preston had known him, he had only heard Colin raise his voice on perhaps four or five occasions. His restraint was legendary throughout their circle.

Throwing his hands into the air, Colin rolled his eyes heavenward. "Whatever possessed you to bring that scheming Haverland female here? If you only knew what trap she has laid for me, you would understand the trouble you just escorted through my front door!"

Perplexed by Colin's seemingly overblown reaction, Preston raised a restraining hand to his friend's shoulder.

"Calm down, old man. I am fully aware of the so-called compromising position you found yourself in with our beloved Beatrice.

"And no," he warded off Colin's protest, "Bea has not yet made it common knowledge to the *ton*. I have my sources, you know. When I got wind of her intention to come to Sorrelby, I insisted, as the gentleman I am, on escorting her here. She had no choice but to accept my generous offer, but I assure you the vixen has been spitting nails the entire trip."

Preston shook his head, recalling the five hours of agony he had to endure in a coach with the thwarted Haverland.

"Lady Beatrice naturally assumed that arriving at your

country estate without an appropriate chaperon would clench the deal.

"You need not worry about the gossip yet, either. I believe that she is hoping to reel you in without exposing herself to that type of scandal. But do not underestimate the woman. She will definitely use it if she feels it necessary to force a proposal from you."

Steering them over to a pair of wingback chairs, Preston motioned for Colin to sit down as he poured two glasses of gin from the sidebar. After handing a glass to Colin, he sank into the luxurious leather and flashed his famous twisted smile.

"Call me skeptical, but I sincerely doubt that Beatrice is the reason for your unprecedented display of temper."

Colin scowled into the pale liquid. "Sorry for the outburst, Pres. I don't know what got into me. You saved me from certain disaster and I am grateful. I cannot imagine how Lord Wotbane allows his daughter to go skipping about the country with little or no supervision. By God, she would have really had me then, wouldn't she?"

Massaging his temple with the heel of his hand, Colin slumped deeper into his chair. "No, you're quite right. Beatrice comprises, at most, an annoyance. My ill humor is entirely due to the contrary Miss Olivia Knowles."

Preston's charmingly crooked smile quirked downward in disappointment. With a sigh of resignation, he commented, "I knew that I could not be so fortunate as to discover that delectable little morsel as yet unclaimed. Is she leading you a merry chase, then?"

A short bark of humorless laughter preceded Colin's response. "My reputation would be destroyed if the fellows at White's knew the hoops I've been jumping through. I've offered the girl marriage, and she's refused me twice already!"

Preston's languid pose vanished for an instant as he sat up, stiff and unbelieving in his chair.

"The devil, you say! Marriage?"

Colin nodded his head affirmatively. "I've considered the matter rather thoroughly, and it seems a practical solution to my dilemma. Since inheriting this title, and wealth, I have been plagued with the likes of Beatrice Haverland and hordes of other fortune-hunting misses. You understand, of course, how inconvenient this is in light of my active social life."

Preston smirked. "Indeed. During your absence, I have received at least six separate inquiries from your latest love interests as to your whereabouts. Naturally, I claimed complete ignorance.

"Which reminds me," he added with a wicked gleam and a speculative air. "I quite fancy the widow Chesterhaven, myself. Are she and you still *intime?*"

Colin waved his hand distractedly. "Nothing between us for months. You're welcome to her."

"Glad to hear it." Preston sipped his gin. "But, about your bewitching Miss Knowles. If she is reluctant to marry, certainly someone else would suffice. An attractive woman of good breeding, willing to become a countess, cannot be so difficult to unearth."

Colin's jet eyebrows lowered in consternation.

"I want Olivia. I want her very much," he baldly proclaimed. "She is the perfect candidate for my wife. She is witty, intelligent, and beautiful; she is from this area and will maintain a good rapport with the locals when I am in London. She dislikes London and its trappings, which I consider a definite attribute. Further, she has impeccable bloodlines that tie to the Forster name."

"My, my," Preston clucked, setting his glass down. "The great strategist has homed in on his quarry and is moving in for the kill. If I may be so bold, Colonel, you have overlooked one trifling issue. Your intended does not appear the type to sit by quietly while you dally in London."

"I can be discreet," Colin defended himself, jumping to his feet. Pacing back and forth, he explained, more to himself than to Preston, "I have not bothered in the past simply due to the fact that I was a bachelor. There was no reason to discourage the talk before."

"Inasmuch as that is true, old chum, frankly, she does not strike me as the malleable sort. I cannot picture that fiery-haired woman condoning *any* trifling on your part."

"I can handle Olivia," Colin growled, silencing the opinionated Lord Campton.

With a smirk Preston answered, "Well, best of luck to you then," and poured another round of gin.

The evening meal was an awkward affair, for Beatrice would not stop her thinly veiled attacks upon Olivia. Lady Forster and Lord Campton made numerous attempts to engage Beatrice in more innocuous topics, yet she always returned her attention to her targeted victim. Olivia, although tempted to retort in kind, recalled her uncle's many sermons about controlling her explosive temper, and thus either ignored Bea's barbs or responded with strained patience.

Despite his mother's subtle prodding, Colin disregarded Lady Beatrice's impertinence, oblivious to the strained undercurrents being passed with the mint jelly. Having been raised with three younger sisters, Colin had long ago learned to turn a deaf ear to female squabbling. Little did he realize that his silence was costing him greatly in the eyes of the persecuted Olivia as Bea's taunts grew more vicious. Preoccupied as to how best to pursue his courtship, he consumed an unusually large amount of wine, a fact which did not go unnoticed by Lord Campton.

Olivia, though grateful for Lady Forster's and Lord Campton's intervention, began to silently fume when she realized that Colin was not going to rebuke Beatrice for her increasingly rude remarks. Drawing her own conclusions, Olivia attributed Colin's reluctance to censure his gorgeous houseguest to the fact that he most likely planned to slip into Beatrice's room later that evening. She seethed as she pictured their two dark heads together, locked in a heated embrace. By the time the meal concluded, Olivia's temper was well whetted.

The ladies excused themselves, under Lady Forster's lead, and left the two gentlemen to their cigars and port. The younger girls were sent to bed, leaving the quartet of ladies to retire to the parlor.

Determined to evade Lady Beatrice's caustic tongue, Olivia sat down at the pianoforte. Sliding her long fingers across the cool ivory keys, she closed her eyes and breathed in the familiar lemony scent of the highly polished wood.

"Your mother was a gifted pianist," Deirdre spoke behind

her, in a reminiscing voice. "She began playing when she was but five and it was immediately evident that she had been blessed with talent. Play something for me, Olivia. Please."

Obligingly, Olivia struck up a pretty Irish ballad, singing the words beneath her breath, and yielding her tension to the lighthearted melody. Miss Osborne and Lady Beatrice whispered on the sofa while Deirdre Forster stood next to the piano, gently swaying to the familiar air.

Irked that Olivia appeared unruffled despite her best efforts, Bea approached the piano, compelled to set the girl down a few pegs.

Beatrice stood for a few moments, toying with her diamond pendant, her head tilted as if studying the music. "What a strange air!" she commented, frowning. "Did you learn it in some tavern?"

"Lady Beatrice!" Deirdre reproached her, a slight Irish lilt evidencing her anger. "That tune is well loved by the Irish people and one of my personal favorites."

Bea widened her thickly lashed eyes in mock bewilderment. "I do apologize, Your Ladyship. My musical training did not include folk tunes. I am curious, however," she asked spitefully, throwing caution to the wind as she glared at Olivia with a malicious sneer, "where a harlot would learn to play the piano."

Aghast, Lady Forster's sharp intake of breath echoed in the deathly silence of the room as Olivia's fingers fell mutely upon the keys. Rising regally to her feet, without the aid of her crutches, Olivia stared tranquilly into Beatrice's smug face.

"Where did *you* learn to play, Lady Beatrice?"

Nellie gasped, but her cry was eclipsed by the sharp ringing of Bea's hand making contact with Olivia's cheek. Olivia staggered under the vicious blow, and Lady Forster leaped forward to assist her. At that very moment the parlor doors swung open and the two men entered, the clap of the blow still resounding throughout the room.

Colin and Preston stood momentarily upon the threshold, confounded by the tableau at the piano.

"What's going on here?" Colin demanded.

Though hindered by a slight limp, Olivia strode past him without a word, her ears ringing.

Deirdre hurried after her, pausing at the door to cast a condemning look upon her unfortunate son, before climbing the stairs in pursuit of Olivia.

On the sofa Miss Osborne nervously fiddled with her skirts, tears threatening to fall on her pale face. Bea had turned her back to the door in order to compose herself before facing Colin.

"What is this all about?" Colin demanded again, his face a dark thundercloud as he marched across the floor to confront Beatrice and Nellie.

Nellie began to sputter, but was instantly silenced by Beatrice's menacing countenance.

Her voice thin with false brightness, Bea answered, "I daresay Miss Knowles was tired. She didn't even have the courtesy to excuse herself."

Preston and Colin exchanged knowing glances. Annoyed, Colin acknowledged that he was not likely to pry the truth from Beatrice's lips, and Nellie looked as if she might faint dare he question her directly. Recalling the withering looks he had received from the two departed ladies, he resignedly determined to discuss the incident with his mother tomorrow. Aggravated that his wooing of Olivia was to be interrupted by Beatrice's meddling presence, Colin scowled at his uninvited guests before gruffly bidding them good night.

"Olivia"—Deirdre knocked—"may I come in?"

At the murmured assent Deirdre walked in expecting to find Olivia in tears. Quite to the contrary, Olivia stood before the open window, the frigid night breeze flowing around her, molding her thin gown against her youthful form.

"I'm cooling off," Olivia explained as she rubbed her hands over the prickly skin of her chilled upper arms. "I'm forever fighting my quick-tempered nature, you know, so I decided I ought to cool down before I marched back downstairs and gave Lady Beatrice a lesson in good old-fashioned fisticuffs!"

Olivia shook a fist at the silvery moon overhead, and Deirdre chuckled with relief. "And here, I thought you'd be in need of a consoling shoulder to cry on!"

Still facing the starlit sky, Olivia answered, "I might not have use for a shoulder but I am in need of your help. Could you see that two letters are delivered as soon as is possible?"

"Certainly, dear." Deirdre frowned. "I'll ask O'Shea to deliver them at first light."

"Thank you. If you could wait just a moment." Olivia turned away from the window and took a pen and parchment to the table, rapidly penning two notes. The first missive she addressed to Mr. Whitehead, advising him of her plans to inform Lord Sorrelby of the embezzlement. She urged him to explain the circumstances surrounding the theft to the earl, assuring the steward that the earl was a man of compassion. Olivia determined that she could send a letter to the earl in a day or two, advising him of the theft and begging him to be lenient on the unfortunate Mr. Whitehead. If Mr. Whitehead chose to flee the area instead of facing Colin's wrath, at least he would have a few days' headstart, she reasoned.

The second note was for Henry, directing him to come around in the morning as early as possible to retrieve her and her baggage. She was ready to come home.

The next morning Olivia awoke at dawn with the headache, a sore ankle, and an unusual brightness to her left cheek. Memories of last night's scene with Beatrice did little to alleviate her discomfort, so when Polly knocked to see if she wanted breakfast in her room, she requested a medicinal herbal tea. By the time Polly returned with the teapot, Olivia had already gowned herself in her best lavender daydress.

"Polly, could you please pack my clothes for me? I'm returning home today."

The maid's cherubic face fell in disappointment. "Oh, miss, I'm sorry to see you leavin' us."

"Thank you, Polly. You've been simply wonderful." She hugged the startled servant. "I'll miss you and your sunny disposition."

Biting her lip, Olivia contemplated saying goodbye to Smythe, O'Shea, Deirdre, and her daughters. And Colin. Olivia had not yet informed Colin of her plans to return home, and she knew cowardice to be the reason.

Beatrice Haverland might offer a justification for Olivia's decision to flee Sorrelby Hall. The woman obviously had her sights set on Colin, and she certainly would not allow Olivia to interfere in her scheme. But, to be honest with herself, as much as Beatrice needled and baited her, Olivia deflected Beatrice's scorn with relative ease. The woman was not worth losing her temper over. Should Colin actually be interested in Lady Beatrice, perhaps it would be to the well and good for her to return to Mossgate, Olivia rationalized.

As valid as that argument might be, it was increasingly difficult for Olivia to deny her *true* reason for wishing to be gone from Sorrelby. Before learning of her association to the McClellan family, Olivia had been able to employ Colin's noble birth as a shield, behind which she could hide her burgeoning feelings for the irresistible earl. Ignorantly, she had pretended that she was incapable of caring for, much less marrying, a member of the upper class. Now that pretext was no longer available to her since she, herself, was a duke's descendant and had learned that social position had little to do with the quality of one's character.

No, to be honest, Colin affected her too greatly. He had merely to glance in her direction, and her pulse began to race. A casual touch set her atrembling. Determined to wed her, he had exercised all his considerable charm and wit these past days trying to convince her to accept his proposal. Their interlude in the greenhouse yesterday had almost been her undoing.

Olivia's cheeks flushed with warmth as her breast swelled in blissful recollection of Colin's hands touching her. Butterflies flitted in her stomach, reacting to the memory of his passionate kisses. Olivia pictured his handsome face leaning over her, his purple eyes glistening with ardor, a wayward black lock falling low over his forehead.

No, she thought, I would not be safe from myself if I were to stay here one more day. In Colin's arms she forgot reason and reality. When he held her and kissed her, she thought only of him.

Slamming her small fist into a pillow, Olivia groaned to

herself. If only things between them had been different. If only she did not melt at his lightest touch. If only he were not the most famous womanizer of the nineteenth century. If only he could consider their marriage a joyous union, instead of an intelligent business decision. But it was not to be. Her safest course of action would be to get away from Colin and his devastating charm, and to get away fast.

After gathering a few personal items, save a bracelet she had left with a note for Polly, Olivia left her suitcase in her room and walked downstairs for breakfast.

Certain that Mr. Browning would not approve, Olivia had abandoned the crutches after her flight from the parlor last night. Granted, her ankle still pained her somewhat, but not enough for her to resume use of the unwieldy walking aids.

Entering the breakfast room, she sighed, gratified to find only Lord Campton at the table.

"Good morning."

"And good morning to you, Miss Knowles," Preston greeted, rising to his feet to pull out her chair. "Are you always such an early riser?"

"Yes, I am. Thank you," she added as he seated her.

Lord Campton, like Colin, she noted, preferred understated attire. His forest-green jacket and buff-colored pants complemented his fair hair. He looked vigorous and athletic this morning, belying his lazy grin.

Passing the kippers and toast, Lord Campton commented with a small smile, "I dismissed Smythe. Told the old fellow I could pour my own coffee, so I hope you do not object if I pour for you?" And he raised the pot invitingly.

"Not at all." She proffered her cup. "Lady Forster has not yet come down?"

"Not to my knowledge. Beatrice and Nellie will probably be abed for another good hour or two, and Colin left early for a ride on Dublin."

"Mmm. What a pity," Olivia murmured, torn between relief and disappointment. Elaborating, she explained, "My cousin Henry is arriving this morning to take me home. I have not yet thanked Lord Sorrelby for his hospitality."

"Does Colin know that you intend to leave today?" Lord Campton inquired pleasantly.

Squirming ever-so-slightly in her seat, Olivia confessed, "No, he does not. With his family's arrival, and then your arrival . . . and other events . . . everything has been so hectic, I haven't informed him of my intentions."

With a wan smile Olivia looked to Lord Preston, mutely beseeching him to accept her lame excuse. He merely looked at her over the rim of his coffee cup.

A pang of guilt spurred Olivia.

"I could always leave a note if he does not return before Henry arrives."

"Yes, I suppose that you could," he responded noncommittally.

Cursing her faintheartedness, Olivia nonetheless leaped from her chair, babbling, "Well, it has been a pleasure, Lord Campton. I have so many people to speak with before I go that I must hurry. If I don't see Lord Sorrelby, I will leave a note, but would you please also extend to him my most heartfelt appreciation for his generosity in allowing me to recuperate here?"

"Of course," he responded, a hint of humor coloring his deep voice.

Olivia hastily made her exit.

Twenty minutes later, after having made all her goodbyes, save one, Olivia sat in the greenhouse, awaiting Henry, her battered traveling case at her side. Through the glass walls she would be able to see the cart when he drove up, and she did not want to waste any time jumping into the vehicle and urging forward the horse.

Lady Forster had shed a few tears when Olivia had sought her out to tell her of her imminent departure. The two women had grown very close during the past few days, and Olivia solemnly promised to correspond with her and the girls on a regular basis.

Both O'Shea and Smythe urged her to stay on a day or two more, for once, the two men in agreement.

"Ah, lassie, wouldna Mr. Browning feel better if ye rested a wee bit longer?" O'Shea asked.

"Quite right," Smythe agreed. "It would not be wise to overexert yourself before fully healed."

Olivia assured them that she was in fine health and, with hugs and kisses, told them that they were always welcome at the vicarage.

"There you are, Livi," Henry called, entering the greenhouse via the door to the manor.

Starting, Olivia exclaimed, "But I didn't see you drive up, Henry. Where's the cart?"

"In the stables. I arrived early. Thought I might be able to see Katherine, but she's not yet downstairs."

"Henry, you goose," Olivia scolded affectionately. "You cannot call on young ladies at eight in the morning. According to Lord Sorrelby, most ladies in London never arise before noon."

Henry scratched his golden curls and walked over to Olivia's bench.

"You don't say," he mumbled. "At any rate, Liv, it's just as well. I wanted to talk with you before I saw Katherine again."

Henry sat down and Olivia stood.

"Cannot we discuss this at home?" Olivia implored, casting furtive glances toward the door.

"It's fairly urgent business, Liv," Henry softly pleaded.

Undone by Henry's doe-eyed appeal, Olivia sank back onto the bench, folding her hands together with resigned patience. She forced an expectant smile to her face and resolutely turned her back to the door.

Henry self-consciously cleared his throat.

"I considered discussing this with Maggie at first, but then I thought that you know Katherine better than Mags does. And mayhaps Katherine has revealed to you her opinion of me."

Henry questioned her with a hopeful look.

Olivia shook her head. "Katherine and I have not shared many confidences, Henry."

He shrugged. "Not that it matters, I guess."

Drawing a deep breath, he expelled his words on a rush,

"What I need to ask is how does a fellow know if he's in love or not?"

"Henry!" Olivia exclaimed, unable to mask her shock. "With Katherine?"

He hung his head bashfully for a moment, then looked up at Olivia, spreading his arms in a helpless manner.

"Ah, Liv, you know me. Gadgets and contraptions, nuts and bolts. These, I understand. Love isn't as easy to piece together. I think that I'm in love with her, and I *believe* that she cares for me, but I just can't be sure. She says one thing and acts another way, and I really don't know what she wants from me.

"Growing up with you and Maggie, you might think that I would at least understand women"—Henry frowned sadly—"but, I don't."

Olivia patted Henry's hand consolingly. "Dear Henry, I assure you that I am no expert on the subject of love, but perhaps I can offer you a woman's perspective."

Gazing into the distance, Olivia spoke dreamily, unaware of the door behind her suddenly flying open and then being caught in a strong brown hand before it could slam against the wall.

"I think that love is a very complicated emotion. Not only does it bring joy, but it can also bring great pain. To love is to desire that person's happiness even above your very own. To thrill when that loved one enters the room; to die a tiny death when he leaves.

"When I think of loving a man, I imagine someone honest, stalwart, and compassionate. He would have to be able to laugh and to make me laugh. He would be a playmate, a friend, a husband, and a lover." Olivia shone her liquid green eyes into her cousin's face, her voice throbbing with pent emotion. "I believe, Henry, that you know it is truly love when you cannot bear the idea of continuing your life without that person by your side."

"Bloody hell!" a deep voice swore viciously. Olivia and Henry swiveled around to find, what looked to Henry, a demonic avenger swooping down upon them. Attired in black, his dark cloak swirling about him, Colin's furious glower lent credence to the netherworldly allusion as he came to stand, legs widespread, only a few feet away from the couple on the bench.

Caught in an early morning shower, Colin's wet hair was slicked back on his head, revealing more clearly the rage evident in every line of his noble face. He held his body rigidly, the damp clothing molding to his finely sculptured chest and arms. His tense physique trembled, the threatening violence barely bridled beneath the bulging muscles.

"I so hate to interrupt this intimate conversation," Colin said between clenched teeth. "But my houseguest neglected to bid me adieu before sneaking off with her baggage."

Shooting a withering glance at the hapless Henry before piercing Olivia once again with his glare, he continued sarcastically, "Of course, I understand your hurry to rush back into the arms of your lover, my dear, so by all means, let us make our goodbyes quickly so that you two can find a secluded corner for your lovemaking."

As Olivia's lips fell open in astonishment, Colin reached down and grabbed her by one wrist, hoisting her to her feet and into his arms. With savage intensity, his mouth took possession of hers, crushing her tender lips against her teeth and sucking the very breath from her. Olivia's chin was held immobile in one large palm, while Colin's other hand gripped her buttocks, pressing her against his hard maleness.

Although the kiss was harsh, Olivia did not struggle and within seconds the angry nature of Colin's embrace yielded to the familiar passion that thrived between them. The kiss softened, and when Olivia's lips would have clung to his, Colin sharply turned his head away and stepped back from her.

At first dumbfounded, Henry finally found his voice as the two separated. Angrily he demanded, "Now, see here—" but Olivia's staying hand cut short his tirade.

Colin's eyes briefly devoured Olivia. Near growling, he warned, "I *still* mean to marry you. Lover or no lover." And he spun about on his heel and stalked out of the greenhouse.

Shakily, Olivia raised her hand to her eyes and struggled for breath. Henry placed a comforting arm about her.

"My God, Olivia, the man is completely uncivilized. I cannot fathom how you have endured his company these past weeks. Has he . . ." Henry paused and squared his shoulders manfully. "Shall I call him out, Liv?"

Olivia half laughed under her breath. What a scene! Poor Henry, thinking of demanding satisfaction from that . . . that savage!

Regaining her senses, Olivia felt the quick rise of anger swelling in her breast. How dare he, she fumed. How dare he maul her in front of Henry? And to presume that she and Henry were lovers! Did he think that she was intimately involved with every man she sat with on this greenhouse bench?

Wrenching her case off the floor, Olivia stormed, "Let's go, Henry. I've had quite enough of Sorrelby Manor and its master!"

In his study Colin poured himself his second gin and slammed the crystal decanter onto the sidebar. None of his London compatriots would have been able to recognize him had they witnessed his behavior of a few moments ago. Easygoing, slow to temper, charming, possessed of a quick wit and a lighthearted character. Those were generally the terms used to describe Colin Forster. Before he met Miss Olivia Knowles, that is.

Awash with self-loathing, Colin threaded his fingers through his dark, wavy hair and tugged painfully at the roots. What was it about that woman that drove him to distraction? What happened to a cool head and detached involvement?

Colin sat down behind his desk and drummed his fingertips in a monotonous rhythm. Approach this rationally, he told himself. First, his life had undergone major upheaval in the last month, when you considered the inheritance and all its ramifications. Certainly enough to shake anyone's composure, he reassured himself.

Second, he had chosen a bride. A reluctant one, at that. She teased and titillated him, yet balked at marriage. What man would not be rattled by such a difficult pursuit of a woman? he asked.

When he had returned from his ride, Preston had advised him, with ill-concealed amusement, of Miss Knowles's precipitate departure. Livid that she was so eager to be gone from him,

Colin charged through the hallway in his wet riding clothes and into the greenhouse to discover her tête-à-tête with the handsome Henry. He noticed the especial pains she had taken with her appearance: her finest daygown, the stylish coiffure, and the irresistible crown of sweetpeas adorning her red-gold curls. Breathtaking. But for whom had she so coquettishly arrayed herself?

Then, overhearing her words of love, Colin's normally keen vision had become obscured by a fiery-red haze of anger and jealousy. Jealousy. Of a sudden, Colin caught himself up short in his contemplation. His fingers ceased their strumming. Had that invidious emotion been responsible for his outrageous conduct? Had jealousy disturbed his generally unshakable equilibrium?

Unfamiliar with the concept, Colin allowed himself a few minutes to dissect the idea. To his thinking, Olivia was his fiancée. He had decreed that she would be his wife, and thus, for all practical purposes, she was his. So, in finding her with another man, his inherent reaction was to guard that which was his. A simple matter of protecting one's territory. Nothing more complicated, he convinced himself, merely a question of ownership.

However, his precious little redheaded piece of property had just deserted him. Undoubtedly her sentiments toward him were not too favorable at this moment, either, after his cavemanlike behavior in the greenhouse. Well, he thought, he would give her a few hours to calm down, and then he would go after her. And this time the irresistible Colin Forster would do the wooing, not the hot-tempered stranger from the greenhouse.

Chapter Eight

❦

THREE DAYS THE earl rode into town to see Olivia and three times he was informed that she chose not to receive him. Although curious, Aunt Joan and Uncle Nathan held their tongues and bridled their curiosity, for despite closeting herself in her room during the earl's visits, Olivia appeared otherwise to be in fine spirits.

A fever outbreak had kept their household busy. One case had become two; two cases had become four; suddenly a small epidemic threatened Mossgate. Uncle Nathan supported families in prayer, and Aunt Joan prepared casseroles by the dozens for those too ill to cook for themselves. Margaret and Olivia assisted Mr. Browning, although the physician kept the young women away from the sickbeds for fear of their contracting the dreaded illness.

On the fourth day of Olivia's homecoming, she was walking back to the vicarage after delivering one of Aunt Joan's stews to an ailing neighbor. The morning was muggy, as the sun played hide-and-seek with threatening rain clouds. Olivia had enjoyed little sleep of late, and she felt as if the heavy, humid air weighed her down. Fatigued, she shuffled her feet along the dusty path, lamenting the condition of her soiled hem and yet too tired to lift it.

The tiny cottages bordering the thoroughfare, their appearance improved over the last weeks thanks to the recent influx of the earl's money, proudly flaunted bright coats of paint and mended fences. Olivia was halfheartedly admiring Mr. Grayson's freshly whitewashed porch when a large, dark shadow engulfed her own. Turning about, she saw Colin astride his black stallion, Dublin.

Her heart leaped to her throat, but Olivia deliberately subdued her fluttery reaction. Refusing to acknowledge him, she increased her stride as Colin slid from the saddle to stroll alongside her. Obstinately Olivia doubled her pace.

"Olivia, please," Colin began. "I must speak with you."

The mere sound of his voice unleashed an indescribable warmth in Olivia's veins. As usual, his impeccably tasteful and conservative dress emphasized the strong, lean lines of his athletic form, though Olivia did not allow her eyes to linger. Clutching her basket more tightly, she marched straight ahead, looking neither to the right nor to the left.

"I most humbly apologize for my atrocious conduct the other day. I cannot express strongly enough to you my extreme remorse."

Olivia turned past the white picket fence onto the vicarage's brick walkway, and Colin was forced to let her go ahead as he quickly looped Dublin's reins over the riding post. Running down the path, he caught up with her at the doorway and followed her inside.

"Olivia, hear me out," he pleaded, his baritone voice filling the small parlor.

Without looking directly into his spellbinding eyes, Olivia laid her basket upon the gleaming sideboard.

"I've heard you. Apology accepted. Now, please leave." An imperious finger pointed him toward the door.

"You don't look very forgiving," Colin teased with a playful pout, violet orbs twinkling.

"Hhmph," Olivia huffed, folding her arms across her chest. Her face was shadowed by the largest straw hat that Colin had ever seen. A green satin bow lent a modicum of charm to the headpiece while Olivia's thick gold and auburn braid trailed out from the tattered back. Colin grinned to himself, thinking that he had never seen her look more desirable.

Attempting to peek at her expression beneath the sheltering brim, Colin leaned over. He was not encouraged by her thin-lipped smile.

Blast him, she thought. *How dare he act the charming*

penitent when I am simply furious with him! Defiantly Olivia strove to hold on to her anger, for she knew that once she let down her guard, she would be forced to face the tumultuous emotions bubbling just beneath the surface of her ire. Admittedly, she had been incensed by his Neanderthal act in the greenhouse, but if the truth were to be told, she had already forgiven him.

Frankly, her anger stemmed from the fact that she had been unable to sleep nights, her dreams were so full of Colin. Haunting memories of his kisses caused her to toss fitfully in her once comfortable bed, her skin itching and tingling for his touch. Further irritating was the fact that Olivia lay restless and alone in Mossgate while Beatrice, the single-minded, husband-hunting miss, resided at Sorrelby Hall. Not only was Olivia miffed at Colin for tolerating the woman, but she was especially peeved at herself for being envious of someone like Beatrice Haverland. And if Olivia risked asking herself *why* she envied Beatrice, she knew the answer would not be to her liking. She was jealous of Beatrice, plain and simple. Time and time again, Olivia pondered Colin's proposal of a platonic union, recalling the sound, sensible reasons he had given her. Would he consider such a logical, pragmatic marriage to Beatrice? Or would passion and love drive him into the fair Beatrice's arms?

At any rate, Olivia tried very hard to sustain her indignation as Colin dropped to one knee in front of her, his hat in hand.

"Olivia, allow me to explain," he cajoled. "Although, I recognize that my conduct was inexcusable, I was beyond the pale when I discovered you with another man. I behaved irrationally. I"—Colin ground his teeth—"I should have known that I was not your sole suitor."

Pique prevented Olivia from correcting Colin on that point. Let him believe that I am well sought after, she thought. That I am showered with nosegays and sonnets. I certainly do not have to settle for a marriage of convenience because it suits him!

Rising to his feet, Colin continued, "I also spoke with mother, and she told me of Lady Beatrice's assault upon you. You need not concern yourself with her. Beatrice is of no significance whatsoever. A spoiled child, accustomed to getting what she wants. Unfortunately"—Colin shrugged—"she believes that she wants me, my title, and my fortune."

"She is welcome to them, as far as I am concerned," Olivia shot back.

"I sincerely hope you do not mean that, Olivia," he answered solemnly. "Lady Beatrice plans to tell all and sundry that I have compromised her, thus forcing me to offer for her."

"Well, have you?" Olivia demanded sharply, suddenly advancing upon him like a stalking tigress. "Have you compromised her?"

Taken aback, Colin stumbled over his words. "No! Well, er, technically perhaps, but certainly not intentionally."

"Ah-hah!" Olivia exclaimed with heat, her emerald eyes flashing dangerously. "Yet again, 'The Devil's Darling' conquers another unsuspecting female. Well, let me tell you something, Lord Sorrelby"—and Olivia began jabbing Colin's iron-hard chest with her finger as she emphasized each word with a forceful poke—"Beatrice Haverland may have you and your *sensible* marriage! I want none of it!" and she whirled on her heel and flew upstairs to her bedroom sanctuary.

Colin would have pursued her, but at that moment Henry entered the cottage through the back door, his arms laden with flowers from the garden that his mother had cut and asked him to bring inside. Seeing the handsome, tawny-haired Henry with what Colin assumed to be a love-offering for Olivia snapped the man's tenuous hold on his temper.

Choking on the most violent of oaths, Colin stalked out to his horse and roughly threw himself up into the saddle. The sun had lost its battle with the moisture-laden clouds, and now the gray, overcast sky aptly reflected Colin's dark mood. He raced back to the estate, relentlessly pushing his thoroughbred over the dangerously pitted road. The wind bitterly stung his eyes as he flew across the valley and up the small hill approaching the estate.

Anger and frustration spurred him on, and he literally charged into Sorrelby's stable on the winded and salt-lathered Dublin. Tossing the reins to a startled stableboy, he roughly admonished the lad to tend to the exhausted animal. Colin's black, wind-swept hair stood on end, and he bolted across the lawn, up the stairs and into the manor.

He flung upon the doors of the parlor to find it empty. Whirling on the threshold, he cursed and ran into the fragile Smythe, who barely managed to stay on his feet.

"May I be of assistance, my lord?" he inquired with concern.

"You may!" Colin thundered. "Where are they?"

Nervously Smythe smoothed his few gray hairs atop his head.

"If you refer to your houseguests, my lord, the ladies and Lord Campton are in the courtyard. Your—"

Smythe's sentence was left unfinished as Colin sped past the butler. Sensing trouble, Smythe followed the pounding of Colin's boots on the marble floor to the patio.

Lady Beatrice lay languidly upon a chaise, her ample bosom threatening to fall from the small piece of cloth that comprised the bodice of her dress. Miss Osborne sat in a chair to her side, reading aloud, while Lord Campton lounged in another chair, sipping from a glass and admiring the view so generously afforded by Beatrice.

The rising breeze ruffled the pages of the book that lay in Miss Osborne's lap, disturbing a pair of sparrows pecking at crumbs upon the patio. The monotonous hum of Miss Osborne's voice lulled her listeners into a tranquil, half-dozing state.

". . . something other dearer still than life," Miss Osborne read tonelessly. "The darkness—"

"Campton," Colin interrupted, his voice harsh against the still afternoon. The trio quickly came to attention. "Kindly see that the ladies have the benefit of your escort back to London this afternoon."

"Wh-what?" Beatrice exclaimed after a brief, stunned silence. As his words sank in, her lovely face contorted with indignation. "Are you throwing us out?"

Staring down at the slack-jawed beauty, Colin answered, his voice tight with angry impatience. "Your visit has been most enlightening, my dear, but I have decided it's time for you to be on your way."

Rising to her feet, Beatrice placed her fists on her hips and threatened, nearly shouting, "But you can't do this! Have you forgotten what took place in your town house courtyard, Lord Sorrelby?"

Mockingly, Colin raised one finger to his temple as if striving to recall.

"Oh, yes, I had almost forgotten. It wasn't that memorable, was it?"

Beatrice gaped, her mouth working futilely, struggling for words. Her vanity could not fathom his indifference; she, Beatrice Haverland, the most beautiful woman in England, forgettable!

"Well, I never!" she huffed, her indignation giving way to anger. "Mark my words, you'll live to regret this!" Gathering her skirts about her, she barked an order to Nellie, and the two ladies marched away in grand style, Smythe trailing in their wake.

Chuckling, Preston arose. "Not a pleasant woman to have on your bad side, old chum," he warned good-naturedly. "I think I'll ride alongside the coach on the return trip, if you'd be so good as to lend me a mount. Tantrums hold little appeal for me, you know.

"Any luck today in the village?" he continued merrily, slapping Colin on the back.

Preston and O'Shea had divined the reason for Colin's daily jaunts into Mossgate, and judging by the earl's black mood these past days, both had determined that Miss Knowles had not yet softened her attitude toward their unfortunate friend.

"I spoke with her at least," Colin dryly conceded. "She told me in no uncertain terms that Bea may have me."

To conceal his "I-told-you-so" smirk, Preston rubbed his jaw in a cogitating manner.

"Mmm, I see. Jealous, is she?"

"Jealous?" Colin frowned curiously at his friend. "Do you think so?"

"Well, you are more experienced than I in matters of the heart, old fellow, but, generally, when a woman throws another woman's name in your face, jealousy is the reason."

Colin nodded his head slowly.

"You might have hit the nail on the head, Pres. Good thing

I sent Bea packing. Perhaps once she exits the scene, Olivia will come around."

Preston shook Colin's hand in farewell, his trademark sardonic smile tinged with both amusement and a hint of envy. "Good luck to you then, Colin. In my estimation, your Miss Knowles is a prize worth winning."

Olivia did not feel much like a prize, lying across her bed, crying into the pillows to muffle her sobs. She felt simply wretched. Never having been prone to crying spells, she found the experience miserable. She did not weep prettily like Margaret, but rather sobbed her heart out till her eyes were red and swollen and she was convinced that she had squeezed out every drop of water to be had in her body.

Exhausted from the emotional storm, Olivia did not at first hear the gentle tapping on her bedroom door.

"Olivia," Margaret called. "Olivia, may I come in?"

Wiping her face upon Aunt Joan's handcrafted quilt, she answered hoarsely, "Yes. Come on in, Mags."

Margaret entered, quickly registering her cousin's distraught appearance. "I heard the earl was here again today," she ventured, seating herself upon the white iron bed next to Olivia.

With a slight hiccup, Olivia answered dejectedly, "Yes, he was here."

"Darling, I've never seen you cry like this. Why don't you tell me what troubles you so?" Margaret's round face creased with tiny lines of worry.

"Oh, Maggie," Olivia cried, throwing her arms around her sympathetic cousin. "I have done the stupidest thing imaginable. I fear that I have fallen in love with the Earl of Sorrelby!"

Not surprised by the confession, Maggie patted Olivia consolingly. "Ah, sweetie, there, there. He is very handsome and very charming. Who could blame you?" With a halfhearted attempt at humor, she joked, "I'm afraid that even Mother is slightly enamored of the dashing earl. Have you noticed the way she dresses for tea lately?"

Olivia groaned and buried her face in her hands. "Precisely. Women fawn over him. He has only to crook his little finger, and any number of women fall over themselves trying to win his favor."

"But you're not just any woman, Olivia. You're beautiful and intelligent and kind," Margaret argued. "And do not forget that you are also his social equal. The granddaughter of a duke! Why, I'm certain that if you set your mind to the task, you could have him on his knees begging for your affection!"

Olivia laughed recalling only this morning, Colin on bended knee, imploring her forgiveness. And in her temper she had shunned him, sending him back to the waiting arms of Beatrice Haverland.

Misinterpreting Olivia's feigned laughter, Margaret asked compassionately, "Has he shown no interest in you, then?"

With a cryptic smile Olivia answered, "Well, he *has* asked me to marry him once or twice."

Margaret blinked, then blinked again. "Are you serious?"

Olivia nodded, uncertain whether to laugh or to cry again in the face of Margaret's apparent bewilderment.

"I-I don't understand, Liv. Why are you crying? He wants to marry you? My heavens." Margaret distractedly chewed on a fingernail.

"Yes, but for all the wrong reasons. He wants a wife so that the marriageable London misses will shift their attention elsewhere. He says that he grows weary of their pursuit," Olivia explained. "The earl is looking for a suitable wife to reside at Sorrelby so that he may live the life of a bachelor in London without the worries of bachelorhood. He does not love me, Maggie. He wants a marriage of convenience."

"Are you sure, Liv?" Margaret persisted, a small frown settling between her blue eyes.

"Absolutely. He was most precise in detailing his needs."

"But"—Margaret blushed at broaching the topic—"surely he desires an heir."

Olivia paused and cocked her head, her braid spilling over her shoulder. In a matter-of-fact voice she responded, "He did not make mention of it."

Turning pink, Margaret reflected on the few, brief kisses she had allowed Leonard. With puzzlement she asked, "Has he . . . has he not attempted even to kiss you?"

It was Olivia's turn to redden. "Well, yes. He has done that. But he proposed the marriage as a solid business arrangement, so I don't see how he could anticipate any . . . intimacy."

Margaret did not look convinced. "Could you not persuade him to fall in love with you?"

Despite her loveliness, obvious to everyone but herself, Olivia remained far from conceited. She sighed discontentedly.

"Beatrice Haverland wishes to wed him, and you, yourself, have seen her beauty. After my rashness of this morning, Colin has most likely already placed a ring upon Bea's finger."

Margaret pounced on her words. "What do you mean, your rashness of this morning?"

Olivia winced slightly, remembering her harsh words. "I told the earl that as far as I was concerned, Beatrice Haverland could have him and his fortune."

"Olivia, you didn't! How could you sentence the man you love to a lifetime with that shrew?"

"I was angry," she confessed. "But better that," Olivia argued, "than I wed a man who does not love me. Imagine, Maggie, what torture it would be to endure a loveless union while your husband sought out the company of other women. I could not bear it," she added sadly.

"Nor could I," Margaret affirmed. She hesitated a moment, thinking of her sweet, tender Leonard. "And yet . . . neither could I imagine choosing a life without the man I love."

Grasping Olivia's hand, she looked deeply into her friend's troubled green gaze. "Consider this, Olivia. If you were to marry the earl, he might come to love you . . . with time. Whereas if you forsake him now to Lady Beatrice, you shall never know."

Olivia gratefully squeezed Maggie's hand, sighing heavily.

"But how could I endure the pain should he never return my affection?"

Margaret had no answer.

After having watched Beatrice and Nellie flounce wrathfully into their coach, all the while Beatrice loudly condemning Preston for his decision to ride, Colin dropped the curtain from the window, silently wishing them Godspeed and good riddance. Relieved to be rid of Beatrice's cloying flirtatious mannerisms that had so irked him these past days, he walked down the hallway to his study and poured himself a celebratory drink.

He had spent only a quarter of an hour or so reviewing the latest financial reports when he was interrupted by his mother. Deirdre Forster appeared agitated as she rushed into the room, biting her lower lip to still its telltale trembling.

Aware of her distress, Colin arose from his chair and quickly came around the desk.

"What's wrong, Mother?"

"It's Katherine. She had complained of the headache, so I urged her to lay down for a rest. After a few hours, I grew concerned and crept into her room to check on her."

Raising her worried face to her son, Deirdre spoke in a near whisper. "She's burning up and her breathing is labored. I think she has the fever."

Colin swore quietly under his breath, not wishing to further alarm his mother.

"Don't worry, Mother," he calmed her. "I'll send O'Shea to Mossgate for Mr. Browning, and he'll be here within the hour. He's been very successful in treating the cases in the village. He'll know what to do."

Colin did not add that he knew the physician to be struggling to keep up with the overwhelming number of patients he already had to care for. Nor did he inform his mother that despite Mr. Browning's best efforts, two villagers had already succumbed to the illness.

Within a few minutes O'Shea was riding off to the village while Colin and Deirdre tried to soothe Katherine's feverish brow.

The Nicholson family sat at their tea when the knock came upon the door. Olivia stiffened, unable to believe that the earl would return after their confrontation of that morning. She and Margaret shared an eloquent non-verbal exchange before Joan Nicholson stated haltingly that she would answer the door. Aunt Joan paused a moment under the pretext of smoothing her apron, giving Olivia the opportunity to flee upstairs should she so desire, but the young girl remained steadfastly at the table.

"Sorry to disturb ye, Mrs. Nicholson, but I'm lookin' for the doctor and he's not at home. I thought he might be here."

"Mr. O'Shea, please come in. May I offer you a cup of tea?" Aunt Joan invited, leading him into the parlor. "In answer to your question, sir, Mr. Browning is not here, either. He has been back and forth between the Harris family and the Dickermans' most of the afternoon. Both families have grievously ill children, and we're all terribly concerned."

She gestured toward the tea table as Margaret poured a cup for their guest.

"You know my husband, the vicar, don't you, sir?"

O'Shea nodded his head in greeting, and the vicar arose to shake his hand.

"And of course, you know Henry and the girls," Joan added. "Margaret and Olivia have spent the past few days assisting Mr. Browning," she explained, clasping her hands together. "The good doctor hopes that the worst is over, and we pray that his hopes are realized."

"What brings you searching for the physician, Mr. O'Shea?" Olivia asked, forcing down her budding anxiety. "Is all well at Sorrelby?"

"'Fraid not, Miss Olivia. Miss Katherine has the fever, and Colin told me to fetch Mr. Browning as fast as I'm able."

"Katherine?" Henry repeated hoarsely, his face stricken. "Katherine is ill?"

"Oh, dear me," Aunt Joan moaned. "I am so sorry to hear that, Mr. O'Shea. I don't see how Mr. Browning can get away when those two children are barely clinging to life."

Olivia stood up.

"He cannot leave them now, Aunt Joan. You're quite right. But I can tend Katherine. I've seen the proper treatment.

"I'll collect a few things upstairs while you drink your tea, Mr. O'Shea, and I'll be with you in a trice."

"I'm coming with you, Liv," Henry declared stoutly, jumping to his feet.

"No, you are not," she contradicted, pausing at the foot of the stairs. Weary from her crying bout of the morning and her endless hours of toil assisting Mr. Browning, light violet circles arched beneath Olivia's eyes. She knew, however, that she dared not reveal her fatigue, or Aunt Joan would adamantly reject her decision to go to Katherine.

Drawing on some hidden reserve of energy, Olivia straightened her aching shoulders.

"I've been exposed to the fever, and fortunately, I've remained healthy. You might not be so lucky." She glanced around the room, adding, "Besides, you know that Mr. Browning cannot spare any of you."

Studying Henry's ashen face, she walked over to him, murmuring in his ear, "I'll take care of her for you, Henry. I promise." And she ran up the stairs to her room.

Within five minutes Olivia joined O'Shea outside. Aunt Joan squeezed her tightly, begging her to take care of herself, while Uncle Nathan smiled benevolently behind his glasses, his warm look expressing his love and approval.

With no time to waste, Olivia straddled the borrowed horse and waved goodbye. As the two galloped down the dirt road, Olivia caught O'Shea's stare. Agog, he gawked at Olivia's long legs, scandalously exposed by her hitched skirts.

With a shrug of apology, she explained, "I never learned to ride sidesaddle."

O'Shea stared for a moment longer, then shrugged himself. Sidesaddle or astride, Miss Olivia was a true lady, he thought with a smile.

Chapter Nine

✧

Dusk descended as the pair arrived at Sorrelby Hall. Olivia jumped down from her horse in front of the main steps, allowing O'Shea to lead her mount to the stables. Bounding up the stairs, her bag in hand, she stopped at the imposing double doors and patted her disheveled hair. Prior to leaving, she had pinned up her braid, but a few escaping tendrils curled casually around her oval face.

As she raised the knocker, the door swung open and Smythe greeted her, his thin, lined face gaunt with concern.

"Miss Knowles. Have you arrived with Mr. Browning?" He attempted to peer around her for the awaited physician.

Stepping inside the door, Olivia explained, "He cannot leave Mossgate yet, so I came to nurse Katherine."

"Well, then, we're glad to have you here, miss."

Smythe led her upstairs to Katherine's room. The scene that presented itself to Olivia tugged at her heartstrings.

A single lamp illuminated the pale figures as twilight infiltrated the hushed bedroom. Colin and Deirdre sat on either side of Katherine's bed, alternately mopping her brow with a cool cloth and replacing the blankets that Katherine threw off in her feverish struggles. The heavy cream-colored bed hangings appeared gray in the shadowed room, enclosing the threesome in a despondent darkness, reflective of the somber ambience. Not a word was said as Olivia entered to stand beside Lady Forster.

Quietly she asked, "How long has she been feverish?"

"Four or five hours, I believe," Deirdre answered.

Laying her hand on the older woman's shoulder, Olivia suggested, "Why don't you check on Eleanor and Tori? They must be frightened." Meaningfully, she added, "Tell them Katherine is going to be just fine."

Deirdre turned her head and looked up into Olivia's face, searching for reassurance. Her tearful amethyst gaze read the confidence and commitment in Olivia's expression, the strength of will and determination stamped across the young girl's features. With a nod of acquiescence, Deirdre arose, surrendering her chair to Olivia.

Across the bed Olivia met Colin's eyes. Instinctively she longed to rush to him, to soothe the lines of worry from his brow, and to wrap her slender arms around him. Instead, she offered a tentative smile.

He returned the smile and whispered softly, "Thank you."

Olivia did not know if he thanked her for reassuring his mother or for coming to Katherine's aid. She did know, in that instant, that she loved him with every fiber of her being. And she swore that she would not allow his sister to die.

Into the late evening and through the wee hours of the night, Olivia nursed Katherine. Methodically she bathed her hot, parched skin, anxiously searching for any sign that the fever might soon break. With Colin's help, she forced a specially prepared brew past Katherine's cracked lips, hoping that the meager amount of liquid would be enough to sustain the ailing girl.

Katherine moaned and tossed, her words incoherent. She struggled when the cup was raised to her lips, but so weakened, she could not long resist. Olivia soothed her with whispered words of comfort and her own cool hands. She plaited Katherine's long, dark hair, marveling at its texture, so similar to Colin's silky jet locks.

The night stretched interminably and Olivia's fears grew. The oppressive stillness disturbed her as she and Colin sat on either side of the bed a few hours before daybreak. Unbidden, her thoughts turned to the fragility and uncertainty of this world as evidenced by Katherine, so strong and vital but a few days past, now lying precariously near death's door. How tenuous our hold on this existence, Olivia brooded as she considered those issues cluttering her own life.

"Colin, I do not know if I should broach this subject now or not, but I need to talk with you about Mr. Whitehead," she began hesitantly.

Colin smiled thinly, having completely forgotten about Olivia's involvement in the theft of the ledger and her indecision about reporting the incident. Matters had been smoothed out with the steward to Colin's complete satisfaction, and the issue of the embezzlement was now ancient history.

"If it's regarding the embezzlement, Olivia, I know all about it and have already resolved the matter with Whitehead."

Surprised, Olivia exclaimed, "Did he confess?" thinking that perhaps her note had spurred the steward to make a clean breast of it.

"Not exactly." At her anxious expression he added, "Don't worry, Olivia, he is still in my employ and I understand what prompted him to steal the money."

Sinking back into her chair, she breathed with relief, gratified to have cleared her conscience. "I knew that you would understand."

Shaking his head, Colin asked, bemused, "Do you always think the best of people? Believing in Whitehead, believing in me?"

Olivia recalled her early impressions of Colin as an irresponsible playboy and jaded dandy and answered ruefully, "I am sorry to say I do not."

Colin saw her face register some unnamed emotion, but did not question her as she picked up a cloth and began bathing Katherine's forehead once again. Scrutinizing Olivia's solemn profile, Colin declared, "Since we're making confessions, I would appreciate an opportunity to explain about Beatrice."

Olivia paused in the bathing of Katherine's brow, but did not look up. Colin took her silence as an invitation to continue.

"It was Beatrice who prompted me to sojourn to the country by appearing one evening, uninvited, at my London town house. I was returning home from my club, after having enjoyed a few rounds of spirits, and Graves, the butler, told me a lady awaited me in the garden." Colin rolled his shoulders as if trying to rid himself of some invisible weight.

"To make a long story short, she grabbed my hand and placed it inside her gown at the precise moment that Nellie arrived to witness the exchange.

"I vow to you that I made no advances toward Beatrice. She had been pursuing me with a mind to marriage, and I assume that my lack of interest pushed her to such an extreme act."

Olivia finally glanced up from her ministrations, and Colin felt compelled to seek absolution in her eyes.

"You must believe me, Olivia. I have never been, nor ever will be, interested in Beatrice Haverland."

"No need to carry on, Colin. I believe you," she answered him easily.

Baffled by her simple statement, Colin could only stare blankly at her bent head. She had seemed so angry yesterday morning. He had been prepared to beat upon his chest and swear on his father's grave, if necessary. Instead, his word had sufficed. She believed him. Remarkable.

Through the window Olivia watched dawn approaching, praying that the new day would bring an improvement in Katherine's condition. The dark-haired girl lay quietly now, after having thrashed in her delirium throughout most of the night. Laying her hand along Katherine's forehead, Olivia bit down hard on her lip as she realized that the fever was still unabated. If anything, Katherine felt hotter than she had even a few hours earlier.

The day wore on and Olivia tirelessly maintained the routine; she bathed the girl's fevered skin, forced the herbal concoction past her patient's lips, and prayed. In desperation Olivia had altered the ingredients in the herbal remedy, hopeful that she might somehow stumble upon a miracle cure, but Katherine's fever did not lessen.

Colin remained with her every minute, and as he watched the shadows deepen under Olivia's eyes, he ordered her to bed, but she refused. In her exhaustion she had come to believe that only her presence was keeping Katherine alive.

The patient's raspy breath was the lone sound in the room as

Olivia looked out the window at the advancing twilight. The familiar pond nestled cozily in the green meadow, its waters reflecting the last rays of daylight. How often had she gazed upon those cool waters from her own sickbed, yearning to throw herself into its refreshing depths?

Abruptly Olivia jerked up from her position over Katherine. Her sudden movement startled Colin, a pained expression flashing over his face, as he assumed the worst. He darted a glance to the chair where his mother dozed, but then relaxed when he heard Katherine's labored intake of air.

Olivia answered his questioning frown, her voice urgent. "Colin, I need water from that pond," and she pointed out the window to its blue-green surface. "Enough water to fill a bathtub. Make certain they collect the coldest water they can, the icier the better."

Unquestioning, Colin arose and hurried out the door to see to her bidding. As Olivia waited, she stared down at the face so similar to the one she loved. Glancing to Deirdre, asleep in the corner, Olivia thought how strong the resemblance was between the three of them. A family united by love. She thought of Henry and his heartfelt confession and wondered if he would have a chance to join this family.

She tenderly stroked the girl's raven hair off her hot brow. Katherine, she silently pleaded, you cannot die. So many people love you and need you. Deirdre, Colin, Eleanor, and Victoria. Henry. And me.

Although Katherine's behavior toward her had often been uncharitable, Olivia had nonetheless grown fond of the girl. She saw beyond the jealousy and petty jibes to the frustrated young woman beneath the hard-edged veneer. She could not help but love Katherine when the girl reminded Olivia so much of her older brother.

"If you're half as tenacious as your brother," she whispered encouragingly to the unconscious Katherine, "you'll hold fast to this life."

Deirdre awoke when a half-dozen men struggled into the bedroom, each carrying two heavy buckets of water. They were followed by two more footmen, hefting the bathtub, and Colin, also laden with two pails of pond water.

Olivia gestured for the men to fill the tub, then waved them out of the room.

Noting Deirdre's consternation, Olivia explained her reasoning. "We simply must lower her temperature, for I doubt her body can withstand such a high fever much longer."

Understanding the severity of Katherine's condition, Deirdre tightly squeezed shut her eyes, cloaking her fear.

"I see," she finally said.

The three then lifted Katherine from the bed and lowered her, still clad in her bedclothes, into the frosty bathtub. Their patient stirred in the tub, yet remained unconscious while Olivia gently cradled her head above the water.

After five or ten minutes Olivia laid her palm against Katherine's forehead once again and, nodding to Colin and Deirdre, suggested they return her to the bed.

When they lay the dripping Katherine upon the bed, Olivia began to dry off the girl's face. Reaching for a clean cloth, she was gently patting the damp skin along Katherine's neck, when she froze. Tiny beads of perspiration were gathering along the girl's silky hairline. Not daring to believe what she saw, Olivia wiped away the small drops, only for them to reappear. Tears welled in her tired eyes.

Her voice shaking with joy and relief, she informed Colin and Deirdre, "Her fever has broken. She's going to be well."

Overcome, Deirdre wept into Colin's shirtfront while Olivia calmly completed the task of stripping off Katherine's wet nightgown and slipping a dry sheet beneath her cooling body.

Olivia offered a silent prayer of thanks, gazing upon the night-darkened pond. She was still staring out the window when Colin's deep voice broke through her meditation.

"I've sent Mother to her room. I will stay with Katherine while you rest. You look on the verge of collapse."

For once, Olivia did not argue with him, for she knew he was correct. She questioned whether her own legs could carry her exhausted form down the hallway to her old room.

"Yes, I think I will rest for a bit," she conceded. 'Call me, however, if her fever rises again."

Colin shook his head, amused. "She's going to be fine. You said so yourself, lady physician."

Olivia mustered a feeble smile. "Yes. I did say so, didn't I?"

Exhausted, yet ever so satisfied, Olivia dragged herself down the hall and pushed open the door to "her" room. Nostalgia washed over her as her gaze fell upon the worn silk coverlet and the lacy white pillows.

"Ah," she groaned contentedly, falling onto the bed and into a deep, exhausted sleep.

In London an ornately decorated coach, its curtains drawn, pulled up alongside the waterfront docks. The footman, attired grandly in black and gold, jumped down from the coachman's seat, anxiously clutching a pistol beneath his uniform's jacket. Uncomfortably he surveyed the unsavory crew of cutthroats lurking in the shadows of the seedy taverns and ramshackle warehouses that populated this section of London.

Muttering beneath his breath about "the chit's foolishness," the footman knocked on the carriage door. Garbed in a black cloak, the mysterious lady occupying the coach spoke from beneath her concealing veil.

"Over there." She gestured to two men hovering near the exit of a noisy pub. "Bring them here."

The footman looked over his shoulder.

"Ye want to speak with the likes 'o them, milady?"

"Yes. Now go get them," she ordered. "And remember, if you value your position, not a word to my father."

"Aye, milady."

Peeking from beneath the coach's curtain, she watched the footman scamper over to the designated duo. He spoke rapidly to the pair while nervously casting his eyes back and forth as if expecting a knife in his back at any moment. She saw the footman gesture toward the coach, and as he turned, the two men followed.

The coach door opened, and the woman quickly raised her perfumed kerchief to her nose to prevent herself from gagging. The stench from the two men nearly overpowered her as they climbed into the coach and sat on the opposing seat, their filthy clothing marring the pristine crimson velvet interior. One of the men was so large that his greasy hair nearly scraped the coach ceiling.

Perfect, she thought to herself, surveying the miscreants. Dirty and bedraggled, they appeared to be men of few scruples and a limited purse. One slight and wiry, the other much heavier and stockier, their aspect alone was thoroughly menacing. The large fellow's beady dark eyes sent a shiver up the young woman's spine, and she had the unfortunate feeling that he could see straight through her cloak and gown.

A hideous scar transfigured the smaller man so greatly that the woman was forced to avert her gaze to the enormous, beady-eyed man, although his lascivious stare unnerved her.

The scarred man spoke first.

"Wot do ye wants wit' us fancy gents, me fine laidy?"

The larger one laughed slightly at his cohort's wit.

Glad that her veil concealed her expression of revulsion, the lady addressed the scarred cutthroat.

"I want you to do a job for me. Are you interested?"

"That depends. Wot kinda job?"

"I want you to frighten a woman. Threaten her in such a way that she will leave the area. She is a nuisance to me, and I want her gone."

"And whar is this laidy?"

Breathing into her lacy handkerchief, the woman in black answered, "Her name is Olivia Knowles. She lives in Mossgate, a small village four or five hours outside London. I want her far from Mossgate; specifically, I want her away from Sorrelby Hall."

The woman removed her gloves and slipped from her finger a diamond-encrusted ring. Passing it to him gingerly, she dropped the ring into his hand so as not to actually make contact with the disfigured creature. Astutely she noted the flare of avarice in his eyes and commended herself on choosing well from the shadowed figures outside.

"When you have succeeded in driving her off, matching earrings will constitute your final payment."

The hideous character examined carefully the ring in his palm before asking, "Ye ain't inter'sed in bein' rid of 'er fer good, eh?"

"No!"

Alarmed, the woman raised her hand to her bountiful chest

and repeated, a note of trepidation evident in her husky voice, "No. You are not to harm her, only scare her away. Is that understood?"

"As ye like, m'laidy, eh, Howie?" He nudged his oversized mate in the ribs.

Howie at last spoke, and the woman understood his previous reticence. His high-pitched, girlish voice contrasted sharply with his burly size, undoubtedly rendering him the subject of much ridicule among his coarse contemporaries.

"Heh-heh, right, Burnsie. Wot the laidy wants."

Relieved, she watched as Burnsie reached for the door handle and the two men stepped outside. Before shutting the carriage door, however, he leaned inside.

"We'll be in touch after taikin' care of yer Miss Knowles," and he offered an exaggerated wink of his bloodshot eye.

"Fine," the lady curtly replied, eager for the odorous fellows to exit her immediate breathing area.

As the two men slunk back into the dockside shadows, Lady Beatrice Haverland leaned back against the velvet upholstery. Gleefully she wriggled her white, uncallused hands into her gloves.

"With that wench out of the way, I'll bring Colin Forster to the altar yet," she mused. "Even if I need Father's help to do it."

Colin had just climbed out of his bath when Smythe entered carrying a tray. Grabbing a towel, Colin rubbed himself down while Smythe laid out breakfast and poured his master a cup of coffee.

"By the way, my lord, Miss Knowles awoke and checked on Miss Katherine before requesting that Polly send Mr. O'Shea to her."

"What? Damnation!"

Colin snatched his britches off the bed, muttering, "I should have known. She's going to enlist O'Shea's help in sneaking off the estate again."

Smythe sniffed and continued unruffled. "Of course, I asked Polly to delay sending the message."

Colin arrested his frantic attempts to dress himself and sat down on the bed, laughing. "Smythe, you're an invaluable asset, old man."

"Thank you, my lord," the butler acknowledged, passing his master the steaming coffee. "I further instructed the kitchen to send up a breakfast tray for Miss Knowles."

"Most thoughtful of you, Smythe." Colin toasted the servant with his cup.

"Thank you again, my lord." Smythe allowed himself a tiny grin of satisfaction before closing the door behind him.

Colin finished dressing in a more leisurely fashion, then went in search of Olivia. After peeking into her room and determining that she had already dined, he found her at Katherine's bedside.

Olivia turned her head as he opened the door, then admonished him to be quiet with a finger against her lips. Rising, she tiptoed away from the bed, meeting Colin at the door. She gestured to the hallway, and Colin backed out of Katherine's room.

"She's resting peacefully. No fever, thank heavens. She will most likely sleep for some time as her body recovers from its ordeal."

Colin grasped Olivia's hand and raised it to his mouth. "Thanks to you, Olivia." He pressed her palm against his lips, breathing deeply of her naturally floral scent.

Skittish, Olivia withdrew her hand. "I did nothing deserving of your thanks. Katherine, herself, fought back. She'll probably be on her feet in a matter of days."

"Olivia . . ." Colin placed a finger beneath her chin, tilting her face up to his. "I wish to repay you for saving Katherine's life. I know, I know. You do not feel that your actions merit any thanks, but I disagree. Mother and I both believe that you rescued Katherine from near death. Mother has mentioned that you expressed interest in searching for your grandfather's family in Ireland. I would like to help you by retaining an investigator, a friend of mine, who can assist you in the search. You realize, of course, it will take time, but if you still have family in Ireland, he can find them for you."

Excitement bubbled in Olivia's veins and shone in her smiling eyes. "Really, Colin? You would do that for me?

I . . . I do not know what to say. My fondest desire has always been to learn more about my mother and her family. I thank you and gratefully accept your kind offer."

"And now?" Colin prompted, his hooded gaze warmly raking Olivia's flushed face.

"And now I shall return home," she answered simply, although her heart was doing flip-flops inside her breast.

"Home," Colin repeated, thinking that home for him would never be the same without this young woman. "Olivia, I know that I have not conducted myself well during this courtship, but I pray that you have found it in your heart to overlook my transgressions. At the risk of repeating myself, do you think that you could forgive my foolishness and do me the honor of becoming my wife?"

Olivia felt her breath leave her body, and the air around her became unnaturally still. She felt that time ceased as Colin's question hung in the silence between them. Margaret's words suddenly echoed in Olivia's ears.

If you marry him, perhaps he will learn to love you, in time. If you leave him to Beatrice Haverland, you will never know.

Then her own words came to her.

But how could I endure the pain should he never return my affection?

Olivia clutched her fist to her breast in an effort to subdue the ache there. She loved him so much! Good God, could she live without him? Could she tolerate seeing him take another for his wife? Years from now would the pain be any less when she saw him with his children, borne by another woman?

Olivia thought of Katherine and her own reflections of the past nights. Life was so precious, dare she waste a single moment that she might be able to share with this man? No, she must seize this chance. Imploring the fates to be kind to her, Olivia knew that she would have to take the risk. Perhaps he would never love her, but what choice had she? Her love for him was so all-consuming, the possible reward outweighed the peril.

Gazing into his eyes, Olivia tried to see directly into his soul. Was there any hint of love there? She saw the glitter of passion and the keenness of anticipation. But what other emotion flickered briefly there before being hidden by a sweep of black lashes?

In a voice she would not have recognized as her own, Olivia answered him.

"Yes, Colin. I will marry you."

Colin had not realized how tightly coiled he held himself until Olivia's words freed the paralyzing tension gripping him. A bolt of lightning shot through him, akin to joy, before he swept her into his arms.

His mouth came down hungrily upon hers, and for the first time Olivia held nothing back. She poured the emotion she dared not verbalize into her response. Colin plundered her mouth, his passion heightened by his sense of victory.

Olivia would be his! His and his alone. He branded her with his mouth and hands. He had never felt more powerful. This woman, whom he desired above all else, would soon be his wife. Colin's hands roamed freely over her yielding body, glorying in her feminine response to him. He felt intoxicated and invincible.

Olivia's knees started to buckle beneath her, and Colin's arm wrapped more tightly around her. Reluctantly withdrawing his mouth from hers, he lost himself in her passion-dazed emerald pools. The colorful clarity of her eyes reminded him of something else.

Not releasing his hold upon her, Colin reached into his coat pocket with his free hand. Deftly he withdrew the diamond-and-emerald ring that he had first selected from the jewelry collection.

Amazement showed on Olivia's face, prompting Colin to disclose, his deep voice caressing her, "I have not been without this ring since first I offered it to you."

Slipping it easily onto her finger, he added with a kiss, "I never gave up hope that someday you might accept it."

Chapter Ten

"Oh, Maggie! What if I've made a terrible mistake?"

"Come now, Livi, that's no way to talk on your wedding day," Margaret gently admonished, rearranging the gossamer veil that fell from the crown of white roses, nestled among Olivia's golden locks.

"But it's not too late!" Olivia declared near hysteria. "Tell O'Shea that I have to see Colin. Now. Hurry, Maggie!"

The floor-length mirror reflected the contrast between the two women. Margaret, arrayed in a sky-blue silk, lent to her by Eleanor, epitomized calm and composure. Even her blond curls rested serenely against her neck as she carefully tended the bride. Meticulously she arranged each and every fold of the voluminous veil, smoothing her white hand across any imperfection that might mar her cousin's fairy-tale presentation.

And Olivia did look like a princess from some ancient legend. Her wedding gown, a present from Colin's mother, had arrived only a few days ago from London. Deirdre Forster had sent a courier to the capital to contact one of London's most exclusive couturieres with explicit instructions on the type of wedding gown that must be fashioned for her son's bride.

Initially Olivia had protested such an extravagance for their small country wedding, but Deirdre had insisted, and when the gown arrived, Olivia secretly rejoiced at Lady Forster's perseverance. Never, Olivia thought, had she seen such a beautiful dress. The white silk gown dipped low, its neckline embroidered with tiny pearls. A wide satin sash hugged tightly beneath her breasts, the iridescent fabric falling straight to the floor. Petite cap sleeves were complemented by the elbow-length satin gloves that Deirdre had ordered with the dress.

However, no pearl-encrusted gown could disguise the alarm evident in the face staring back at Olivia in the mirror. Only a thin rim of green was visible outside Olivia's panic-stricken, oversize pupils. Her face was so pale that the gown appeared colorful by comparison. She looked like a frightened fawn, paralyzed by the glint of the hunter's gun.

Margaret's nimble fingers continued their ministrations as she inquired soothingly, "And what would you say to the earl, dear?"

"I-I'd tell him that I've had a change of heart."

"Has your heart changed, Olivia?" Margaret questioned quietly. "Do you doubt your love for him?"

Olivia closed her eyes against her inner turmoil, her thick auburn lashes resting against her pallid cheeks.

"No, Maggie. I do not doubt that I love him. I only doubt that he will ever love me."

"Olivia, you must have faith. I have seen the way he devours you with his eyes when you are unaware of his observation. He is far from indifferent to you, I assure you," Margaret spoke knowingly.

Olivia did not respond but allowed her mind to replay the events of the past week. Not surprisingly, Colin had demanded that the wedding take place almost immediately. Olivia thought, at first, that he planned to marry her that very day, but thankfully, a special license had to be procured from London, and Deirdre had insisted upon a proper wedding and a proper wedding gown. When Colin had asked with frustration how long it would take for the gown to be sent from London, Lady Forster had informed him that surely the couturiere would need at least a week. Brooking no argument, Colin had then set the date for exactly one week from the day that Olivia had allowed him to place the emerald ring upon her finger.

Although the wedding guest list was small, comprised of the Mossgate villagers and the Sorrelby staff, much needed to be accomplished during those few brief days. Aunt Joan's needle flew like the wind as she let out the seams on her one formal gown. She had also volunteered to take in Katherine's dress, since the young woman had lost substantial weight during her illness.

Margaret and Olivia packed together Olivia's treasures for her move to Sorrelby Hall. Many childhood mementos were anointed with tears before being carefully stowed between tissue and placed in Olivia's single trunk.

Colin seemed especially busy, visiting Olivia but once during their week-long engagement. His visit was enjoyable, although it left Olivia with a number of haunting and unanswered questions.

Naturally, he was his charming self, causing Aunt Joan to blush with his effusive compliments and charitably allowing the vicar to defeat him in a chess match. Knowing Colin's unprecedented skill at the game, not to mention his fierce competitive spirit, Olivia smiled to herself as Colin appeared to blunder with a poor move by his castle in the final throes of the match. The vicar happily captured Colin's king, inviting him back at a later date for a rematch.

After luncheon in the garden, Colin and Olivia took a brief stroll along the riverbank for a few moments of privacy. They meandered along the path in comfortable silence, their footfalls muffled by the thick, newly sprung grass underfoot. Colin politely inquired as to the wedding preparations, and Olivia responded with the same stilted courtesy. She studied the birds in the trees, the creek's mossy rocks, anything but the visage of the man who would be her husband in two short days. Colin followed her example, occasionally commenting on miscellaneous flora and fauna that crossed their path.

His unusually restrained manner provoked Olivia to wonder if he belatedly regretted his proposal to her, but she had not the courage to broach the subject. Her own feelings regarding the impending betrothal swung back and forth between elation and horror, making her loath to discuss the topic.

They walked a fair distance from Mossgate, leaving its straw-thatched cottages and curious residents behind. Once far from prying eyes, Olivia expected Colin to take her into his arms and recreate that private heaven she experienced when his lips captured her own. But he maintained the same impersonal conversation for the remainder of their walk, bestowing a brotherly peck upon her cheek before leading her back into the vicarage garden.

Now, only minutes away from her trip down the aisle, Olivia considered that innocent kiss upon her cheek. Mentally she shrugged, conceding that she had been correct regarding Colin's intentions toward her. As his wife, she would share his name, his home, his friends, but apparently, not his bed. Olivia suppressed a momentary flash of disappointment, assuring herself that she would not welcome that sort of attention from a man who did not love her in return. Physical intimacy and emotional intimacy must go hand in hand, Olivia reasoned. Surely, Colin would not expect anything different.

If, some day, love blossomed in Colin's heart, then perhaps the normal, physical side of marriage could be shared between them, Olivia told herself. But until then he would most likely avail himself of his London "lady friends" for that variety of entertainment. Olivia shuddered at the thought, dreading the day he would seek out another woman.

With fierce determination she refused to pursue that line of thinking on her wedding day. Elevating her firm, little chin a notch, she took a deep breath to calm herself. Regarding her reflection in the mirror, she nodded her head approvingly, and accepted the bouquet of roses and lilacs that Margaret held for her.

Through her bedroom window Olivia could hear the melodic strains of the church organ, welcoming their guests. Margaret's expectant pose told Olivia that the hour had arrived. Emulating her friend's example, Olivia strove for the same poised composure. She hugged Margaret to her, despite Maggie's remonstrations about wrinkling the immaculate bridal gown and veil, and the two girls walked downstairs, their arms intertwined.

Entering the church, Olivia's first thought was that Aunt Joan and Mr. Drysdale, Sorrelby's head gardener, had outdone themselves. Every nook and cranny of the picturesque country chapel spilled forth with an abundance of peonies, tulips, irises, lilies, sweet peas, and forget-me-nots. The profusion of perfume and color led her to believe for a brief instant that they stood in Aunt Joan's garden instead of in Uncle Nathan's house of worship.

The pews overflowed with Mossgate's natives, their good wishes and smiles fortifying Olivia's quaking limbs. She set her eyes toward the end of the aisle and saw her beloved Uncle Nathan awaiting her. To his side, elegantly attired in a dark blue coat, stood Colin. Olivia felt something catch in her throat as she gazed at the tall, raven-haired man soon to be her husband. Although she felt incapable of movement, his over-powering presence seemed to pull her toward him, and Olivia found herself slowly advancing down the aisle.

Arriving at the altar, she heard the final notes of the organ rise and then float away into the highest beams of the small chapel.

She tried to concentrate on the vicar's words, but could not. In a daze she examined the lilies in her bouquet, recalling the day that Colin had compared her to such a flower. Trancelike, she watched the flickering pattern of hues glancing off the sun-splashed stained-glass windows, convinced that Colin's eyes were the very color of Saint Francis's robe.

She started slightly when Uncle Nathan prompted her response to the vows, but nonetheless repeated the declaration in a clear, carrying voice. From a distance she heard Colin's distinctive voice echo the pledge. When Colin slipped the wedding band upon her left hand, Olivia met his gaze for the first time during the ceremony. She had not known what to expect.

Certainly not the laughter-tinged lavender eyes, crinkling at the corners in such a blatantly amused manner. Olivia frowned up at him, confounded by his apparent humor. He answered her with an audacious and exaggerated wink that for some un-earthly reason made Olivia want to laugh. She restrained her laugh but grinned up at him the way one would grin at a mischievous choir boy. He, in turn, flashed her a bright, boyishly disarming smile that so enchanted Olivia, she found her nervousness and anxiety slowly evaporating.

By the time Uncle Nathan pronounced them man and wife, Olivia's earlier trepidation had faded to the point where walking back down the aisle on Colin's arm, she could wave cheerfully to her friends and neighbors, returning their congratulations.

A crepe-festooned carriage awaited the newlyweds outside the church to transport them to Sorrelby Hall, where the wedding feast was to take place. After climbing into the carriage and taking her seat beside Colin, Olivia located Margaret in the throng and, with unerring accuracy, launched the bouquet into her cousin's arms. A roar of approval went up through the crowd, and O'Shea flicked the horses into a trot.

"All right," Olivia said, laughing, "what did you find so amusing?"

"Perhaps the fact"—and Colin playfully tweaked her pert nose—"that my countess was daydreaming of Francis of Assisi instead of me throughout our wedding ceremony."

Olivia tilted her head coquettishly to one side, whispering conspiratorially, "Don't let on, but I was a bit nervous back there."

Colin widened his eyes with feigned surprise. "No! I do not believe it."

"Oh, yes," she replied with an emphatic bob of her head. "Quite true."

Smiling, Colin linked his fingers behind his head and leaned back against the upholstered banquette, tilting his bronzed face up to the brilliant spring sun. Closing his eyes, he assured her, "Don't fret, my love. None were the wiser."

Olivia thrilled at the casual endearment, absorbing her husband's noble profile. Marriage must suit him, she thought to herself, for she had never seen him appear happier.

If Olivia had been able to read Colin's mind, she would have been flabbergasted by Colin's "happy" thoughts. At last, she is mine, he sang to himself. Only a few more hours, he calculated, and Olivia would be his, completely and irrevocably. No battlefield victory nor bedroom conquest compared to the rush of satisfaction he experienced in anticipation of his wedding night.

Even now he was tempted to dip his fingers into her inviting pearl-edged décolletage, where her creamy breasts thrust up from the satin sash. However, if he yielded to the temptation, he would never be able to let her go until he had enjoyed his fill. And upon their arrival Sorrelby would be overrun with hundreds of guests, feasting and fêting, so there would be little chance of whisking Olivia upstairs prior to the appointed time. But, he promised himself, the next couple of hours of restraint would be rewarded over and over again this evening in his massive four-poster bed.

Colin had spared no expense on the lavish wedding dinner, and Sorrelby sparkled in welcome as the carriage rolled up the drive. A tent had been set up on the far lawn, where the guests had already begun congregating. Flowers, food, and wine vied for space on the groaning buffet tables while the servants circulated with glasses of champagne, partaking themselves as they wound through the crowd.

After two glasses of champagne, Olivia was thoroughly relaxed, dancing and chatting and accepting marital words of wisdom from the village's most experienced wives. Colin, the object of much attention, found himself struggling to find time with his new bride. The villagers were eager to bend the earl's ear with thanks and congratulations, and he good-naturedly responded, all the while watching his wife flit happily along from one well-wisher to the next.

From the shadows of the nearby oaks, two poorly dressed men, reeking of rum, spied upon the wedding celebration.

"Well, now, wouldn't our foine laidy be surprised to find that 'er Miss Knowles is hitched?" Burnsie whispered out of the side of his scarred mouth.

Howie frowned, his beefy paw rubbing his head as if it pained him.

"I reckon we ain't gonna be gettin' them fancy earbobs then, huh, Burnsie?" he asked, his high-pitched voice tinged with disappointment.

"Whatcher talkin' bout, mate?"

"Well, we cain't 'ardly scare 'er off if she's got a damned earl for 'erself," he argued, scratching at his greasy pate.

"Aagh, Howie," he snorted in disgust, "ye never did learn t'think. This 'ere's our golden opportunity. We'll not only git the bobs from Lady 'igh 'n Mighty, but we'll git some silver from the earl asides."

Rolling his black eyes at Howie's obvious lack of understanding, Burnsie lowered his voice and outlined his nefarious
plan to his cohort.

The afternoon flew by in a festive blur of music and
champagne, surprising Olivia when the fading sun gilded the
revelers with its copper glow.

In conversation with the Widow Pickley, a firm hand
suddenly grasped Olivia's elbow, and a puff of warm breath
tickled her ear.

"My dear, I believe it is time for us to retire. Evening
beckons and our guests are eager to see us off to our wedding
chamber."

Olivia blushed at his low-pitched words, thankful that
Widow Pickley's hearing was not as acute as it used to be.

Nodding her assent, the earl called for his guests' attention,
thanking them for sharing this memorable occasion with him
and his lovely new countess. Olivia pretended not to see the sly
looks and wistful glances that followed the pair as they wended
their way to the manor.

Colin escorted her upstairs, throwing open the door to an
unfamiliar room. Apparently, thought Olivia, Lady Forster was
not the only one sending to London for goods. A thick,
rose-colored carpet graced the floor, and recently hung damask
curtains framed the view-affording windows. The coverlet
upon the bed bore none of the telltale fraying of the one Olivia
used in the guest bedroom down the hall, nor faded were the
roses, gracefully embellishing the new wallcovering.

"Why, it's lovely, Colin!" Olivia proclaimed, her gaze
skipping across the room from the gleaming rosewood armoire
to the silver toilette set.

"I did not want my bride's new home to be anything less
than she deserves," he stated with a low, sweeping bow. "I only
regret that I was unable to select each piece personally."

"I love it, truly," Olivia assured him. "Thank you."

Colin shifted uncomfortably as his manhood reacted to the
warmth in her jade-green eyes. Good God, but he was eager to
have her under him! He drew in his breath sharply, telling

himself that he must not rush her. An innocent and trusting wife warranted a proper wedding night.

"I'll send Polly to you right away," he offered, backing out the door.

"Mmm . . . good idea." Olivia stretched her arms overhead, stifling a delicate yawn. "It's still early but I'm positively drained."

Colin quirked an eyebrow, but made no comment as he closed the door behind him.

Shortly, Polly arrived with a light supper tray and hot water for a bath. After the footmen had left with their empty buckets, Olivia disrobed behind the hand-painted screen, lovingly caressing the folds of her gown as she lay it carefully over the screen.

Luxuriating in the lavender-scented water, she scooped a handful of water into her palm, watching it trickle through her fingers. The firelight caught the brilliant emerald-and-diamond ring, and Olivia brought it closer to her face to study it.

The stones twinkled up at her, and Olivia lost herself in their clarity. How odd, she thought, are the vagaries of fate. Since meeting Colin Forster, her quiet little existence had been turned upside-down. Here she sat, in a shiny copper tub, pampered and cosseted, a countess of the realm. What's more, she had fallen madly in love with the most handsome, most clever, most dynamic man on earth. Olivia could not resist a sigh of supreme satisfaction. If only Colin loved her, she thought, her life would be nothing short of perfect.

The cooling waters finally forced Olivia from the tub. Polly returned and assisted her into a filmy, silk nightgown that Olivia privately considered most impractical, but she was too fatigued to quibble with Polly's selection. Glancing down at the diaphanous gown, Olivia nearly blushed to see herself so exposed.

"Is there anything else I can get for you, my lady?"

"No, I think not. Thank you, Polly." Olivia pulled her waist-length hair over her shoulder and began to plait the heavy tresses.

"Oh," Polly protested, "don't braid your hair tonight, my lady. It's so beautiful down."

Frankly, Olivia did not understand how that would signify, but again she was so tired, she laid off the tedious task.

"All right, Polly. Not tonight," she conceded with a wan smile.

"Good night, my lady," and Polly giggled, letting herself out the door.

Olivia crossed over to the luxurious rose-covered bed and climbed into its feather-down depths. On the nightstand she espied a pile of books, and curious, she reached over and picked them up to examine.

Reviewing the titles, she smiled, realizing that Colin had selected them for her pleasure. So considerate, she thought. Although he could not personally choose the furnishings for her new bedroom, he still set his own personal touch upon the chamber with the books and, Olivia smiled again, the vase of lilies upon the stand.

Olivia was thumbing through a book of poetry when Colin entered through the connecting door. Slightly startled, as she had not even noticed the door previous to this, she jerked, losing her place in the book.

"Hello again," she greeted, a note of surprise lacing her voice.

Carrying two snifters of brandy in his hand, Colin paused momentarily on the threshold.

"Ah, hello," he answered, a bit tentatively.

"Have you brought me a drink?" Olivia asked. "That's good of you, but you know I don't favor brandy all that much."

"Perhaps next time we'll try port," he rejoined, crossing the room to her.

Dressed in a wine-colored velvet robe, his hair was slicked back off his forehead, still damp from his bath. Dark, curly hair peeped out from the triangle of his naked, sculpted chest, the sight of which elicited a funny, tight feeling in Olivia's abdomen. Discomfited, she averted her gaze to the book in her lap.

Colin passed a snifter to her and, seating himself upon the bed, raised his glass in salutation.

"Let's toast, shall we? To our favorable union."

"Our favorable union," Olivia repeated and sipped at her

brandy. "I must be developing a taste for this wretched stuff. It doesn't taste nearly as noxious as before."

"Lord, I should think not," Colin answered, affronted. "This brandy is the finest that France has to offer."

"Really?" Olivia hazarded another sip. Patting the book of poetry, she said, "I want to thank you for your solicitude, Colin. The room, the flowers, the reading material. You've been most thoughtful. I greatly appreciate your efforts to make me feel comfortable at Sorrelby."

"Well, of course, I want you to be comfortable here. This is your home, Olivia."

"Yes . . ." She sighed and fell back against the pillows, cradling the snifter between her palms.

Colin's eyebrows met in a concerned frown.

"Are you troubled, Olivia?"

"No, not really." Her sweet, wide-eyed gaze pierced him like an arrow. "I'm just so grateful for all that you've done, I don't want you to overly concern yourself with me."

As Colin's frown deepened, Olivia struggled to explain. "What I mean is . . . I realize that our marriage was a pragmatic and sensible decision on your part and that you have other important matters that require your attention. I know that you're a very busy man with the estate and your business and . . . other things . . . and I don't want you to feel that you have to bother with me. I can take care of myself." Her face brightened with prideful determination. "With Smythe's help, I'll soon learn my duties as mistress and to manage the household, so don't feel as if you must watch over me."

Colin grew more uncomfortable with each word Olivia uttered. *Pragmatic, sensible, bother with her?* What impression had she fostered regarding this marriage?

Removing the brandy goblet from her hands, Colin placed their glasses on the bedside table.

"Olivia, you're not to consider yourself a bother to me, do you understand? I assure you that I'll enjoy watching over you," and his voice deepened huskily, his gaze sliding from her face to her thinly cloaked breasts.

He reached out and caressed her, then kissed her fully on the lips. Despite the passion overriding her senses, Olivia knew that she would have to bring a halt to Colin's caresses. As much as she enjoyed his kisses and his touch, he did not love her. Colin did not love her. The words had a startlingly sobering effect.

Colin felt her stiffen and raised his head. She smiled weakly at him, the best she could muster between her still panting lips.

"Don't be afraid, Olivia. I won't hurt you," he murmured.

"I am not afraid, Colin," and her voice was soft and sure and unafraid. "I just think that it is time to say good night." Before he could speak, she rushed on, "We both know that our marriage was not a love-match, so . . . I don't believe either of us would be content with insincere lovemaking."

Colin felt as if he'd been poleaxed. Nothing about the need coursing through him seemed the slightest bit insincere. By God! What was she saying?

He still leaned over her, propping himself up on one arm. He fought down the madness in his blood, striving for the logical, reasoning side of his nature as he studied her flushed face. No fear or pleading lay in those emerald depths. Perhaps the lingering fire of passion, but naught else.

Breathing deeply, he sat up while Olivia self-consciously arranged her nightgown. She watched him intently, hoping he would not be angry with her.

For his part, Colin was incapable of speech, chewing over her words of the evening. She had made many perplexing statements that he had not fully evaluated. Recognizing that he would be unable to think clearly while his palm itched to fondle her and his head spun with his need, he rose unsteadily from the bed.

In a passion-hoarse voice he said, "Perhaps you are right, my dear. Good night and sleep well."

Moving stiffly, he tightened the belt on his velvet robe and left via the connecting door.

Olivia snuggled into her pillow, replacing one of the linen-encased cushions in her dreams with Colin's hard-planed body. Due to the champagne and excitement, she slept soundly, unaware that next door, her husband sat beside the fire, a bottle of brandy at his side.

The reddish-orange flames danced provocatively in the fireplace, reminding Colin of the way Olivia's unbound hair curled luxuriously down her back. He took another gulp of brandy.

Cursing softly, he replayed their conversation in his mind, searching for clues to her rejection of him this evening. Although Olivia claimed that theirs was a loveless alliance, Colin knew beyond a shadow of a doubt that she desired him as much as he wanted her. Her immediate response and labored breathing left little uncertainty as to her state of arousal. Furthermore, she had made no attempt to disguise the potent desire in her glittering gaze.

Unbidden, a vision of Henry sprung before him. Olivia had admonished Colin not to concern himself, that she could take care of herself. Did she hope that once Colin was away from Sorrelby she and Henry could strike up a discreet "friendship"? If so, then why had she married him? To gain access to his wealth?

Colin shook his head in self-derision. Olivia did not crave his money, of this he was certain. When she had accepted his proposal, he had believed that her own physical hunger for him had driven her to yield, but now, of course, he must question that theory. If desire had propelled her into this marriage, she most certainly would not have pushed him away from her this night.

Growling in frustration, Colin reached again for the decanter, replenishing his glass. Tapping his fingers against the crystal goblet, he recalled the terms she had employed to describe their marriage. On more than one occasion she had used those same words—*businesslike* and *practical*—in referring to his proposal of wedlock. Reluctantly he admitted that he might have blundered in his initial approach with her, but surely his actions of late would have convinced her that more lay to their association. Unless, he thought, unless she secretly yearned for another man and thus wished to keep their union platonic.

Within the hour Colin had depleted the contents of the brandy decanter. Finally, in the early hours of the morning, sleep came to him and he slumped lifelessly in the fireside chair, visions of Olivia tormenting his sleep.

Chapter Eleven

NURSING A HANGOVER, Colin awoke at dawn, deciding on a long and vigorous ride around the estate to clear his foggy brain. He left for the stables, after peeking through the connecting door at his slumbering wife. She slept with one hand beneath her ivory cheek, her petal-pink lips slightly parted, the very picture of childlike innocence.

The stableboy unsuccessfully tried to hide his surprise at finding his lord and master awake so early the morning following his wedding night. He kept his tongue, although he wondered at the earl's bloodshot eyes and unshaven beard.

Colin ignored the groomsman's curious stare and threw his leg over Dublin's back.

"I'll be out for a few hours," he gruffly informed the man.

"Aye, my lord."

Colin rode hard throughout the morning, skirting the boundaries of his expansive estate. The mist-laden valleys and crisp morning air successfully dispersed the brandy's effects, and it was with a clearer head that he rode back to the manor.

Directing Dublin into the stable, Colin noted that a strange horse occupied one of the stalls. The groomsman was absent, so he could not inquire as to their early visitor. Striding across the cobblestone drive, he marched up the entrance stairs and into his house.

Entering, he thought he might choke on his fury upon sighting the figure who stood in the hall. His fists clenched as he bit out furiously, his voice like a whiplash, "By God, man, she was only wed yesterday! Couldn't you keep yourself from sniffing about her for at least one day?"

Menacingly, he advanced, jealousy curdling his common sense.

"Damnation, this is my home, and I won't have some young pup hankering after my wife, do you understand?"

Katherine and Smythe, descending the staircase, froze in their tracks, horrified at Colin's outburst. Never had Katherine seen her brother so angry, his handsome face contorted with fury. Mouth agape, she feared that Colin was going to fly at Henry's throat any minute, so licking her dry lips, she called out, "Colin, may I speak with you, please?"

Both Henry and Colin turned to locate the speaker, while Smythe hurried down the stairs to remove Henry from Colin's dangerous path.

"One moment, Katherine," Colin said through clenched teeth, his gaze not leaving his prey.

"Colin, I must insist that I speak to you *now*," she emphasized.

Smythe steered Henry into the parlor, Colin muttering threateningly behind Henry's back, "I'm not through with you."

Katherine descended the stairs, trailing her brother's furious steps into his study. She closed the door behind them, leaning against the oaken portal.

Only half-stifling his irritation, he questioned, "What is so urgent, Katherine?"

Katherine grinned humorously in the face of her brother's gruffness.

"I fear that you have made a mistake, dear brother."

Colin arched a sardonic brow.

Lazily Katherine pushed away from the door and moved to seat herself in one of the leather chairs. She bobbed her ankle up and down, relishing a chance to upend her know-it-all brother for a change.

"If Henry is sniffing around anyone, as you so 'eloquently' phrased it, it is I who am the 'sniffee.' Apparently, you have not noticed, but Henry has been courting me and plans to ask you for my hand. And"—she wagged a finger at him—"you will accept on my behalf."

Staggered, Colin sank into the chair opposite.

"You?" he questioned, stunned.

Katherine frowned with annoyance. "You need not look so astonished, you big dolt. I am certainly of marriageable age."

"But I thought his intentions . . ." Colin's voice trailed off.

Pursing her lips, Katherine rejoined acidly, "Yes, I heard exactly what you thought. Are you so blinded by jealousy, then? Really," she admonished, "Olivia and Henry are like brother and sister. You could not have believed that they—" She broke off her statement, realization dawning.

"Colin," she rebuked, "have you gone addlepated? Olivia loves you. How could you have mistrusted her so and still married her?" She rolled her eyes dramatically. "And you were supposed to be the levelheaded thinker of the family. Lord help us."

Raising his head sharply, Colin skewered his sister with a penetrating look. "What makes you believe that Olivia loves me?"

Katherine threw up her hands with a derisive laugh.

"Oh, this is rich. Colin Forster, the intuitive statesman and observant espionage agent, has yet to ascertain that his wife adores him. Dear heavens, who would believe it?"

Softening the edges of her ridicule, Katherine asked him with a frown, "Tell me, dear brother, what did she say when you professed your love for her? I cannot believe that she did not answer in kind. It is obvious to anyone that she loves you. Very much, I believe."

Moaning, Colin dropped his head into his hands. "Oh, Katherine. I have been such an idiot. The veriest of fools."

Suddenly everything clicked in Colin's brain. He had desired Olivia so intensely that he had never stopped to examine the reasons for his relentless pursuit of her. Even after his jealous outburst in the greenhouse, he had not been able to see into his heart for the deeper emotion lying therein. He wanted Olivia not only for physical rewards, but primarily for emotional and spiritual ones. He loved her as he had never loved another living soul, and she, poor woman, believed that he had wed her for an entirely different set of reasons.

Hell, no wonder she had turned him away last night. She wanted him to come to her with love, not only passion.

Grinding the heels of his hands into his eye sockets, Colin considered how best to remedy the situation. If he went to her now with protestations of love, she would doubt his sincerity, assuming his sole motivation was to entice her into his bed. He would simply have to convince her of his feelings. He would woo her.

Opening his eyes, he saw his sister watching him with an expression both pitying and amused. Heaving a deep sigh, he thanked her quietly. "Katherine. I offer my most humble regrets for my inaccurate assumptions. You have done me a tremendous service by stating the right of the situation.

"I assure you that when Henry approaches me regarding your hand, I will grant him the answer you seek. And a generous dowry, besides."

Blithely Katherine arose. "Well, it was the least I could do for Olivia, considering she saved my life. What a mess you might have made of your marriage, I shudder to think." Katherine placed a sisterly peck on Colin's head and sashayed out the study door.

Standing, Colin pulled fiercely upon the bell, and Smythe appeared almost instantly.

"You rang, my lord?"

"Yes, indeed, Smythe. The countess and I leave this afternoon for London. See to it that our trunks are packed before teatime. I want to arrive in London before dark."

Smythe clicked together his heels and smiled benevolently. "It will be as you wish, my lord," and he was off on his mission.

Colin discovered his mother, his younger sisters, and Olivia in the breakfast room. They had obviously already eaten and were huddled around a settee, discussing an array of fashion templates.

"This would be absolutely divine on you, Olivia," Eleanor

commented admiringly, pointing to a simple, yet starkly elegant ball gown.

Olivia stammered, "I-I don't plan on—"

"I concur, Eleanor, and applaud your fashion astuteness," Colin interjected from above them. All eyes turned to the masculine voice, Olivia blushing slightly at her warm reaction to his handsomeness. Bending over, Colin placed a chaste kiss upon her startled lips.

"Good morning, lady wife. And Mother," he greeted. "I suggest you quickly select your favorites from among those templates, my love, because tomorrow we shall begin shopping for your new wardrobe."

Speaking to his mother, but watching Olivia from the corner of his eye, Colin explained, "Olivia and I shall spend our honeymoon in London, procuring certain necessities, attending a few balls, introducing her to friends. We will be leaving this afternoon."

Turning to his wife, he tenderly placed a finger beneath her chin, closing her lips together as they had fallen open with surprise. Stroking her lower lip with his thumb, he murmured caressingly, "I pray it won't be too great a hardship for you to ready yourself so quickly?"

Dumbstruck, Olivia shook her head in the negative.

"Fine. Mother, you are *au courant* with the latest fashions. Choose a dozen or so that you think might do justice to my exceedingly lovely wife."

Again with a brief kiss, Colin said, "In a few hours, then, my sweet."

Darkness had not yet descended by the time the coach pulled up in front of Colin's town house. O'Shea opened the coach door, and Colin stepped out, offering his hand to his wife.

"Remember, my love, that the town house's previous occupant was a bachelor of moderate means. We will need to refurbish it as appropriate for an earl and his countess."

Olivia laughed at him as they stepped inside to the sparsely, yet attractively, furnished main hall.

"I will try to conceal my distaste, my lord, for the unpalatable accommodations," she haughtily teased, her pert nose in the air, marching forward like the Queen herself.

Graves, the butler, came running into the entrance hall, his generally stiff composure surrendering to amazement and anxiety. When O'Shea had barged into the kitchen, announcing that Lord Sorrelby had returned with a wife, Graves had nearly dropped the silver urn he'd been polishing.

Recalling himself, he straightened his spine, bowing to the lord and lady.

"Welcome home, my lord."

"Thank you, Graves. Olivia, may I present our butler, Graves, an excellent fellow. Graves, my wife, Olivia Forster."

Graves bowed again. "Welcome, your ladyship. Felicitations on your recent nuptials."

"Thank you, Graves." Olivia dimpled prettily.

"Graves, kindly see to our trunks. I want to show Olivia our London abode."

"Immediately, my lord."

A quiet, refined decor reigned throughout the house as Colin led her on a tour of the small town house, ending their circuit in the master bedroom upstairs. Here, also, Colin's unerring good taste had furnished the room comfortably but with a decidedly masculine bent. Royal blue and burgundy warmed the dark oak paneling, and Olivia noted that Colin had selected first-rate quality furnishings, yet had exercised a sparing hand.

As they stood, the footmen entered, depositing both her trunks and Colin's in the corner, beside the armoire. Olivia glanced around, uncomfortably aware that no connecting door led to a separate bedchamber. She did not question the arrangement, for Graves entered before she could speak.

"My lord, O'Shea informed me that you and her ladyship had not yet dined, so I instructed Cook to whip together a repast. I regret that it's not the usual fare, but I pray it will suffice."

"I'm sure whatever Cookie has prepared will be delicious, Graves. Shall we go downstairs, my lady?"

"Yes," Olivia answered, her stomach rumbling indelicately. "I'll need but a moment to wash."

*   *   *

The meal was excellent, and Olivia ate heartily, although her thoughts kept straying to the sleeping arrangements awaiting her upstairs. After supper Colin instructed Graves to send up a bottle of port and, without further ado, assisted Olivia from the table and lead her upstairs.

Olivia hesitated at the bedroom door, but Colin's hand on her elbow gently propelled her into the room before she could invent an excuse for her obvious hesitation. Graves entered, nearly on their heels, balancing the tray of port and glasses. Colin accepted the tray from the butler and bid the servant a good night, ushering him out the room with a raised eyebrow and a nod toward the door.

Colin loosened his cravat with one hand while pouring two glasses of port with the other. Sighing contentedly, he took a seat by the fire, glass in hand.

Olivia stood awkwardly for a moment, then decided to join her husband for a libation. After all, there was no harm in that, was there? She picked up the second glass and, moving over to the hearth, sank into the companion chair.

Colin eyed her speculatively over the rim of his glass, aware of her thinly veiled distress. Clearing his throat, he drew her gaze to him.

"Olivia, as I said before, the town house was designed for a bachelor, not a family. There are guest bedrooms down the hall, but it might look peculiar to the staff should you take a room so far removed from this one.

"I swear to you that I will behave honorably if we share this bed. I would never wish to force unwelcome attention on your person."

Olivia squirmed slightly under his steadfast stare. She understood what he asked of her, but honestly questioned whether she could withstand her own traitorous body in such close proximity to Colin.

Colin saw her hesitation. "If you are uncomfortable with that arrangement, I could sleep in a guest room—"

"No," Olivia interrupted. "That won't be necessary. I trust you."

Colin lowered his head in acknowledgment of her faith in

him. "Well, then, I'll leave you to some privacy. I regret w
have no lady's maid on staff, but if you so desire, we can locate
someone tomorrow."

"No, I've dressed and undressed myself alone for years," she
reminded him with a humored twist to her lips. "I will manage.
Thank you."

After Colin left, Olivia drained her glass of port, telling
herself she would need the extra fortitude this night to keep her
own passions at bay. Walking over to the armoire, she searched
for a nightgown, the servants having unpacked their trunks
during supper. Vainly she sifted through the clothing, but was
unable to find any of her old, plain cotton nightgowns. The
only nightwear that had been packed for her was the filmy,
cream-colored silk negligee she had worn the night before.
Biting her lip with vexation, she carried the flimsy slip over to
the dressing screen and shrugged out of her gown. Dropping
the silk shift over her head, Olivia moaned as the delicate
fabric molded to her own soft curves. It felt positively delicious
against her skin.

She had just settled into the foreign bed when Colin knocked
softly upon the door.

"It's all right," she called. Colin entered, carrying a lamp,
which he set on the fireside table and snuffed out with one
breath. Moving around to the bed with his usual silent tread, he
also blew out the lamp there, and then, navigating solely by the
light of the fire, moved behind the privacy screen.

The tiny scrapes and small raspings as Colin removed his
clothing unnerved Olivia to no end. She could not help but
envision with each sound her glorious husband untying his
stock, removing his jacket and shirt to reveal his broad,
well-honed chest. Then the thud of his boots dropping on the
floor, followed by him slipping out of his pants. Olivia felt as
if she were subjecting herself to some inhumane torture,
especially when the bed tilted under Colin's weight and he
eased himself under the covers.

Neither of them seemed to breathe, and but for the crackle of
the dying fire, the room would have been quiet as a tomb.
Finally Olivia could bear it no longer and expelled a long
breath. With that exhalation she attempted to relax, but her

ody was too aware of the one that lay next to hers. She lay awake for a long while, until she heard the cadence of Colin's breathing change. Ultimately, worn out from the tension of holding herself stiffly away from him, she succumbed to slumber.

"Hmm-mm," Olivia purred, snuggling more closely to the warm body wrapped around hers. Sunshine poked through the curtains, urging her to awaken, and yet, sleep had never been more enjoyable. Groggily she found consciousness, enjoying the pleasurable feelings seeping through her body.

A large palm possessively held onto her right breast, its thumb lazily stroking back and forth. Rhythmic breath brushed past her ear, its pace slowly quickening. It was the quickening breath that ultimately roused Olivia from her dazed sleep. The body pressed against hers was unclad, she realized, its rough hair rubbing sensuously against the silk of her nightgown. Turning a furious shade of pink, Olivia discerned what pressed so urgently in the cleft between her bottom cheeks.

Colin, who had been awake a good half hour, felt Olivia's body stiffen as she came fully conscious. Without any apologies he murmured, "Good morning, sweet wife."

Olivia thought she might jump out of her skin. Her voice cracked, answering, "G-good morning."

They remained as they were until Olivia tentatively shuffled her posterior away from Colin. He did not pursue her, but still held on to her breast as if it were perfectly natural for him to awake in such a position. After a few moments Olivia realized that Colin would be utterly content to remain as they were for the remainder of the day. Knowing the inevitable conclusion to remaining abed any longer, Olivia matter-of-factly slipped out of the bed, nonchalantly strolling over to pick up her robe.

When she finally mustered the nerve to turn around and face her husband, she found him sitting up against the pillows, bare-chested and smiling.

"I trust you slept well, my love."

"I did. And you?"

"Never better," he assured her. "Why don't you ring for our breakfast? By the looks of it, morning is half over."

Compliantly Olivia rang, tearing her eyes from the mat of ebony curls on her husband's bronzed chest.

They breakfasted in their room, the intimacy of the setting playing havoc with Olivia's heightened awareness of her husband. The immodest fellow had not even donned a shirt for breakfast, so Olivia was forced to hide her longing for him behind her breakfast napkin. Colin ate like a trencherman, his appetite as hearty as his disposition. After patting his flat stomach appreciatively, he left her alone to dress.

Olivia chose her best gown and made a speedy toilette. Colin was eager to commence their shopping excursion, and he had admonished her to make haste.

Madame LaForge's boutique, situated in a fashionable locale, catered to the most exclusive clientele of the *ton*. Colin was hailed as a long-lost friend, and when he introduced Olivia as his wife, Madame LaForge effusively complimented "the countess's flawless figure and unparalleled beauty." Glancing down at her best lavender frock, Olivia felt somewhat embarrassed, recognizing that even the couturiere's dress outshone her shabby cotton gown. Fortunately, Colin took charge from the moment they entered the couturiere's establishment.

Madame LaForge, not surprisingly, agreed with the earl that the countess was in dire need of a complete wardrobe, and they decided to begin with the underclothes and work their way out. Silk, lace, linen, and cotton were paraded by for Colin's eagle-eyed inspection. When pressed for a decision, Olivia generally deferred to Colin's judgment, although she recognized the fact that at some point, she would need to make these decisions on her own. She couldn't rely on her husband to dress her for the rest of her life!

The templates that Deirdre Forster had sent along were discussed, and bolt after bolt of material appeared in the arms of the junior seamstresses. Valiantly Olivia attempted to follow the debate over organza or chiffon, velvet or brocade.

Colin had commissioned at least a dozen gowns, with Madame's enthusiastic approval, when he abruptly asked, "Now, Madame, I understand that you will need some time to complete these costumes, but the countess will need a few items in the interim. What can you provide us today?"

"Ah, my lord, I have only a few pieces—" she demurred.

"Nonsense," Colin interrupted. "One ball gown, three morning dresses, and a riding costume, minimum." He waved his hand. "And of course, all the pertinent frippery."

Madame LaForge disappeared into the back of the boutique, and Olivia seized the opportunity.

"Colin," she protested. "You have been much too extravagant! Honestly, I need only a dress or two. Certainly not—"

He hastily cut her off with an abrupt hand movement as Madame returned, her plump arms burdened with a rainbow of fabrics.

"*Mon Dieu,* my lord, I shall have to invent some excuse for the marquess's mistress when she comes to collect these tomorrow."

Suavely Colin bestowed his most earth-shattering smile upon the Frenchwoman.

"I am sure you will think of something, dear lady. Naturally, I will recompense you for your inconvenience."

Colin ignored the elbow jab he received from his wife, and he and the couturiere hashed out the final details on Olivia's behalf.

And so the afternoon went at the milliner's, the bootery, and the parfumerie. After pleading exhaustion, Olivia convinced Colin that gloves could indeed wait another day, and they climbed into the heavily laden coach and headed home.

Overwhelmed, Olivia hardly knew where to begin. Throughout the day she had tried to curtail Colin's lavish expenditures, but each time he had brushed aside her protests with a kiss and a wave of his hand. Now she tried again.

"Colin, this is insane!" she argued. "I do not need even half of what you have ordered. The purchases today"—she gestured to the top of the coach where two dozen boxes had been strapped—"are more than sufficient. Honestly, how many ball gowns will I need for gardening or linen inspection at Sorrelby?"

Colin reached over and took Olivia's hands in his.

"Olivia, I don't intend to imply that we have money to burn, but my skinflint grandfather has left me a veritable fortune. The purchases made today are not even a drop in the bucket compared to what I plan to spend on you, my love."

"But, why?" Olivia persisted, frustration clouding her eyes. "Why spend a fortune on a wife whom . . . whom . . ." Olivia paused, uncertain what words could describe the role she held. In reality, she was not his wife; certainly nothing more than a friend or companion. Their marriage had not been consummated and could still be easily annulled at a moment's notice.

Sighing deeply, Colin realized that he would have to lay bare his heart in the hopes that Katherine had not misjudged Olivia's own feelings toward him.

"Olivia, I had wished to wait a day or two more, to ascertain myself your sentiments, but I think the time has come for me to clarify a few points regarding our marriage." Speaking slowly, he explained, "Initially, when I proposed to you, it was with the intention of procuring a suitable, compliant wife to reside at Sorrelby and relieve me of the burden of bachelorhood." Detecting Olivia's withdrawal from him, he held fast to her wrists, his fingers soothingly stroking the surfaces of her palms. "I genuinely regret that the impression I gave you at that time has endured, despite the fact that my feelings have radically changed since that time."

Olivia stopped in her struggles to pull her hands away. Her green eyes became guarded, her long lashes dropping to obscure their expression.

"Olivia, I have behaved like an idiot. Wildly jealous of Henry, I insulted you with my barbaric conduct. Too blind to question my own actions, I fumbled on, pressing you into marriage against your will—"

Olivia's head jerked up, and she opened her mouth to remonstrate, but then reconsidered and tightly snapped her jaw closed.

"The only rationalization I can offer for my supreme stupidity"—and Colin lowered his voice to a sensuous rumble, his eyes searching hers—"is that love has rendered me a thoughtless cretin, motivated solely by the need to possess you, body and soul."

"Wh-wh-what?" Olivia stuttered, her heart beating furiously beneath her jacket.

"God forgive me, Olivia, for I know I don't deserve you, but I love you. I love you more than you can imagine."

For a heartbeat Olivia sat dazed. Then, shrieking with delight, she threw herself into her husband's arms, nearly unbalancing him and sending them both to the carriage floor. Heedless of the open curtains, Olivia plastered her lips to Colin's mouth, her lips and tongue devouring him. Startled, yet far from displeased, Colin fervently returned the embrace as he half-lay across the bench cushions, his exuberant countess nearly strangling him with her ardor.

Gasping, Olivia came up for air and, between grins and giggles, rained tiny, moist kisses all over Colin's face. She punctuated each peck with an ardent "I love you" or "I adore you" until their boisterous laughter drew the attention of a passerby. Stopping at a corner for traffic to pass, an elderly gentleman stood not three feet from the carriage window. His astonished "I say" brought a brief intermission to their playful necking while Colin, with a lascivious wink to the affronted octogenarian, pulled shut the coach curtains.

Returning to his seat, Colin wrapped his arms around his bride, whispering into her red-gold hair, "Katherine told me that you loved me, but I dared not believe her."

"Believe, believe, dear husband, for I have loved you from the moment I first saw you. I did not understand the reason I shook and shivered whenever you came near, but now I cherish every goose bump you incite."

Laughing, Colin grabbed her arm. "Where are those goose bumps, then, my lady?" and he trailed a path of kisses along the sensitive skin of her inner elbow and upper arm.

Melting, Olivia leaned into him, prepared to beg for more, when the carriage came to an abrupt halt. The vehicle swayed slightly as O'Shea jumped down from the driver's perch, allotting Olivia a second to pat her disheveled hair into place.

O'Shea threw open the carriage door and offered his hand to Olivia. Although her expression was composed, her rosy face betrayed her, and as she mounted the steps, O'Shea shot a satisfied beam in his master's direction. Colin saluted his friend in return and chased his wife's swaying skirts up the stairway to their home.

Chapter Twelve

THE PUNGENT SMELL of coffee roused Olivia from her sleep and, stretching languidly, she rolled onto her back. Inhaling deeply of the aromatic brew, she recalled her uninhibited behavior of the night previous and smiled with delight. No woman, she was convinced, had ever been so thoroughly loved. After matching Colin's passion on the hearth rug, she had been carried to their bed where Colin had cradled her in his arms as they dozed off to sleep. Sometime during the night, he had awakened her with his caresses and transported her once again to the heights of ardor, then replete, the two had fallen into a blissful sleep of exhaustion.

"May I offer you a cup of coffee, my little passion kitten?"

Opening her eyes, Olivia smiled into her husband's face. He was propped against the pillows, leaning over her, love shining from his eyes.

"I would dearly love a cup."

Noting the breakfast tray on the bedside table, and the pile of correspondence that Colin was sorting through, Olivia glanced toward the window, measuring the daylight.

"Is it late?" she asked, accepting the coffee from Colin.

"Not quite eleven," he answered, tossing aside an envelope.

"Heavens, eleven o'clock!"

Olivia sat up in bed, careful not to spill her cup.

"I've never slept so late in my life!"

Colin turned to her, admiring her bare breasts above the sheet resting upon her lap.

"You had an arduous night, my love, and needed your rest," and he pecked her playfully upon the cheek.

Following his gaze, Olivia self-consciously reached for the sheet, but Colin's hand stayed her.

"No need for modesty, my love. I very much relish the idea of eating breakfast while admiring your loveliness."

Olivia would not have believed it possible that she could blush after all that transpired between them last night, but nevertheless she felt a pink glow blossoming under her ivory skin. She did, however, leave the sheet upon her lap.

She sipped at her coffee, glancing over to the breakfast tray. "I'm rather peckish. What is there for breakfast?"

Colin returned the correspondence to the sidetable and reached for the tray.

"A veritable feast for your pleasure, my lady."

Biting hungrily into the biscuit Colin handed her, Olivia shot a sidelong glance at her husband.

"Somehow, we overlooked our evening meal last night," she teased.

Pretending surprise, Colin answered, "Surely you forget, but I assure you I dined exceptionally well. On the most delicious fruit." His eyes cast down to her exposed bosom.

Olivia laughed. "You really are wicked, you know."

"Ah, yes, and you love me that way, don't you?" and he leaned over to lick a drop of marmalade off the corner of her mouth.

Beaming, she assured him, "I most certainly do."

Attacking his breakfast with gusto, Colin gestured with his fork to the stack of mail. "As much as I would love to spend the remainder of our honeymoon in this bed, I also want to show off my breathtaking countess. There's a ball tonight at Almack's that I would like to attend, if you have no objections."

Olivia froze in the midst of chewing, her happiness rushing out of her like air from a balloon. Colin detected her abrupt stiffening.

"Would you prefer not to attend?"

She swallowed her biscuit, pushing it past the sudden lump in her throat. She simply wasn't prepared; she didn't know anything about proper social decorum or balls or what to say or whom to say it to.

"Colin, I don't wish to embarrass you," she pleaded. "What if I commit some hideous gaffe?"

"Sweetheart, you could do nothing to embarrass me. Just be yourself. But we don't have to go tonight if you're uncomfortable."

Pushing her breakfast around her plate with her fork, Olivia deliberated. Just be herself, he said. Well, she thought, I ought to be able to manage that; I've had a lifetime of practice. And, most important, if Colin wanted her to go with him, then she'd go.

"No, I am going to enjoy myself," she answered, determinedly cheerful. "Almack's, after all. *The* place to be introduced into polite society," and she squared her firm, feminine jaw with the look of a Christian entering the lion's den.

Charmed by her stoicism, Colin chucked her softly on the chin. "That's my brave little countess. You'll see, you'll be the talk of the ball."

"A vision, my love. You are simply beautiful."

Olivia swirled around, affording Colin a complete view of her gown, her hair, her shining face. She had never felt prettier, not even on her wedding day. Then she had been too nervous, unsure of herself and unsure of Colin, whereas today she knew herself to be a woman well and truly loved.

"Madame LaForge must be possessed of psychic powers. This gown could only have been designed for you."

"Thank you, Colin." Olivia smiled demurely, skimming her fingers over the shimmering aqua silk. The blue-green gown complemented the deep richness of Olivia's hair and enhanced the alabaster purity of her skin. Diamonds from the Sorrelby collection glittered at her throat and in her coiffure, reflecting Olivia's vibrant blues, greens, golds, and reds. She literally sparkled with vitality.

In his elegant jet-black evening attire, Colin provided the perfect foil to Olivia. His wife honestly believed him to be the most attractive man in all of creation and she wondered how many other women would think the same of him tonight.

Hopeful that she wouldn't have to beat them off with a walking stick, she took Colin's hand, and they descended to the carriage.

Almack's already teemed with the social elite, although the hour was still relatively early. Planning to make the obligatory appearance with his bride, shake hands with the well-wishers, and then sneak off, Colin aimed to be home in bed with Olivia within a matter of hours.

Staring down at his breathless bride, Colin cursed the latest fashion which decreed that a gown's neckline dip nearly to the nipple, revealing, in Olivia's case, an astonishingly ample display of bosom. In the privacy of their bedroom Colin had thought the gown lovely, but in Almack's ballroom, he found it almost indecent. Surveying the room, he conceded that his wife's gown was no more revealing than most, and certainly more modest than some on show this evening. Nevertheless, he bristled as introductions were made, and gentlemen braved a quick glance at Olivia's cleavage, until Colin's threatening glare brought their eyes up and forward.

Within twenty minutes of their arrival, Olivia was surrounded by a circle of fawning gentlemen, both married and unattached. Colin resolutely kept at her side, although his role was more that of a guard than a husband. Occasionally a scrap of conversation was thrown his way as a gesture of politeness, but it was Olivia who held the crowd in the palm of her hand.

Naturally, if Colin had been willing to abandon his wife to the wolves, he, too, could have enjoyed a similar popularity among the women, but wild horses could not have dragged him away from her enchanting laugh and precocious banter. Fortunately, when Olivia requested a glass of lemonade, dozens of volunteers fought for the honor, thus enabling Colin to adhere to his post.

After an appropriate interval, Colin, sufficiently annoyed with the lisping compliments and lascivious stares, laid his hand possessively on Olivia's arm.

"Excuse us, gentlemen, but I see some other friends my wife has not yet had the opportunity to meet."

Steering her through the group of crestfallen expressions, Colin began circulating the room, introducing Olivia to the haut monde. As he anticipated, people instantly warmed to her, even the ladies who were secretly gnashing their teeth in envy of her beauty. Had Olivia been unwed, undoubtedly the young ladies would have been less hospitable in their reception, but since Olivia posed no competition in the marriage market, they could afford to be generous with their friendship.

Making their way around the room, Olivia noted that the circle of people ahead of them appeared to be abuzz immediately prior to Colin and her joining their company. Between introductions, Olivia asked Colin about the phenomenon.

"Darling, have you recognized how everyone is chattering away until we join them?"

"Olivia, you are so delightfully naive. They are talking about us, dear. You may not be aware, but the knowledge that I have married is causing a bit of a sensation. That, coupled with the fact that I have wed a golden-haired goddess, supplies this evening's revelers with much meaty gossip to digest."

"Oh." Olivia frowned. "What do you think they're saying?"

"Well, the men are probably speculating as to where I uncovered such a gem as yourself, while the women, most likely, are debating how you trapped me into marriage."

At Olivia's outraged appearance Colin smiled placatingly.

"If only they knew the truth, hmm? That you fell out of a tree into my lap, and then I had to beg you for weeks to coerce you into marriage."

Smiling, she agreed. "I guess truth is stranger than fiction."

Suddenly from the masses of people, a striking blond woman dashed up to Colin and laid a wet kiss directly upon his lips.

"Colin, darling, where have you been? It's been far too long," she chided, batting her eyes, innuendo thick in her voice.

Stepping back a pace, Colin saw Olivia's arm raise, as if prepared to do combat, and he smoothly grasped her hand in his own.

"Samantha, allow me to introduce my wife, Olivia Forster, the Countess of Sorrelby. Olivia, Lady Samantha Kilgarry."

Obviously, the news of their wedded state had not yet reached Samantha's ears, for she appeared genuinely mortified by her conduct. Recovering, she greeted Olivia, her chagrin plain, "My lady, excuse my familiarity. It is a pleasure to make your acquaintance."

Darting a brief look of apology at Colin, Samantha quickly spun around and disappeared into the throng.

Wryly Olivia commented, "I hope word of our marriage is soon widespread so that we may avoid further incidents such as those."

Cringing slightly, Colin concurred with fervor, "As do I, my dear. As do I."

Moving along, Colin greeted an elderly couple, and they passed a couple of minutes in conversation. While speaking with the gray-haired marquess, Olivia surprised herself by realizing that she was honestly enjoying the ball. She liked meeting new people, with the exception of Colin's ex-lovers, and the music, flowers, and generally festive air imbued her with an indescribable buoyancy.

Reflecting on her high spirits, Olivia recognized that she had not really attended many parties during her lifetime. Mossgate affairs, while merry, more closely resembled family gatherings. Everyone knew everyone else, and discussion usually revolved around whose child had recovered from mumps or which crops were likely to fare well that growing season.

The newlyweds had almost completed a full circle around the ballroom, and were talking with a military acquaintance of Colin's, when heads turned in inquiry to the announcement of new arrivals.

"The Earl of Wotbane, Lady Beatrice Haverland, and The Honorable Nellie Osborne."

Standing so near the entrance, Colin and Olivia were easily espied by the threesome as they entered the ballroom. Their varied reactions would have been comical in a different situation perhaps, since the apparent emotions telegraphed by the newcomers ranged from fright to annoyance to outrage.

Nellie, unnaturally pale, quaked as she recognized the formidable Earl of Sorrelby who only a few weeks ago had banished them from his home. Not blessed with a strong constitution, she would have fled if not for the fact that Beatrice intimidated her even more greatly than the earl.

Bedecked in rose chiffon, Beatrice's cheeks flamed with

similar color upon perceiving Colin's companion. Mentally berating the two waterfront blackguards for not yet having disposed of the troublesome chit, she assured herself that Burnsie and Howie would have sufficient intelligence to follow Olivia to London and see the job done. At least, she conceded, it would be easy for the girl to become lost in London, once the two cretins scared her away from Colin.

With vicious satisfaction she watched her father's reaction, assured that, at last, with his "assistance," Colin would be encouraged to offer for her hand.

Lord Wotbane, who was often compared to a bulldog, both in appearance and temperament, glared ferociously at Colin, his face purpling with fury. The ivory-tipped walking cane he employed for his gouty leg was raised menacingly in Colin's direction as he limped his way toward the earl and countess.

After having been expelled from Sorrelby, Beatrice had been in such a snit that, on returning home, she had tearfully sought out her father and divulged to him Colin's beastly behavior. To soothe her father's ire, she had admitted that she favored the earl, but that he refused to offer marriage after having compromised her. Understandably, the enraged Lord Wotbane swore to see justice done and his daughter's honor restored.

Although reading the murderous intent in Wotbane's eyes, Colin held his ground, a placid smile resting upon his granite features.

"Damn your eyes, you insolent pup!" the aging earl bellowed, approaching Colin. "You've got your nerve, parading around town in the guise of a gentleman!"

A hush fell upon the buzzing throng as Lord Wotbane's roar reached into the far corners of the crowded ballroom. All eyes turned to watch the melodrama play out, people jostling for better position to view the confrontation.

"Don't think I don't know what you did to Beatrice, you rounder! She thought to protect you and yet you scorned her! No man treats my daughter the way you have. You will wed her, by God, or my name isn't Virgil Haverland!"

Initially stunned by the man's tirade, Olivia bristled, listening to him rain down epithets upon her husband's head. Nothing could have surprised her more than Colin's cool response to Lord Wotbane's diatribe. Countless times, she had unwittingly provoked him to anger and thus had thought him as quick-tempered as herself.

"Sorry I can't accommodate you, Wotbane, but I am already married," Colin answered, smooth as silk, flicking an imaginary piece of lint from his jacket sleeve.

Nellie actually swooned, clutching to Beatrice's arm, while Beatrice wrenched free of the grasping hand. Her look of dazed shock clashed with Olivia's fiery-green gaze.

Choking upon a barely audible "No," Beatrice reached out her hand and tried to pull her father away, but he would not budge.

"Married?!" Wotbane nearly bawled. "Then you'll bloody hell get it annulled and do right by my daughter!"

Valiantly attempting to keep a lid on her simmering anger, Olivia's temper reached its zenith at that last pronouncement.

Stepping around in front of Colin, she spread her feet wide, belligerently folding her arms across her chest, her stance that of an Amazon preparing for war.

"That's out of the question." Her voice rang out, easily audible to the absorbed crowd of listeners. "Our marriage has been fully and completely consummated to our mutual satisfaction, and you damn well cannot obtain an annulment if I'm carrying this man's child."

Gasps and titters broke the silence, but Olivia heard them not as she ranted on. "But since we're discussing legal action, I'm of a mind to sue your daughter for compromising my husband! The truth of the matter is that she and her accomplice"—Olivia shot a look at Nellie—"snuck into Colin's town house where Beatrice then forced her attentions upon *him!*"

The murmurs increased in the background.

"Should you have any doubt that I speak the truth, I'm certain that Miss Osborne would prove an edifying witness once placed in front of a judge, would you not?"

Nellie's panicked gaze flitted from Olivia to Colin to Beatrice and then, with a fatalistic sigh, she collapsed in an unconscious heap at Beatrice's feet.

Lord Wotbane appeared for a moment as if he would follow suit, his florid face now ashen. Quivering, he looked to

Beatrice, saw the truth written in her remorseful expression, and felt as if a knife were twisting in his gut. Imperceptibly he shook his head, ashamed of his own ignorance and his daughter's duplicity. By God, the girl had gone too far! He had spoiled and cosseted her, granting her every desire, but to what end? A selfish, unthinking young woman had replaced his cherubic, darling, curly-haired child, and no one was to blame but himself.

Slowly raising his head, he scanned the silent faces of his peers, aware of the shame he had brought down upon his family. Forcing himself to straighten from his defeated, slump-shouldered posture, he hoarsely addressed Colin. "I apologize, Lord Sorrelby. Naturally, you shall want satisfaction. Send your man around tomorrow with your requirements."

Olivia momentarily tensed at the idea of Colin meeting this aged man upon the dueling field, but she breathed easier on hearing Colin's response.

"No need, Wotbane. Your apology is accepted."

Dismissively turning his back on the Haverlands and the unfortunate Miss Osborne, who was being administered smelling salts, he spoke softly to Olivia.

"Well, little hellcat, shall we call it an evening?"

Olivia placed her hand in his and mutely nodded.

Chapter Thirteen

❧

MEEKLY OLIVIA DONNED her wrap and stepped into the coach awaiting them outside. Colin had not spoken a word to her since they departed the ballroom abuzz with gossip. Neither of them had afforded a look backward to ascertain the fate of the hapless Haverlands.

Colin had paused outside the coach to speak with O'Shea, indicating to Olivia that she should proceed him. Squirming on the edge of the banquette, she dreaded the stern lecture she was certain she would be receiving. Colin stepped inside the coach, and Olivia apprehensively bit down on her lip. Before he had even seated himself upon the bench, she launched into her explanation, her words rushing together breathlessly.

"Now, Colin, it wasn't really my fault. I had warned you that I would likely commit some unforgivable faux pas, but you wouldn't believe me. And then when that horrid man began hurling insults and accusations at you, I tried to keep a lid on my temper, but then he used the word *annulment,* and I just lost control, I was so angry and I . . . I'm sure you're wishing that you had never married such a hotheaded creature as myself."

Colin listened patiently to her speech, one hand casually loosening his immaculately tied cravet.

"Are you quite finished?" he asked when she finally paused.

Miserably she bobbed her head.

"Good, because I'm not in the mood to talk."

Dejected, Olivia thought, *he doesn't even wish to discuss the incident, I have humiliated him so.* Thus, when Colin's large hand reached out under her wrap to slip her thin cap sleeve from her shoulder, she jerked in surprise. Looking up at him, she saw the fire in his liquid eyes and her skittishness dissolved as relief swamped her. Angry or not, Colin desired her, and abruptly her nervous tension gave way to pulsating, physical tension.

Tentatively she asked, "You're not too angry with me, then?"

Covering her lips with his, he spoke into her mouth, "No talking, remember?"

Smiling, she answered by pulling his head closer to her.

They clung together and Olivia's anxiety eased as Colin's kiss assured her of his love.

He lifted his head and the glint in his violet gaze warmed her while he pulled her close for a hug.

"I shan't forget this evening," he teased her with a smile. "The night my warrior wife defended my honor."

Olivia cringed. "Was I abominable?"

"On the contrary, my love, I thought you magnificent. The picture of the golden-haired Amazon squaring off against the indomitable Lord Wotbane shall surely be the talk of the *ton*.

"Frankly, I wouldn't have been surprised to see you pull a spear from the folds of your gown and launch it through poor old Virgil."

Knowing that he jested, Olivia curled her lips mockingly. "No spears tonight, although I'll speak to Madame LaForge about it.

"Seriously though, dear," she persisted, a worried crease between her brows, "will we ever be able to show our faces in London again?"

"Sweetheart, you don't understand. You are a heroine. Every hostess in town will want you to grace her dinner table. I assure you that tomorrow we will be literally inundated with invitations."

"I didn't embarrass you?"

"Embarrass me? You made me proud. Throughout the years I have had to take care of myself. When you suddenly leaped to my defense this evening, I remembered how nice it is to have someone else look out for me, too.

"Especially touching, I thought, how you placed your body in front of mine to ward off attack," he teased.

Olivia threw her arms around her husband, rubbing her face into his neck. Ah, she loved the scent of him. Brandy and leather and something uniquely Colin.

"The only attack you need fear, my lord, is from yours truly," she promised.

Smiling, Colin wrapped his arm around her while knocking on the coach ceiling, the signal that he was ready to go home.

The faint rustling outside their bedroom door awakened Olivia, and glancing at her slumbering husband, she was relieved to find his sleep undisturbed. Quietly easing off the four-poster bed, she donned a silk nightrobe before tiptoeing to the door.

Judging by the filmy sunlight, the hour was still relatively early, and Olivia wondered who dared disturb the master of the house at such an hour.

On their return from Almack's last night, Colin had ordered a cold supper to be sent up, and they had dined *au naturel* in front of the fireplace. Reclining upon the plush rug, Olivia had playfully trickled a few drops from her champagne glass onto Colin's chest, watching the bubbly pool down his flat stomach into his recessed navel. He had insisted, of course, that she clean up her mess, and her playful slurping around his belly button had led to more champagne being "spilled" in the most intimate of locales.

Shoving her heavy hair away from her face, Olivia smiled, questioning her bright spirits in light of the lack of sleep she'd benefited from these past nights. Resolving that love must be as nourishing as rest, she tightened the sash to her gown and opened the bedroom door a crack.

Hovering in the hallway, one of the kitchen lads fidgeted, nervously bobbing up and down on his long legs. A comely youth, Olivia recognized him as the servant who had delivered their late supper last night. He appeared uncommonly nervous, Olivia noted, no doubt in a quandary as to awakening the earl.

She peeked out from the bedroom door, and the young man nearly fell over his feet in his haste and relief.

"Milady, I hates to bother you, but there's a man at the kitchen door who says he carries an important letter from Miss Margaret Nicholson. I told him to give it to me, and I'd have it sent up to you, but he said he was told to only give the note to you."

A pang of alarm shot through Olivia. Uncle Nathan or Aunt Joan must have taken ill or suffered an accident. Quelling her apprehension, she looked down at her silk wrap and realized she would have to dress before going downstairs.

"Have Graves see the—"

"Sorry, milady, but Graves is at market," the lad interrupted.

"Oh." Olivia frowned. "Ask the messenger to wait just a moment. Tell him I'll be right down."

The lad bobbed his head and loped down the hallway toward the stairs.

Olivia moved noiselessly to the wardrobe and snatched up the first dress her hand touched. With shaking fingers, she buttoned the blue-and-white-striped morning gown, cautious not to awaken her exhausted husband. Leaving her hair unbound, she found a pair of slippers for her feet and silently left the bedroom.

Her thoughts flitted back and forth between a variety of dour possibilities as to the note's contents. For Margaret to send a special messenger, something very serious must be afoot. Had someone else fallen prey to the lung fever? Or perhaps one of Henry's experiments had gone afoul and he had injured himself?

Entering the kitchen, she spotted the cook bustling about in the rear of the pantry, but otherwise the kitchen was deserted. Hurriedly she crossed to the back door, looking for the messenger. Goodness, he couldn't have already left, she worried. She had only been a few minutes throwing on her gown, and she had sent word that she was coming.

Stepping down the stairs and into the alley, she called out, "Hello! Hello!"

A heavy fog hung above the street this morning, and Olivia narrowed her eyes, peering down the length of the misty gray alley. She shivered as a shifting of air flowed over her, and then, without warning, a large beefy arm seized her from behind.

She was pulled hard against a wall-like physique, the muscled arm wrapped tightly around her stomach, causing the air to *whoosh* out of her lungs. She labored to draw breath back into her body so that she could call out for help. Her cry of alarm was cut short by a dirty rag being stuffed into her mouth while she struggled against the unseen assailant. Olivia kicked and writhed, but her captor did not release her.

When a flour sack dropped over her head, she redoubled her efforts, jabbing her elbow into his unyielding midsection as she felt herself being dragged backward in the giant's grasp.

My God, Olivia panicked, *I'm being abducted!*

Her mind's eye flew to the vision of Colin, his tousled black curls against the snowy white pillow, one bronzed arm thrown over his eyes, a muscled leg stretched out from the rumpled sheets. What would he think when he discovered her gone? And what were her abductor's intentions? Would she ever see her husband again?

Winded from the man's viselike hold, her own struggles, and the constricting rag in her mouth, Olivia panted inside the confines of the sack. She must not panic, she told herself. She must gain her freedom. The man continued to drag her down the alley, and Olivia could hear the soft neighs of an impatient horse. Knowing she had only a moment before she was spirited away from the house, she abruptly allowed her flailing form to go limp. Caught by surprise, her abductor stumbled over his enormous feet and, in falling, loosened his grip upon Olivia.

Her rump bounced painfully on the cold cobblestone street, but she wasted no time in soothing her bruised posterior. Jumping to her feet, she began running in the direction of the house, the flour sack over her head. She had only taken two or three strides when she heard the sharp ringing of the man's boots upon the cobblestones as he set out after her.

Flying as if on winged feet, Olivia dared not spare even a second to remove the sack, although she did manage to spit the offensive rag from her mouth. With a sinking heart, she knew she would have to slow down to pull the sack over her head or risk running pell-mell into a brick wall. Even as the realization came to her, she was abruptly wrenched backward and caught in the arms of her oversize kidnapper.

Too breathless even to scream, she thrashed around in his arms and sank her teeth into human flesh. She chomped down as hard as she could to assure the bite penetrated the sacking, and was rewarded by a choked howl of pain.

With difficulty she sucked a deep breath into her burning lungs, prepared to let loose a tremendous scream, when the steely prick of a blade pierced her side.

A lower, more menacing voice, hissed at her, "'Nuff shenanigans, laidy, if ye value yor life."

Tears welled in her eyes as she sagged against her assailant, a light trickle of blood flowing from the wound.

"Thanks, Burnsie," the large man holding her muttered. "Gor, but she's a wild one, ain't she?"

"This knife'll keep 'er in line, won't it now?" the other man threatened.

From beneath the sack Olivia swallowed hard against the tears of defeat, saying nothing. Quickly the two men hustled her back down the street and unceremoniously thrust her inside a dank-smelling coach. Terrified, Olivia scrambled to sit upright on the bench, imploring herself to remain calm.

Heaving a shaky sigh, she concentrated on the sounds wafting to her as the coachman whipped the horses into a brisk trot. She strained her ears, listening for clues to their destination, the *clip-clop* of the horses' hooves, the call of street merchants, voices raised in argument.

Her abductors remained silent, and for this, Olivia was grateful. By the accents spoken on the streets and the smell of saltwater permeating the coach, she deduced that the coach was approaching the wharf district. Panic flooded her again, and she prayed that her kidnappers would not be placing her on a ship bound for some Godforsaken foreign land.

She bit down hard on her lip to control its quivering and then spoke out in a loud, confident tone, "What do you want with me?"

A grunt of surprise preceded indiscernible mumblings and then the fellow with the menacing voice answered, "No talkin' lest ye want me t'poke ye agin."

"I'm not afraid of you," Olivia lied from beneath the sack.
"Tell me what you want."

"Hell's bells, but she's a bold wench," the higher-pitched
voice commented with awe.

"Aye, that she is, Howie, me boy," the other man answered.
"Awright, yer grace, if ye wonts to know. We figger to make
some blunt off ye. Figger the earl 'll pay us to git his lovely
laidy back agin."

"How did you know to use Margaret's name?" Olivia
demanded, her voice gaining strength.

The man chuckled unpleasantly. "We've bin followin' ye
'round fer a while now, even in Mossgate. At yer weddin', no
less. Lovely affair, weren't it, Howie?"

Howie giggled girlishly.

Olivia quieted, digesting the fact that these two ruffians had
been trailing her for at least a week. But why? Surely, easier
prey was to be had here in London without traveling to tiny
villages such as Mossgate to seek out qualified victims.

The coach halted and the one named Burnsie whispered
threateningly as he caught hold of her arm, "Don't try nothin',
yer laidyship, or I promise ye, ye'll feel my blade.

"Howie, ye go first t'make sure the coast is clear."

Olivia felt the coach heave beneath her as the heavier man
climbed out and wished she dared remove the sack to determine their exact location. But the threat of the knife prevented
her from taking such a risk.

"Awright, Burnsie," Howie called.

Burnsie roughly gripped her upper arm and pushed her down
the coach steps. Olivia nearly gagged on the overpowering
smell of refuse, rum, tobacco, and saltwater as she stood in a
puddle awaiting Burnsie's directions. She heard the clink of
coins as Burnsie paid off the coachman.

"Ye never seen us, right?" Olivia heard him prompt the
coachman. A low murmur was followed by the clink of more
coins, then the clicking of the horses' hooves informed her of
the coach's departure.

"Move 'long, now," he told her, shoving her up a flight of
stairs, his hand bruising her upper arm. Hindered by the sack,

Olivia blindly negotiated the stairs, stumbling often, but Burnsie kept her upright, pushing her quickly up the wooden staircase.

At the top of the landing, Olivia was led down a hallway, and then she paused, listening to the creak of a key turning in a rusty lock. Roughly thrust inside, her shins cracked against the side of an iron bed before she could regain her balance. Blindly she spun about but heard the door close, Burnsie cackling, "Make yerself comfortable, yer grace. Ye might be here awhile."

Olivia immediately pulled the sacking over her head to survey her whereabouts. Dark and dusty, the highly pitched roof suggested that her temporary cell occupied the attic space of the building. The floorboards were thick with dust, and the furnishings consisted only of a chamber pot, the iron bed, devoid of any blankets or linens, and one rickety wooden chair that Olivia would not have trusted to bear her weight.

Sitting gingerly upon the black iron bed, Olivia closed her eyes, concentrating on the faint sounds drifting up from below. The low murmur of voices was occasionally punctuated by a shout or roar of laughter, and Olivia conjectured that she was being held in a tavern or inn near the docks of the Thames. Thrusting her fear to a corner of her mind, she focused solely on her dilemma, believing that somehow she would arrive at a scheme to free herself from these ruffians.

Hopeful that neither Burnsie nor Howie stood guard outside the door, she stood up and decided to test the lock. She grasped the doorknob, giving it a good shake, and, when she heard no grumbling from the other side, sank to her knees to more closely scrutinize the corroded lock. Although it squeaked when previously opened, it appeared to Olivia that the lock was too strong for her to force open the door without the aid of the key.

Nonetheless, she threw her shoulder into the door, her hand firmly twisting the doorknob back and forth, employing her hip as a battering ram. She shoved and twisted, but to no avail, and after a few minutes of fruitless attack, she abandoned her efforts.

Frowning, she dusted off her soiled skirt and hands, looking for an alternative exit. One small window, on the opposite wall, admitted a meager amount of daylight, its panes filmy with grime and grease. Although the window was quite narrow, Olivia optimistically calculated that she might be able to squeeze through it if only she could reach so high. Walking over to the windowed wall, she stood on tiptoe and stretched her fingers, estimating that the window stood half a body length above her own head. Chagrined, she sank back onto the bed, considering her options.

Eventually, she thought, someone would have to return to provide her with nourishment and drink. If she were able to overpower that person, perhaps using the chamber pot as a weapon, then she could escape via the back stairway without drawing attention to herself.

Or, if unable to subdue that person, she might be able to steal the key away by causing some kind of diversion. Olivia wrinkled her nose regretfully, concluding that it was most unlikely her captor would not discover the loss of the key, for he or she would wish to lock the door on exiting.

Again, Olivia's eyes strayed to the tiny window. *Yes,* she mused, *I do believe I could squeeze through that opening, if only I could manage to devise a ladder.* With disappointment she once again scanned the sparsely furnished room. Even if she were able to scramble up the posts of the iron bed and somehow balance herself atop one of the newels, the bed was too far from the window to be used as a ladder and certainly too heavy for her to move by herself.

Almost as if he were there beside her, Olivia heard Colin's resonant voice softly echo inside her head. *What about using the bed ropes?* The bed ropes! Olivia hopped off the bed and dropped on her back to the floor, looking beneath the thin straw mattress. There they were! Perfect. Her eyes flew to the window, and she realized she would need to secure the rope to an anchor. Since the wall was empty, she would have to toss the rope over one of the rough beams crossing the ceiling. Anxiously Olivia examined the bed ropes, praying they were sufficient to construct a long-enough length of rope. She would have to tie them together carefully so as not to waste any of their valuable length.

Jubilant, Olivia scooted beneath the bed, coughing on the dust clouds she disturbed. Her fingers grasped the first knot, and she struggled with it until it finally came loose in her fingers. The second knot took even longer, and Olivia's fingers started growing raw from their chafing against the coarse hemp, but she persevered.

She had just released the third knot when she heard heavy footsteps rapidly thumping down the hallway. With mercurial speed, she slipped out from beneath the bed, coughing and sputtering against the heavy dust-laden air and had barely managed to shake out her dress and hair when the key turned in the creaky lock.

The large fellow who lumbered in with a tray could only have been her abductor, Howie. Although Olivia had been blinded by the sacking, the breadth and width of this man was so uncommon that she correctly assumed him to be the man she fought against in the alley outside her home.

"Here's somethin' fer ye to eat," he addressed her in his uniquely girlish voice. He held the tray out to her, and Olivia moved forward to take it from him, eager for him to be away.

She accepted the tray, and still he stood in the open doorway, watching her.

"Yer a lovely li'l piece," he commented, his beady eyes raking her from head to foot.

Nervously Olivia moved away from him, feigning absorbed attention in the unappetizing lunch tray. The boiled meat and cabbage emitted a noxious aroma that turned Olivia's stomach, but better endure the meal's stench than the disquieting intent in Howie's black eyes.

"Burnsie's gonna send a ransom note t'yer husband, the earl, after 'e eats 'n puts away a pint er two," Howie offered.

Bravely Olivia met his licentious stare with her own glacial regard.

"Never fear. I am certain my husband will meet your price as long as I am returned *unharmed*," she emphasized.

Howie shifted heavily, his halting mental faculties digesting her warning. He stood in the doorway a long moment, weighing her words, until grumbling to himself about Burnsie's knife, he turned and plodded out, locking the door behind him.

Olivia heaved a sigh of relief and placed the tray on the floor. Resuming her tedious task, she relentlessly picked at the knots, methodically moving from one length to the next.

For hours, or so it seemed to Olivia, she toiled until she had loosed every piece of roping, all the while her ears anxiously attuned to approaching footsteps. After tying the roping together as neatly as possible, she tried to toss one end over the roughhewn beam. Due to the weight of the rope and the height of the beam, this proved to be no easy task, and Olivia's arms grew fatigued as toss after toss failed to drape across the wooden support.

Wiping her dirty hand across her damp brow, she took another fortifying breath and hoisted the rope into the air, and finally it hooked across the beam with a satisfying *thud*. Wanting to shout with triumph, Olivia scrambled to secure the opposite end to the bedpost, imploring the fates to keep her kidnappers at bay for just a minute or two more.

She gritted her teeth against the pain as her raw, blistered fingers gripped the rope end, and slowly she inched herself up the improvised ladder. Olivia's muscles strained as she pulled herself up, the unifying knots offering a temporary foothold for her to rest between efforts.

Fearful that Howie or Burnsie might return at any moment, Olivia relentlessly pushed her tired body until she came level with the window. Desperately she reached out for the window lever, but the distance was too great. Although burning tears threatened, she refused to give up when she had come so far.

Swinging her body back and forth, she began a pendulous motion, gaining speed. Faster and faster she swung until with a forceful kicking motion, she plunged both feet through the window, shattering the glass, her posterior barely landing on the window casement.

Clinging to the rope, Olivia inched her rump through the opening until her feet found hold on the rooftop a few feet below. Reaching forward with one hand, she pulled her torso through the window, trying to avoid one jagged piece of glass that adhered to the framing.

Carefully she inched out, hoping that the shattering glass had not alerted her captors to her escape. After some careful maneuvering, Olivia stood on a small expanse of roof, gazing down to the alley two stories below. Hysterical laughter bubbled up inside her as she asked, "Now how shall I get down?"

Chapter Fourteen

"TELL ME AGAIN, dammit!" Colin spat at the quaking cook.

"Aye, m'lord," the man repeated, his eyes bulging out from his bald head. He wiped the nervous perspiration from his face with the corner of an apron and cleared his throat, his heavy jowls aquiver.

"As I said before, m'lord, I didn't hear or see anything until I heard a lady's voice yelling 'hello.' She said it twice, 'hello, hello' like she were calling for somebody. I was at the back of the pantry, so I walked into the kitchen to see who it were, but the kitchen was empty. Then I saw the back door open, and I stepped out to the alley. Fog thick as pea soup, and I didn't see a soul, but I thought I mighta heard a muffled cry or shout. When I turned in that direction, I still didn't find anyone, but that there rag."

The poor fellow shrugged helplessly, and Graves patted him consolingly on the back. Colin paced back and forth, crushing the filthy rag in his fist, his heart hammering so loudly that he feared both Graves and Cookie could hear its deafening pounding. He had awakened and discovered Olivia gone. Considering that he had overslept, he had not been too concerned, albeit sorely disappointed not to find her soft, yielding body awaiting his pleasure. Slightly disgruntled, Colin had rung for Graves to demand his morning repast as well as to request that his wife be summoned.

Naturally, Graves had believed the countess to be still in her chambers with the earl and thus had arrived at the master's chambers with breakfast for two. When Graves claimed no knowledge of Olivia's whereabouts, inquiries were made of the staff, and within minutes a search was launched, resulting in Cookie being brought to Colin's study to relate his forbidding tale. Graves had further informed the earl that Freddie, the young kitchen hand, also appeared to be missing.

"Graves," Colin instructed, his deep-timbred voice carefully controlled, "send a messenger for Lord Preston Campton. Tell him to meet me here at once."

"Yes, my lord," and Graves fairly ran out of the room.

Colin marched in front of the study window, his knuckles white and tightly clenched around the sole piece of evidence, the rag. Staring blindly out to the fog-shrouded courtyard, he methodically ticked off each piece of information available to him regarding Olivia's disappearance.

Her wardrobe doors had been ajar, and Colin, having personally selected her wardrobe, rapidly determined that a striped morning gown had been removed. Although Olivia had dressed, both her cape and shawl still hung in the oak armoire, leading Colin to assume that either she had not planned to leave the house or that she had been so hurried that she had neglected to protect herself against the bone-chilling London mists.

Furthermore, she had not awakened Colin to say goodbye nor had she informed any of the servants as to her purpose in leaving. If she needed to perform an errand, surely she would have called for the carriage as she knew London not at all. Where then had she gone?

Racking his brain, he constructed a number of scenarios in an attempt to determine what might have prompted her to go out alone, at such an early hour.

They had passed a passionate evening together in each other's arms and both had fallen asleep well-satiated. He, himself, had slept uncommonly late and thus had not been surprised when he discovered that Olivia was not abed. Had she been hungry and sought out breakfast in the kitchen? But then what had prompted her to go outside?

Colin's thoughts kept returning to the muffled scream Cookie might have heard in the early morning fog, and reluctantly, his eyes fell to the crumpled rag in his fist. *Olivia had not left the house of her own accord.*

All evidence pointed to an abduction. His wife of less than a week, his newfound love, had been stolen from him. Primal fury threatened to overwhelm him, and suddenly he smashed his fist down on the heavy oak desk, relishing the pain that radiated through his fingers and hand. Nothing could compare to the agony he felt this moment, not knowing what had become of Olivia.

The study door opened, and Graves hastily ushered in a disheveled Preston Campton with O'Shea clipping fast on his booted heels. Preston tugged at his jacket and ran a hand through his blond waves in an attempt to complete his hurried toilette.

"This better be important, old chum, for I was literally dragged away from my bangers and eggs."

Colin raised his dark head, and Preston was immediately silenced by the raging emotions clearly evident in his friend's tortured amethyst gaze.

"Anything, O'Shea?" Colin addressed the Irishman, his voice hoarse.

"Not hide nor hair, laddie," the man answered sorrowfully.

Preston frowned. "What's wrong, Colin?"

"Olivia has been abducted."

The lack of inflection, the tonelessness of his voice, told Preston more than he wanted to know.

"Tell me what you have," he requested, and Colin succinctly related the few facts surrounding Olivia's disappearance.

"Interesting about the boy," Preston commented, "I cannot help but wonder—"

"Excuse me, my lord, but Lady Beatrice Haverland is here and insists upon seeing you."

Colin's head whipped around at Grave's interruption.

"Tell her she can go to—" he began to growl.

"She says she has information about the countess," Graves put in meaningfully.

Colin straightened, his spine as stiff as his forbidding expression. He glanced to Preston before answering Graves, "Send her in."

Beatrice Haverland shuffled inside the study, a handkerchief dabbing at her big brown eyes. Attired in black, she appeared to be mourning the loss of her highly coveted social position in the wake of last night's scandalous revelations at Almack's.

She paused within a few feet of the study door, her exaggerated and mournful sighs threatening to toss her bosom from the gown's plunging neckline. As she surveyed the study's occupants, and found no sympathy in their severe aspect, her self-pity yielded to a growing sense of trepidation. Her crocodile tears evaporated when her gaze finally alighted on Colin's demonic visage.

Chaotic black curls stood on end, and the finely sculptured face appeared drawn and pale with anxiety; his ordinarily laughing eyes were an icy, deep purple and cold as death. Against the unnatural white of his face, his eyes glowed eerily, freezing Beatrice to the spot where she stood. Colin's powerful hands clenched and unclenched at his sides, clawlike, while he seemed somehow larger to her, more intimidating, looming over her like a hungry bird of prey.

Beatrice herself grew ashen as she silently rehearsed the story she must confess to this frightening figure. She looked to Lord Campton for support, but he merely watched her expectantly, no gleam of welcome in his gaze. Her eyes then darted to O'Shea, who looked as if he would not hesitate to throttle her himself should Colin overlook the opportunity.

"What do you know of Olivia?" Colin boomed. Beatrice nearly jumped out of her shoes as his furious voice rang out in the cavernous study.

"I . . . I believe I know who has taken her."

"How did you know she was missing?" he lashed out at her.

Beatrice slowly backed up against the study door, nervously licking her parched lips.

"Freddie came to see me this morning and told me that she was missing and that a man had arrived earlier with a message for the countess."

At Preston's inquiring look, she explained haltingly, "Freddie has from time to time assisted me in . . . uh, keeping tabs on Colin. He was the one who helped me sneak Nellie inside the town house that . . . that night."

Colin glowered ominously at the reminder of her attempt to

trap him into marriage, and Beatrice could have bitten her tongue at her clumsiness.

"Anyhow," she stumbled on, "when Freddie described the man, I realized that I knew who it was."

"Go on," Colin instructed, and she gulped, desperately longing to flee.

Strengthened by a measure of righteous indignation, Beatrice continued, her tone bordering on petulant.

"After you so rudely expelled us from Sorrelby, I was simply beside myself, Colin. I had made up my mind to marry you, you see, and I thought you had behaved abominably to me. So"—her voice weakened—"I thought that if I got rid of her, Olivia, then you would come around and do right by me."

Colin growled, "Why, you thoughtless little . . . I'll kill you with my own hands," and he leaped across the room toward the astonished Beatrice.

Preston vaulted from his chair in the nick of time, barely restraining Colin by the lapels of his jacket, as he murmured to his friend, "Easy, old man. She's only a girl."

Beatrice flattened herself against the door, frantically protesting, "But I told them not to hurt her. I made that very clear. I just wanted them to scare her away from you, frighten her away from Sorrelby. I had no idea you were affianced, I swear it.

"When I heard that you two were married last night at Almack's, I nearly fainted. I had no idea, Colin. I thought she was only another one of your dalliances. I swear it."

Colin shook himself free from Preston's hands, his steel-like gaze piercing Beatrice. "You'd better pray that not a single hair on her head has been harmed, Beatrice, for I vow if she has been injured in any way, I shall have my revenge."

Beatrice vehemently shook her head, tears beginning to pour down her face as she pictured the ruthless cutthroats she had chosen for her nefarious deed.

"I told them not to hurt her, I really did."

"What are their names?" Colin bit out from his tightly clenched jaw.

"Burnsie and Howie. They're from the docks. One is huge, with black eyes, and speaks in a high-pitched voice. And the other"—Beatrice shuddered—"is small and wiry and sports a rather . . . disfiguring scar across his face."

Preston grunted his disgust. "You ought to be soundly thrashed, you spoiled wench."

Beatrice's sobs grew in intensity. "I know. That's what Father says. He's sending me off to the country for the rest of the Season. We're leaving this afternoon."

She cried pitifully into her handkerchief, but Colin remained unmoved. "If anything has happened to Olivia," he threatened again, "I will be paying you a visit in the country. You have my word."

Stalking over to the desk, he opened a drawer and withdrew a pair of heavy pistols. After a cursory examination of the weapons, he tossed one to Preston.

"O'Shea, you stay here in case they try to contact me."

"Aye."

To Preston, he ordered, "Let's go," and the two men marched out of the study, leaving Beatrice to her soaked handkerchief and O'Shea's scowl.

Colin and Preston had checked out three or four waterside pubs, gleaning small bits of information regarding Olivia's abductors, but, unfortunately, no one had been able to tell them where they might find Burnsie and Howie until they chanced upon a talkative, rum-soaked sailor at one of the seedier taverns along the wharf.

Choosing a table close to the door, in case they needed to make a hasty exit, they sat down at the soiled table, scanning the occupants of the shadowed room. Although not yet noon, the bar was doing a brisk business, and when the barmaid approached them to take their order, Colin slipped the woman a coin.

"Who here might have information about Burnsie and Howie?"

The dazzled barmaid quickly shoved the precious coin down the front of her dress.

"Gor, mate. Wit' boodle like that, 'e'll deliver 'em to yor front doorstep!" and she gestured over her shoulder to a sailor at a nearby table, hovering lovingly over his drink.

With a nod of thanks to the woman, Preston and Colin arose and walked over to the man's table.

"Mind if we join you?" Colin asked.

The sailor looked up, bleary-eyed, from his drink and raised his bushy eyebrows in surprise at finding two well-dressed gents addressing him.

"All we want is some information. We're looking for Burnsie and Howie."

The sailor laughed raucously into his mug until the unmistakable glint of gold caught his eye as Colin tossed a coin against the man's drink. The laughter stopped abruptly, and the man snatched up the coin, eyeing Colin and Preston with a speculative air.

"They likes to 'ang out at the Black Anchor, but I warns ye, they ain't the friendliest of blokes. 'Specially Burnsie. 'E's a mean one. Ye'll know it's 'im by 'is scar. Got it in a brawl wit' a whore a few years back.

"Heh-heh . . ." The sailor chuckled, gleefully recounting his story. "The doxie didn't wont a thing to do wit' Burnsie, that's fer sure, but he weren't goin' to take no fer 'n answer.

"He threw 'er down on the pub floor, and in front of us all, lifted 'er skirts, 'n made ready to 'ave at 'er. Then, from nowheres, the bit pulls a blade on 'em and slashes 'is face from ear to nose.

"Blimey, but the blood spilt everywheres!" The man cackled. "But Burnsie didn't let goes, 'n bleedin' like a bloody stuck pig 'e were, 'e grabs the knife from 'er . . . well, the li'l blond piece paid fer 'is scar with 'er life."

Colin forced down his revulsion and, tossing the man another coin, motioned for Preston to follow him out the tavern.

"My God," Colin swore once they exited the smoky, smelly pub. "To think that Olivia is at the mercy of such a man." He swallowed the bile that rose in his throat.

"Don't torture yourself, man," Preston advised. "Let's just find her. And quickly."

The two men mounted up and rode for the Black Anchor.

The only glimmer of hope Colin could cling to lay in the fact that the waterfront riffraff with whom he and Preston had spoken widely considered both Burnsie and Howie to be complete and utter muttonheads. As one bloke explained, the only reason Burnsie put up with Howie was that he had finally found someone even more beef-witted than himself.

Trotting along the back alleys, Colin maintained a watchful eye on the shadowed doorways and blind corners, one hand loosely covering his firearm. This neighborhood boded ill for any strangers, but certainly for two gentlemen, expensively clothed riding well-bred mounts. Although the fog had lifted at his town house, it still hovered down near the water's edge, the cool shroud enveloping them in its concealing mist.

Colin rolled his shoulders, striving for a degree of calm and awareness he had mastered through his years of military training. The sangfroid for which he was famous was not so easily maintained as the unsavory stories about his wife's abductors echoed menacingly in his head.

Suddenly the sound of breaking glass caught Colin's attention, and while whirling about to alert Preston, a handful of shards showered down upon the alley directly in front of him. The shattering glass sounded loudly on the still street, and urging his horse forward around the broken glass, Colin glanced up, seeking the source. To his total astonishment, he espied his wife perched two floors above him on a roof ledge.

"Olivia!" he called out, dumbfounded.

"Hello, dear," she waved.

Behind him, Colin heard Preston softly repeat with a laugh, "'Hello dear'?"

"Olivia, what the bloody hell are you doing?"

"Escaping. Isn't that obvious?" she retorted with a hint of sarcasm. *Honestly,* she thought, *what kind of question is that?*

"Olivia, by God, be careful!" Colin shouted, watching her sway so far above him as her foot seemed to slip on the treacherous roofline.

"That ledge is too narrow, and I've had quite enough of you falling from high places," he admonished, his eyes roaming the alley to assure they were still alone.

"I sincerely agree, dear, but I'm afraid that I cannot get down."

"Unbelievable!" Preston laughed softly to himself.

Shooting an annoyed glance at his friend, Colin silenced Preston with a frown. Turning back to Olivia, he studied the window from which she exited and promptly determined that she could not return in that direction, so he removed his pistol from his coat pocket and handed it to Preston.

"Keep watch, Pres," he instructed, hopping off his horse. "I'm going to get her down."

"Naturally," Preston concurred dryly, his face wreathed in amusement at the unlikelihood of the situation.

Colin located an empty keg barrel and rolled it across the alley to place it beneath the roofline, standing the barrel on one end. Jumping onto the barrel, he reached up, his fingertips barely grazing the rooftop. He groped around for an instant to gain a better hold, then, exhibiting uncommon strength, he pulled himself up by his fingers, the muscles in his arms and shoulders bulging and straining beneath his coat jacket. With a grunt of exertion he rolled over onto the roof and came to his feet.

Skimming carefully across the rooftop, he approached Olivia where she stood above him.

"All right, darling, I know it's some distance, but you'll have to jump into my arms."

Olivia peered down to where Colin cautiously stood balanced on the peak of the lower roof. If he should drop her, she would not merely fall to the rooftop, she decided, but she would roll off the roof, probably dragging Colin with her, and they would both fall the full distance to the street below.

Colin saw her hesitate and prodded, "Come on, love, we haven't much time. I won't drop you."

Recognizing that she had few alternatives, Olivia closed her eyes, whispered a quick prayer, and jumped. The air *whooshed* about her, causing her skirts to inflate and balloon around her, the cool, foggy air reaching up between her bare legs. Suddenly she felt Colin's arms close around her and then felt him stagger back and forth beneath her weight seeking sure footing. For what seemed to Olivia an eternity, Colin stumbled backward and forward, two steps back, three steps forward, two more back, dancing dangerously upon the steep rooftop. When eventually he steadied, she slowly opened her eyes and offered him a tentative smile.

"Are we still alive?" she asked.

Colin studied her grimy, dirt-streaked face and sensed something expand in his chest. He thought his heart might explode with pride, love, and relief, he was so happy to have her back in his arms.

"Very much alive, my dear."

Putting her on her feet, he held to her hand.

"All clear, Pres?" he called down.

"All clear," he called back, a pistol directed to either end of the alley.

"Now," Colin explained, "I'm going to jump down, and then I will catch you again, understood?"

Olivia nodded, and Colin released her hand. Jumping from the roof, he landed with all the gracefulness of a jungle cat, quickly spinning about to catch Olivia.

"Here I come," she warned, and this time, Colin had no difficulty in capturing her to him.

"Oh, Colin," she murmured, snuggling into his chest, breathing richly of his unique tobacco and leather scent. She wanted nothing more than to curl up in his arms and go to sleep, when remembering where they were, her head snapped up, spilling her dirty, yet glorious hair about her shoulders. Fear was stamped across her features.

"Colin, we must leave at once! They might discover me gone at any time."

When Colin only held her more tightly to him, she began to struggle.

"Sweetheart, you don't understand. I was abducted by two horrible men, one of whom is the size of your horse! We must be away," she urged him anxiously, her gaze now pinned to the corner of the building, anticipating her kidnappers' arrival at any moment.

"Olivia, I do understand. Perhaps more than you know. Let me first look at you." He gently placed her on her feet, his eyes and hands feverishly roving her beloved figure. Abruptly his hand snaked out to a rusty bloodstain at the side of her gown.

"What is this?" he demanded, his voice shaking slightly.

Olivia had forgotten Burnsie's knife at her ribs, but reminded by Colin's fury, she looked down with horror at the telltale evidence of the kidnapper's blade. Predicting Colin's reaction should she tell him the truth, and wishing only to be gone from this place, Olivia stammered, "It's only a sc-scratch, dear. I might have done it when I broke through the window."

Colin's eyes narrowed. "The blood would not already be dried, Olivia. Tell me. Did they harm you?"

"No, darling! Truly!" she averred, too frightened of Colin facing the two blackguards to care whether she spoke the truth. "It was only an accident. Honestly" — she half laughed — "the worst thing they did was try to feed me boiled cabbage for lunch."

Imploringly Olivia turned to Preston, silently begging him to assist her in her efforts to soothe Colin and to escape a confrontation. What she failed to realize was that Colin would not be satisfied until the two men who had dared steal his wife from his very home were staring down the end of his pistol.

Preston shrugged, offering her a faint, although not encouraging, grin as he placed the pistol into Colin's extended hand.

"No," Olivia remonstrated, grabbing hold of Colin's arm, her eyes wide and pleading. "Please, darling, don't. I am unharmed, save for the scratch." She ignored her burning and blistered palms, bent only on keeping her husband from harm.

Colin paused and gazed down into her liquid emerald pools. Softly he explained, though his firm voice brooked no argument. "You know I would deny you nothing, my love, but in this I have no choice.

"Pres, stand guard. I shall not be long."

Placing a brief kiss on Olivia's protesting lips, Colin turned away, purposefully marching around the corner to the tavern's entrance, his boots clicking loudly in the hushed alley.

"Preston, please, you must help him," Olivia begged, frantically tugging on his jacket sleeve. "He is outnumbered, and I did not exaggerate about the giant named Howie. He's enormous!"

Preston placed a comforting arm around Olivia's shoulders, patting her soothingly.

"Olivia, I have seen your husband in action, and trust me, you need not fear for his safety. He is more than capable of handling those two ruffians."

"But, Preston, you don't understand," she argued vehemently, "they're truly vicious. The worst sort of blackguards! I implore you—go after him!"

With a crooked grin he shrugged. "My dear, I sincerely doubt that your husband would appreciate my intrusion. I assure you that he would prefer to take care of those two on his own."

Perplexed by his lack of concern, she knitted her brows together, wondering at Preston's unruffled acceptance of Colin's capabilities. How could he be so certain? She, herself, while believing her husband to be all that was noble and masculine, still knew him to be merely a man. A man made of flesh and blood, and she wanted none of that flesh marred nor any of that blood spilled.

Nervously worrying her lower lip with her teeth, Olivia paced. She pictured Colin alone in the pub at the mercy of Howie. She had not actually seen Burnsie, so for all she knew, he could be as large as his dangerous crony. And further unsettling, she knew that Burnsie carried a knife and employed it freely as he deemed necessary. If he did not hesitate to use his blade on an unarmed woman, she fretted, he would have little compunction about wielding such a weapon on a man carrying a pistol.

Without warning, Olivia impulsively bolted down the alley toward the front of the tavern, her skirts flying about her as she sped to her husband's aid. She heard Preston shout after her, and his pursuing footsteps, but she refused to turn back. Colin was in danger and she simply could not passively wait in the alley, twiddling her thumbs and praying for his safety!

Rounding the corner of the building at full speed, Olivia crashed headlong into a rock-hard chest. She would have gone flying backward onto her bum if not for the lightning-speed reaction of a strong arm whipping forward to securely grasp her.

"Oomph," Olivia grunted as the wind was knocked from her

sails, and she lurched clumsily backward before being snatched back upright.

Preston came skidding up behind her, grimacing apologetically into Colin's frowning visage.

Still grasping Olivia with one hand, a rope in the other, Colin growled good-naturedly, "I thought I gave you the easy assignment, Pres."

"It might have been easier to take on Howie and Burnsie," Preston commented dryly.

"Yes." Colin gestured with a bob of his head to the two men, bound hand and foot, behind him. "They did not prove overly difficult, as a matter of fact."

Olivia stared, mouth agape, at the two men her husband led by a length of rope. Blood trickled from the smaller man's mouth, and he appeared to have recently lost a tooth or two. As for Howie, both eyes were quickly purpling in their swollen sockets, and he hung his head as if semiconscious.

Olivia whirled around to inspect Colin, and to her utter amazement, he seemed fit as a fiddle. Her anxious gaze traveled his unmarked face from his forehead to his cleft chin. Babbling, she questioned, "But . . . but you were only gone a few minutes!"

Breezily Colin reiterated, "I know. As I said, they did not prove too difficult."

Stupefied, Olivia's gaze bounced back and forth between Preston's satisfied grin and Colin's nonchalant expression.

"W-were you hurt?"

Releasing his hold on Olivia, Colin raised his large hand to his face, his fingers clenched. Pouting slightly, he brought his fist forward for Olivia's examination, muttering plaintively beneath his breath, "My knuckles are slightly abraded."

Preston chuckled while Olivia made a show of soothing the injured digits.

Handing the rope to his friend, Colin said, "Do be a sport, old man, and take these two in to the authorities for me. I need to get my wife home."

"My pleasure," Preston responded warmly and accepted the leash.

*   *   *

"Ahhh," Olivia sighed, sinking into the perfumed bathwater. "This feels positively heavenly. I vow I inhaled a veritable mountain of dust in that filthy old attic."

Colin was lifting the cover from the luncheon tray, but spoke over his shoulder.

"Most ingenious of you, darling, to devise that rope ladder. A bit risky, perhaps, but altogether a rather clever plan."

Soaping her arms, Olivia surveyed her raw palms, the soap and warm water stinging the exposed skin.

"Actually, dear, it was your idea. I could not think of what to do, when suddenly your voice came to me, whispering about the bed ropes."

"Really?" Colin asked, one dark eyebrow cocked. "How extraordinary."

"Mmm," Olivia murmured as Colin picked up a chair and moved it to the side of the tub. Retrieving a plate from the table, he balanced lunch on his lap while pouring them both a glass of claret.

"That looks delicious, Colin. I'm so hungry! Give me a bite, will you?"

Obligingly, Colin leaned forward and plopped a forkful of ham into Olivia's mouth. She lay back in the oversize tub, chewing contentedly, her eyes closed.

"I know I should be frightfully angry with Beatrice, but I can't really blame her. Who knows to what lengths I might have gone to catch you?"

"As I recall," Colin commented sardonically, "I was the one trying to do all the catching."

One green eye opened.

"Will she be in terrible trouble when Howie and Burnsie claim that she hired them?"

"I doubt that anyone will lend their story much credence, my love. You see, when I entered the pub, Burnsie had just finished penning his ransom note to me, a most illegible missive, and I am certain that once the authorities review the note and its demands, they will conclude it to be an open-and-shut case of kidnapping. Anyway, as I understand, Beatrice and her father are planning an extended sojourn to their country estate."

Olivia sighed blissfully, swirling around in the warm water. "The country. I do miss Sorrelby, don't you?"

Colin offered her another morsel, which she eagerly accepted.

"Yes, I do." He picked up his wineglass, studying the ruby colors reflecting off the crystal. "I have always enjoyed London and considered it home up till now. But lately I find myself yearning to return to the peace and quiet of the country."

"Do you, really?" Olivia sat up, excited, unconsciously exposing her rosy breasts from beneath the warm water. "I know you want to make some purchases for the manor, first, but do you think we could go home in a week or two? I don't want to rush you, but there is so much yet to be done at home. Why, we don't even have a nursery!"

Colin laughed out loud and bent over the steaming water to kiss his flushed bride.

Nuzzling her damp neck, he chortled, "There is nothing I would rather do than get to work on furnishing a nursery. With babies, I mean."

Olivia laughed seductively, stroking his dark head. "Well, there's no time like the present."

Epilogue

"OLIVIA! WHAT ARE you doing?"

Colin sprinted across the courtyard from the study's French doors to where his wife sat straddled on the ground, her large belly resting on a pile of freshly dug earth.

Her red-gold hair arranged artfully atop her head, she had to shield her eyes from the sun as she looked up at him from her low-lying position. Her hands were caked with dirt, and the way her legs straddled wide, she greatly reminded Colin of a child making mudpies. The swollen abdomen, however, left little doubt that she was indeed a full-grown woman.

"Hello, love," she greeted cheerfully. "I wanted to divide this lily plant before I forgot, because once the baby arrives, I know I'll be too preoccupied to remember."

Reaching his hands beneath her arms, Colin carefully hoisted her to her feet.

"Sweetheart, you could have asked one of the gardeners to do that for you. You shouldn't be digging in your condition."

Brushing herself off, Olivia smiled up at her husband's alarmed expression.

"I know, but I wanted to do this myself. You once compared me to this very flower, you know, so it holds a special, sentimental value to me." She patted her stomach affectionately. "Since we are multiplying, I thought it might be a good time for the lily, also."

Colin reached down and placed his hand lovingly over her own, adoring the feel of his baby inside his wife. His eyes glowed with love as he pressed his fingers closely against hers

Holding her in this manner, he felt something shift and tighten under his palm. He had often felt the baby move and kick during the past few months and, in fact, had developed a nighttime ritual of falling asleep with his hand closed over Olivia's stomach. But this tightening of her abdomen did not feel like the other movements he had known.

Shocked, his eyes flew to Olivia's, and he saw the small flickering of pain within her green gaze.

"Olivia?" he questioned breathlessly.

"Yes"—she nodded, gracing him with a diffident smile—"the pains have been coming for four or five hours now."

"What?!"

"I wasn't sure at first, but I'd venture to say that your son will be born sometime this evening."

Floored, Colin gawked at his wife, who so calmly informed him, with mud clinging to her hands, that she was in labor. Scooping her up in his arms, he dashed toward the house, bellowing for Smythe and O'Shea.

"Colin, dearest, you needn't hurry so. Babies usually take their time in arriving, at least the first time around."

"By God, Olivia, gardening! If I hadn't found you when I did, you'd probably be out in the exercise yard breaking in my new stallion!"

O'Shea and Smythe nearly collided as they barreled into the hall from opposite directions. Colin's barked orders sent them into another flurry of motion as they scrambled over each other, hurrying to carry out their instructions.

"O'Shea, send a messenger to my mother in London. Tell her that her first grandchild should be arriving shortly. Smythe, send for Leonard Browning. Tell him I want him here *immediately*. Have Polly bring up some hot water and towels."

Ascending the staircase in Colin's arms, Olivia pointed to the row of ancestral portraits.

"Imagine, Colin, our son's portrait will join these one day."

Shaking his head in befuddlement, Colin asked, "I still don't understand how you can be so sure it's a boy, Olivia. You know how desperately I want a daughter."

"Next time," she promised. "Today it's a son to carry on the Forster name."

She groaned as another spasm wrapped its way around her abdomen, causing Colin to suddenly take the stairs two at a time in a mad rush for their bedroom.

Shouldering the door open, he almost ran across the room, flipping the coverlet down in one quick motion.

"Are you all right?" he asked, watching the tension slowly fade from her face as he tenderly laid her back against the pillows.

"Darling, I'm fine," she reassured him, her palm cradling his cheek. "Remember, I have attended many a birth. I know what has to happen."

Colin straightened, running both hands distractedly through his hair, wishing he were half as brave as his wife seemed to be in the throes of childbirth.

Polly bustled in with the water and towels, and after cleaning Olivia's hands and face, she and Colin helped change her into a nightgown. Each time a spasm racked Olivia's swollen body, Colin fought to keep his own distress hidden. Clenching to his hand in a death grip, Olivia breathed through the spiraling pain while Polly gently mopped her forehead. When a contraction subsided, Colin heaved a huge sigh of relief.

Distractedly his gaze kept returning to the door, expecting Mr. Browning to come floating in like a savior angel at any moment. Unlike Olivia, Colin had not much experience with childbirth, and the sight of his wife courageously managing such extreme discomfort tore at his gut.

After what seemed to Colin to be hours, the physician entered, his large leather bag in hand, spectacles perched atop his nose. Walking over to the bedside, he spoke directly to Olivia in a calm, low voice, "How are you doing?"

"It goes well, I think," she answered with a smile. "The pains come rapidly together now."

Stunned by her composed response when only seconds earlier she had bitten her fingernails into his hardened palm, panting through another spasm, Colin looked down at his wife in awe. Even as he marveled at her, another pain gripped her, and she clung to Colin's hand.

Delving into his leather bag, Mr. Browning adjusted his

spectacles, commenting, "Yes, it seems to be moving along rather quickly" as he rummaged around the bag's contents.

Peering owlishly over his lenses at Colin, while fiddling with some instruments, the physician inquired as Olivia subsided back onto the bed, "Are you planning to stay?"

The question took Colin by surprise for it had never occurred to him to leave. He and Olivia had made this baby together, and he had assumed that, together, they would welcome it into the world.

Perturbed by the man's stare and unsure of Olivia's desires, Colin looked down at his pale wife, almost whispering, "Would you like me to go?"

"I would very much like you to stay," she whispered back, squeezing his hand, and Colin sensed all his anxiety and indecision melt away.

"I'll stay," he informed the physician, and Polly actually patted him on the back in congratulations.

Through the late afternoon Olivia labored to bring forth a new life. Colin and Mr. Browning encouraged her, praising her strength and urging her forward, while downstairs the staff paced back and forth, awaiting Polly's hourly reports.

The sun had just slipped over the horizon when Lady Forster hopped out of the coach into the magenta-hued dusk. Not the least fatigued from the wild ride from London, she tripped up the stairway and let herself into the house as a lusty wail heralded both her arrival and that of her new grandson.

Upstairs, Colin heard the answering cheer from below as he cradled his baby son in the crook of his elbow. Tears pricked the corners of his eyes, and he swallowed hard to keep the salty drops from dripping onto the small form he held. The miniature, dark-haired version of himself squalled, punching his thin arms futilely into the air, protesting loudly.

Colin carried the squirming baby over to where his mother lay, her eyes shut, an angelic smile hovering around her mouth. The angry cries of her newborn son forced her eyes to open, and tired, but happy, she held out her arms. Immediately the little fellow began rooting around until Olivia unbuttoned her nightgown and he latched on to his mother's breast.

With one finger she traced the outline of his fuzzy, black

hair, her fingertip curving around the perfectly formed little ear. Nothing, thought Colin, could be more beautiful, and a renegade tear crept out from beneath his eyelashes.

"Shall we name him Reginald for your father?" she asked.

"I would like that," Colin answered softly.

"Oh, Colin," Olivia purred, "isn't he precious?" Bending over the tiny bundle, she cooed, "You're mother's little darling, aren't you? My precious, little darling."

Colin smiled to himself, glad that at least one "darling" in the family was at long last retired.